VEIL OF VENGENCE

VEIL OF POWER SERIES
BOOK 1

SERAFINA MARRON

For more information, or to book an event, contact :

Email: Authorseramarron@gmail.com

Website: https://authorseramarron.godaddysites.com/

Beta Reader: Melissa Smith

Developmental editor: Mel of Write On Editorial

Line&Copy Editor: Mackenzie of Nicegirlnaughtyedits

Cover design by BooksandMoods

For all those who wish to be taken by a hot mafia boss...

AUTHOR NOTE

Hello friend,

If this is the first time you're picking up this book, you might not know that this is my debut novel. I hope it meets your standards for a mafia Romance.

However, please remember that this book may contain explicate and triggering topics. A full trigger list will be included on the next page, please consider it and make sure that you do what is best for your mental health.

Veil of Vengence is the first book in the Veil of Power series. It can be read as a standalone.

Please note that Roma's (Emiliano's younger brother) name has been changed to Matteo.

Don't forget to sign up to Serafina's Newsletter for news about future releases.

TRIGGER WARNING

This book may contain the following:

- Domestic Violence
- Child Abuse
- Abduction
- Depression
- Anxiety
- Violence
- Blood
- Murder
- Torture
- Suicidal thoughts
- Disordered eating
- Sexism
- Misogyny
- Dysfunctional family relationships
- Abusive family relationships
- Abusive parent
- Slut-shaming

- Gore
- Death of family members
- Explicate sex and Mature content

Reader discretion is advised

PLAYLIST

The hills - The Weeknd
Prisoner - Raphael Lake, Aaron Levy, Ryan Murphy
I Wanna Be Yours - Arctic Monkeys
Senorita - Shawn Mendes, Camilla Cabello
The Devil Within - Digital Daggers
Daisy (Instrumental) - Ashnikko
Fire On Fire - Sam Smith
Ride It (slowed + reverb) - Jay Sean
Beautiful Liar - Beyoncé, Shakira
Back To Black - Amy Winehouse
Stormy Weather - Etta James
Until I Found You - Stephen Sanchez

You can find the complete playlist on Spotify.

PROLOGUE
EMILIANO

3 1/2 months earlier

Romiro lets out an exasperated huff for the third time in as many minutes, grating on my last nerves.

"If you're that hot, just roll down the damn window," I say, my patience wearing thin. Shooting me a smirk, his fingers run through his tousled blonde curls.

"While I'm flattered that you think I'm h—" he begins, but I cut him off sharply.

"That's not what I said, you fuckface." I shift my attention back to the desolate road ahead, the stores lining the street already shuttered for the night. Nobody in their right mind would be out at this hour if they value their lives.

"What does the Capo want from you?" Romiro asks, his voice edged with curiosity.

"How the fuck would I know?" I sigh in frustration.

"He is your Dad, after all, you asshole." He makes an indistinct noise in the back of his throat before responding with a hint of sarcasm.

"Just because he's my Pop doesn't mean he'll fucking share a damn thing with me." His irritation is evident as he wipes the sweat from his face.

"Why did he have to choose fucking Ohio, of all places?" he grumbles. I can't help but chuckle at his complaints. Romiro's irritability flares, a clear sign that the sweltering heat is getting to him.

"We're here now, Rom. Just hang in there; there's a working air conditioner inside," I reassure him, as he slaps the broken car air conditioner. The car comes to a stop in front of The Sweet Cinnamon, its illuminated letters flickering. My gaze drifts across the boarded-up stores lining the street beside the strip club. Once the doors close with a solid thud, we both step out and stand in front of the car's hood.

"I don't get why it's called 'The Sweet Cinnamon.' That's a stupid fucking name," Romiro complains. I agree, it is a stupid name. However, there was a unique story behind it—the club had been named after a former stripper who had once worked for my Nonno. Romiro remains blissfully unaware of this fact as he kicks a can along the pavement while we approach the graffitied metal door. Raising my hand, I knock firmly. The discolored metal panel swings back, revealing a pair of piercing gray eyes that bore into us before allowing the door to open fully.

"Hey, guys. The boss is in his office upstairs, waiting for you. Dominico is in one of the back rooms," Silvio informs us. I give Silvio a tap on the shoulder as I pass by him, entering the dimly lit club. Old men fill the tables scattered around the stage, their presence leaving the once-purple carpet matted with dirt. The subdued lighting and sensual music pulsating through the speakers create an ambiance thick with intrigue. In the shadowy corners of the room, seedy-looking men leer at the stripper performing. As we pass the dimly lit stage, the stripper playfully winks at Romiro, the harsh red lighting casting shadows that make her seem older than her years. Determined to stay focused, I press on, leaving Romiro to engage with her as he winks back, lingering at the edge of the T-shaped stage. He's like a dog waiting for a fucking bone. Glancing back at him, I raise an eyebrow.

"You coming, or...?" I ask, my tone laden with impatience. The stripper gracefully descends the pole, her eyes fixed on Romiro as she crawls toward him sensually. He offers his signature smirk, and she responds by licking her ruby-painted lips.

"Oh, he'll be coming, for sure," she purrs with a suggestive double entendre. A nauseating twist churns in my stomach at her words.

"Nah, bro, you go ahead. I'll be right here if you need me," Romiro replies, giving a nonchalant shrug. I nod and continue through the club. Surprisingly, it isn't as crowded as I had anticipated, which suggests that most of our security is likely deployed at our other club across town. As I make my way to the back hallway, the ambient lighting bathes the area in a cool, soothing blue hue. Framed photographs signed by major celebrities, who had visited the club during the sixties, adorn the walls.

I take a moment to roll the tension out of my shoulders before heading upstairs. Moving forward, the plush dark carpet muffles my footsteps. My Pop's office, with its imposing floor-to-ceiling black-accented doors, remains closed, but I can hear muffled voices from within. The walls of the hallway are a muted gray, and the harsh white lighting above irritates my eyes. Summoning my resolve, I open the door to the office, paying little attention to the club manager who stands at the edge of my Pop's desk. Dim lighting accentuates the somber atmosphere of the room, the dark walls only adding to the overall gloomy ambiance. I approach my Pop's desk, where he sits with a proud smile gracing his lips as his eyes remain fixed on me.

"Figlio, why didn't you have Silvio tell me you're here?" His delivery is light, but there is a hint of something deeper in his light blue eyes as he rises from his seat behind the desk. He steps over to me and gives my shoulder a reassuring pat. Then, he turns his attention to Felix.

"Go on, Felix, you can leave," my Pop instructs. Felix's gaze shifts briefly to me before he nods at my Pop. The door closes with a subtle click, leaving just my Pop and me in the room. We settle into the chairs facing his desk.

"What is it you wanted, Pop?" I ask once we're both seated, the air charged with anticipation.

"I'm considering stepping down soon. It's about time you became Capo," my Pop says, his words delivered with a sense of inevitability. I saw this coming for the past couple of months. He has aged, grown more lenient than he'd like to admit. I wait for the other shoe to drop, as it often does with my Pop.

"But..." he continues, and I brace myself for what comes next.

"I want you to get married before that." Jaw clenching, my teeth grind together. My Pop's old-fashioned beliefs are holding back the Camorra, and I don't have the fucking time to cater to a woman's whims. I lean back in my chair, releasing a deep breath.

"Who did you have in mind?" I ask, my curiosity tinged with caution. He wears a shit-eating grin, as if he has me right where he wants me.

"I was thinking about Stefano Gambi's niece," he replies. My lips curl involuntarily at the mention of the Gambi family head, the man who has relentlessly tried to undermine our drug operations in New York. My Pop's laughter fills the room, a twisted sound that matches his character all too well. He may be an ally who supplies some of our weapons, but he is a devil in disguise. The Gambi family has been one of the most notorious illegal firearm traders since World War one.

"No," I declare firmly, unwilling to entertain the idea any further. His eyes narrow, but before he can protest, the sudden commotion downstairs cuts our conversation short. The intercom buzzes, and Silvio's voice crackles through.

"Boss, we're under attack! They shot Dominico, and he's losing a lot of blood. Tommaso is dead." Heart stuttering, a sense of dread washes over me. Fuck, Dad's Consigliere is dead. Dad storms around the table and stabs the button for the intercom behind his chair.

"Who the fuck is attacking us?" His face twists into a snarl and he pulls a gun from his suit pants. Reacting swiftly, I rise to my feet, draw my own weapon, and head for the doors.

"It's The Outfit, damn it. Romiro, get the fuck down!" The

intercom buzzes once more, and Dad moves past me, making his way toward the staircase. I keep pace, my steps echoing loudly as we descend the stairs. When Dad reaches the bottom, the unmistakable sound of a gunshot rings out, and he collapses to the ground with a heavy thud.

A man in a ski mask stands menacingly over Dad's lifeless body, and I aim my gun at him just as he makes a move to shoot. Without hesitation, I fire, striking him in the knees. He screams out in agony, dropping his weapon. Swiftly, I search through the closet near the stairs and find some rope, which I use to bind him securely before knocking him out. Afterward, I reach for Dad's neck, checking for a pulse, but there is none. I close his lifeless eyes and take a moment to clear my thoughts. My hands are soaked with both my Pop's blood and the fucker's who shot him. I run a bloody hand through my hair. I don't know how the fuck I'm going to tell Ma, or even my younger siblings. Lucio and Matteo will probably take it better than Mara; she'll be fucking devastated. Matteo has always been the stronger one between him and Mara, even if they are twins.

This situation is fucking messy, and I need to stay on guard. Moving down the dimly lit hallway, I make my way into the main room, only to be met with a horrifying sight. Dead bodies are strewn about, with most clustered around the stage. The stripper who had been dancing earlier now lay lifeless in a pool of blood, a stark contrast to the sensual atmosphere that once filled the room. The smell of death hangs heavy in the air, and a haunting silence prevails before the sudden eruption of gunshots echoes from the back rooms.

I run in that direction, gun raised, weaving through fallen chairs and tables as I approach the back rooms. Peering inside cautiously, I find Romiro and Dom positioned by the back door, desperately firing at a car speeding out of the parking lot. The lifeless body of a bouncer lay on the floor, surrounded by dark pools of blood. Dominico is holding a blood-soaked rag to his forearm, trying to return fire. His back slides down the wall, struggling to stay on his feet. I step over the fallen bouncer and reach for Dom, determined to get him to safety and to figure out who orchestrated this violent attack.

"Keep it together, cugino. Rom, we need to get this fuckface to the hospital," I say to Romiro, and he gives me a grim nod, still processing how his night got fucked up.

"Glad you care so much, Eli." Dom's voice is strained, his eyes reflecting the pain he's in. Romiro holsters his gun and grabs one of Dom's arms.

"What about Capo? Where is he?" Dom groans.

"He's standing right in front of you. I am the Capo of the Camorra. Alberto Folonari is dead," I say, my voice heavy with grief. Dom inhales sharply, followed by a muttered curse, before losing consciousness. Silvio rushes in and joins Romiro in helping Dominico, urgency weighing heavily on all of us.

"Silvio, make sure Dom gets to one of our hospitals, and send some of our guys to clean up this shit," I order, my tone conveying the gravity of the situation. Silvio nods, supporting Dominico with one of his arms over his shoulder.

"We've got two of the attackers alive; they're tied up in the back," he informs me.

"Good, that makes three of them. Romiro, I want you to take them to one of our warehouses," I instruct Romiro, who responds with a twisted grin before heading out the door with Dominico and Silvio. As I turn my attention back to the unfolding chaos, my phone vibrates in my pocket. I retrieve it and see the caller ID: Costa. The sigh on the other end of the line tells me that I probably won't like what he has to say next.

"Spit it out," I demand with irritation as Costa delivers his report.

"One of your clubs in Manhattan got attacked."

I clench my teeth, my fingers scraping down my stubbled jaw.

"Who?" I ask. My gaze scans the room as I try to assess the extent of the damage.

"Angel's Hell," Costa replies. Those fucking bastards. I'd warned my Pop about them, suspecting they were working with the Outfit.

"It's the fucking Outfit. They'd broken the unspoken peace we've had for the past couple of years," I respond, frustration and anger simmering beneath the surface. I need to know the extent of our losses tonight, and I'm not about to let this aggression go unanswered.

"How many dead?" I demand, my voice tight with concern. Costa sighs in frustration before delivering the grim news.

"Sixty-five are dead. Around forty-five were our men." Fucking fuck. With the call still ongoing, I close and lock the back door securely before stepping into the main club space. The air is heavy with the metallic scent of blood, a chilling reminder of the ruthless attack.

"I'm going to rip the fucking Outfit bastards to shreds," I seethe, my resolve solidifying. "The Capo's dead. The ceremony will happen today."

"That's not possible." Costa's response comes instantly, full of disbelief. I narrow my eyes as I crouch down, spotting a small platinum ring with an emerald tucked away in the corner of the room.

"I don't fucking care what's possible. Get everyone in New York by the time I get there," I bark into the phone, leaving no room for arguments. Without waiting, I end the call, sliding my phone into the pocket of my suit jacket. A soulless smile curls on my lips as my gaze settles on the name engraved on the edge of the ring—*Giuseppe Moretti*. Little Moretti boy, you've fucked with the wrong family. And I'm going to crush you like the rat you are.

My gaze sweeps around the open warehouse, full to the brim with Camorra soldiers, captains, and underbosses. The air is thick with tension, and my echoing steps seem to amplify the collective unease. From the back of the warehouse, I slowly make my way toward the front, acutely aware of every soldier's gaze boring into my back. At the front, my two brothers stand side by side, with Lucio to the right of Romiro, and Matteo to his left. I reach the front, opting to stand before them without stepping up onto the podium. My piercing gaze scans the room, settling on my uncles, their expressions grim probably at the prospect of a young Capo giving them orders. Clearing my throat, I begin, my voice strong and unwavering,

"The Outfit has attacked two of our clubs—one in Manhattan, and the other in Ohio. Our Capo is dead." I observe as some soldiers shift uncomfortably, tension mounting in the room. My voice remains loud and confident as I continue.

"We have lost many loyal soldiers in these brutal attacks." I let the weight of my words sink in before delivering my solemn promise, "I, Emiliano Folonari, swear that no Camorrista's blood will go unavenged. We will seek retribution for the Outfit's sins, and they will pay for what they have done, tenfold." The crowd erupts into cheers and applause. Once they calm down, I move toward the table on my right, where my family dagger rests. I pick up the gold handle of the dagger, feeling the engravings dig into my skin as I return to where I am standing. Following tradition, it should have been Dominico step-ping forward, but in his absence, Romiro took his place. He halts in front of me and extends a small ceramic bowl. My great, great Nonno brought it over to America when they had migrated from Italy over a hundred years ago.

"Do you, Emiliano Folonari, swear that you will place the Camorra above all else as Capo dei Capi?" Romiro intones, holding the bowl steady.

I place my palm over my heart, responding in Italian, as tradition dictates, "Lo giuro."

Romiro continues. "The blood you spill from this palm will bind every Camorrista to you as your family and will bind you to them as their Capo. This blood means we are one family. You live by the Camorra and die by the Camorra." As I press the cool metal of the dagger into my palm, blood wells, forming beads that drip down into the ceramic bowl.

"Entro vivo ed esco morto," I declare solemnly, sealing the vow with the final drop of blood. *I enter alive and I will have to leave dead.* I then smear the blood on the white handkerchief that Lucio hands me. It's time for revenge, and we will start with the traitor who betrayed our location.

1

VALENTINA

Sitting on the carpeted floors of our library, I face my two younger sisters. It's the only place we're able to talk without feeling the need to watch what we say, but we still keep our voices low.

"You realize that is an idiotic plan and if you get caught by Mom or Dad, they wi-" Violette's voice echoes around the large open library, and I cut her off with a hushed voice.

"I know, but I can't take it anymore. We're being watched all the time, and I heard Nonna and Dad talking... They want to marry me off soon." She opens her mouth to speak, but I continue, ignoring the gnawing feeling in the pit of my stomach.

"I heard them, Violette. They want to marry me off before summer starts. That's in eight months." The panic in my voice is palpable. All I want is to feel some sort of control over my life, and it's slipping through my fingers.

She releases a sigh as she leans back onto the heels of her palms. Tilting her head, her shoulder-length blonde hair falls backwards, making her appear angelic. She inherited our Mom's hair color. I, on the other hand, inherited our Dad's black raven hair.

"I know you might not want to come with me, but Lottie, please don't get in the way," I say firmly, my expression pleading.

I turn to face Monica, who is sitting on one of the plush pink armchairs with her elbows on the armrests. She looks up from her phone and only lifts one of her shoulders in a half shrug, her lips pressed into a line, causing her left dimple to show. Before she can say a word, the library door handle makes an ugly screech, which causes us to turn our heads in that direction.

The door opens and Marcello comes tumbling in. But someone stops him when he tries to step forward into the room.

"Marcello, what are you doing?" My Dad's icy demand cuts through the air as he stands in the entrance behind Marcello, making him flinch. His chin trembles with the effort to hold in his tears. Dad has trained him to better prepare him for his induction, but Marco's yet to learn how to hold in his emotions.

"Marco, come here." My voice comes out softer than I intended it to, causing our Dad to send a scathing glare above Marcello's head toward me. His face set in a scowl as he steps into the library, Marcello moving into my outstretched arms.

"I told you this before, you silly boy. You cannot sit with your sisters, or you'll become soft like them. Now come here." Dad's sharp and cruel tone, as usual, makes Marco bury his face into the nape of my neck and a few sniffles escape from his mouth.

Dad's face contorts into one of utter rage at the blatant disregard of his command, and at the fact that his heir is crying and in the arms of a woman. Before I even know what is happening, my Dad leaps across the room and snatches Marco from my hands, holding him up by his arms to be eye level, shaking him.

"Don't you cry!" he screams into his face. At that moment, Mom appears in the open doorway of the library, paling at the sight of Marco in the hold of Dad. Her fingers clutch the fabric of her long-sleeved gray dress, eyes widening and her chest rising and falling rapidly.

"Alvize, please, for the love of God, put Marcello down. He'll behave this time," our Mom pleads with my dad.

"Shut up, Diletta! This is your fault! Look at him! He's weak! How in God's name will he be the future Capo of the Outfit?!" Dad screams. Mom stands eerily still as her gaze darts to us frantically. As soon as Dad drops Marco from his hold, Mom rushes over to him. "Angelo and Giovanni, get in here." His soulless black eyes stare at Mom as she cradles a crying Marcello. Both Dad's bodyguards rush in through the large mahogany door, waiting for an order.

"Marcello will receive punishment," Dad declares with finality.

"Alvize, what are you going to do? He's only five. He'll learn. Just give him time." Mom's eyes glaze over as she regards our dad from her position on the floor, her arms wrapped around Marcello as he whimpers into her neck.

Monica, Violette, and I are paralyzed in our positions. We all hold our breath, waiting for the domino effect that follows with Dad's outbursts. Dad doesn't break the silence, but with a nod toward Marcello, he orders both Angelo and Giovanni to take him.

"He'll spend the next three weeks in the dungeons." A sob breaks from Mom's mouth, her body shaking, but Dad continues. "No one will speak with him, no one will look at him, no one but the guards will be allowed." There's a deep scowl on his face as he directs a searing look at Mom, and then he turns to leave. But Mom jumps to her feet and runs, standing in his way. She clings to his right arm and begs with hot tears running down her face. I cringe at the sight, knowing what's coming.

"Please, Alvize, I beg of you, please don't lock him in the dun—" she's cut off when Dad throws her off, and she stumbles backwards, hitting her head on the edge of the table.

My knees scrape across the carpet as I rush to stand, Violette and Monica right behind me as we grab Mom, inspecting her.

"Mom, are you okay?" I ask in a hushed voice, concerned that Dad might notice us, but she doesn't respond. She holds back her sobs, causing her shoulders to shake.

"Let me go, LET ME GO!" Marcello's demands make us all turn to see him as Giovanni and Angelo drag him out. His face turns red as he struggles to escape their hold. It's no use.

It's been two days since Dad had his guards take Marcello to the dungeons, and we know nothing. Nonna has tried to persuade him to let Marcello out, but he told her to not involve herself in the men's business.

I focus my attention on the screen of my phone, avoiding Violette's demanding gaze. She's trying to dissuade me from leaving during the party. The party is in a couple of days, and I need to figure out the best route to get out and back in before anyone notices I'm gone. I wipe my sweaty hand on my jeans, trying to appear normal and stop myself from shaking.

According to Nonna, Dad has been Capo for the last thirty years and has been the longest ruling Capo in the Outfit. I guess when you're a crime boss of a very powerful family, it means that everyone will try anything to get rid of you. Dad seems to be proud of his achievement, which is the reason why the party is being held in our Chicago club. At the Via Veneto, the largest club in the entirety of the state of Illinois.

I doubt my uncles want to celebrate my Dad's rule over the Sicilian Mafia. I look up just in time to see Nonna enter grimly, and we all stand out of respect. She clears her throat before she orders.

"Violette, Monica, and Diletta, I want you all out. I need to speak to Valentina." Mom's eyebrows reach her forehead at the tone my Nonna uses, but they all obey. I can feel Violette's stare burn the side of my face. They all scurry out of the large wooden doors, and Nonna watches them before her sharp eyes turn back to me. They narrow slightly, something akin to disgust flashing in her gaze.

Her cane thuds against the cream-colored wooden floors as she makes her way toward the corner of the room, where two leather armchairs are facing each other, with a small black round French coffee table. Nonna doesn't wait for me to sit down.

"As a woman, your place is with your husband, and you have been spoken for by someone we want to form an alliance with." Her expression stays the same, even as she takes in my thinning lips, wide eyes, and clenched fists. I grit my teeth, knowing that she thinks of me as a nuisance.

"Your Dad has decided that an alliance with the Colombians is necessary. You will marry the eldest son of the Guerrero Clan. We will announce your engagement to Nicholas Guerrero at the party your Dad is hosting."

My stomach rolls at the idea of being engaged to a man I have never seen, only having heard the cruel rumors plaguing his name like cancer.

"Nonna, please, you cannot be serious about this. I have never even seen Nicholas, and what if we don't get along-" Nonna cuts me off, my cheek stinging with the pain of her slap.

"Be quiet, you silly little girl. Do not delude yourself into believing that because you were born in America and raised here, that you may entertain such devilish behaviors. We are Sicilian women; we carry our pride and honor like a crown, and I will not allow you to taint the Moretti name with such nonsense." Nonna's harsh words do not surprise me at all. I rub a hand over the sore cheek, avoiding her eyes. "Besides," she continues with a sigh, "you should have been married off when you had turned eighteen, but since your Mom insisted that an education is important in today's society, we had put off marrying you. Now the time has come for you to start your own family."

Nonna clearly doesn't think I have anything of value to say, because she leaves once she has finished speaking.

Eyes burning, my vision slowly blurs. I try to take deep breaths to calm myself, but it doesn't work because I can feel my throat closing as if something is choking me. My chin quivers with the effort of not crying, and I rub the heels of my palms into my eyes, wishing for the earth to open up and swallow me.

I stand up, letting out a frustrated sigh. No, I won't sit here and wallow in misery. I need to find a way to get out of this arrangement.

The drawing room is on the bottom floor of our Chicago estate, located in the farthest corner of the villa. Irritation clings to my skin as I make my way through the hallway toward my sanctuary in this hellhole. The library. Taking a breath, I stop in front of the door that would lead me to the hedge maze outside.

Instead of going to the library, I decided to slide the glass doors open and walk down the curving stairs. Pausing at the last step, a cool breeze washes over me. It's kind of warm for an early fall afternoon.

As if the summer is refusing to move on, the leaves are already falling and turning orange. Which I am perfectly content to watch. I think that fall is the best time of the year because you get to see the beautiful change in nature.

A soft breeze blows my hair in my face as I reach the bottom step of the large granite stairs. I watch the sun as it slowly descends on the horizon, casting different hues of colors. My heart thumps as I weave myself through the first few hedges of the maze, some of the sun peeking through.

The sound of leaves crunching fills my ears as my sneakers step over them, something about it easing my racing thoughts. The maze always ends up feeling haunted around October and November, but once December hits, when it snows, it resembles a Christmas wonderland. Doesn't matter when I explore it, though, it brings me a sense of peace every time. And right now, that's exactly what I need.

<hr>

By the time I make it out of the maze and back into the house, dinner is already being prepared and I can hear Dad's angry voice echo down the hallway.

A loud bang sounds from his office, bouncing off the dark gray walls. I pause outside the large mahogany door.

"Your son is going to cost us another war with the fucking Camorra, Benito. I will not have the Outfit suffer for your son's stupidity." Dad must be on the phone with my uncle, and I'm not surprised that this concerns one of my cousins.

"No, your son was initiated two weeks ago. I will punish him for stepping out of line like everybody else..." It must be about Giuseppe.

I don't know what he did, but I am kind of surprised because he's usually the more level-headed one between him and Michele.

"And because he's fucking family, we will discipline him accordingly. I don't tolerate any kind of challenge to my rule, Benito. I don't care if he wasn't initiated when he acted outside of orders. You know this. Giuseppe better be in the dungeons by six tomorrow, or you know what will happen." I doubt Dad waits for a response since he slams something, which I assume is his phone against his table. The carpet muffles the sound of my sneakers as I try to avoid him.

"Valentina, sweetie. Where were you?" *Cazzo!* I clearly didn't walk quickly enough to get away before he opens his door. My dad is usually nice to us when we do nothing he'd deem disrespectful. Well, as nice as a mafia Capo could be. With a swallow, I turn toward my dad.

"Um... I was out in the rose maze, Papa," I say, and I can see his eyes narrow.

"Right, well, go to your Mom. She's looking for you." I nod, but before I can say that I'll go find her, he speaks up again. "Has Nonna spoken to you about your upcoming engagement announcement?"

My jaw clenches involuntarily at the mention of my upcoming prison sentence, or at least that's how I think it'll be.

"Yes, Nonna has made me aware of it." My heart thumps in my ears and my shoulders stiffen as I wait for him to let me go. Dad finally dismisses me with a nod.

I turn and manage to walk three steps before he speaks up again. "And Valentina, from now on, you are to wear heels at all times."

Clenching my fists on the side of my baggy denim jeans, I look down to stare at my sneakers.

"Yes, Papa." I stand there for a beat longer, wondering if he has any other demands, but all I hear is the click of his door closing.

I FIND MY MOM ON THE SECOND FLOOR OF OUR HOME LIBRARY. HER back to me as she rests her head on the window, both her legs tucked underneath her. She must not have been there long; she doesn't enjoy the silence much, not after Dad had locked her for two months in the basement for being a "disobedient" wife. If she could get Marcello out, she would have, but she risks Dad breaking her ribs like last time, and maybe even worse going after Monica as well.

I don't understand what she's looking at since you can barely make out anything from the second floor of the library windows, especially at night.

"Hey, Mom. Dad said you were looking for me?" I keep my voice low to not startle her. She snaps out of her thoughts and turns her head to look at me.

"Mia Cara, come here." She waves me closer, and I make my way toward her. Moving her feet off the bench, she reaches out to hug me, my arms awkwardly wrapping around her as her rose perfume fills my nose.

I'm not exactly fond of physical touch or affection, but I love my Mom and she has enough on her plate. We both have very similar frames, both quite petite, but she is taller. Mom pulls back after a long hug, her eyes distant. They have a suspicious sheen that she blinks away.

"Valentina, sweetie. I want you to know that if I had the power to, I would stop it." She doesn't outright say what "it" is, but we both know what she means.

"But you don't, and you can't," I say to her. There isn't any use in saying "if I could" with things like this, things that are out of our control. We have no choice but to fall in line. I just hope that my sisters are going to have a different life than my Mom's or mine. If my life turns out to be like Mom's, I don't think I'll survive.

"Cara, you know we have little choice, especially being a woman in our world." She shakes her head at me. "I hope Nicholas will treat you right." There is hope in her voice, hope for my future, hope for a marriage I have no choice in, and hope for a monster as cruel as Nicholas Guerrero to be a good husband.

I want to contradict her, but I can't break whatever hope she has for me. It'll be cruel. Mom's already suffering since Dad is punishing Marcello.

"Mom, do you know when Marcello will come out? Has Dad said anything?" I ask her.

She swallows roughly and says, "He'll be let out after dinner. Your Dad is letting him out earlier because he has a speech to make during the party. He wants us to appear as a united front." My eyebrows pull together and my lips twist into a snarl. Dad has always loved flaunting the fact that he has been the longest Capo alive in the history of the Outfit.

"Who's going to be there?" I ask, trying to see if maybe Mia will join us. Mom's face lights up.

"If you're asking if Mia will be there, she will. Your cousin Nicolette will also be there." Oh. My. God. Yes! If Nicolette is coming, that means Aunt Belinda too. Mom and I smile at each other, the corner of her eyes wrinkling. It's been a couple of years since we last saw my cousin and aunt.

Our happiness doesn't last long, because she quickly sobers up and gives me a look. "Mia Cara, I want to give you one piece of advice and I want you to carry it like you carry your honor and pride. Don't let anyone make you think that kindness is a weakness. Look for opportunities to be compassionate and generous. Be aware of people who might deceive you into believing that kindness is a weakness, because in a world like ours, authenticity is hard to find."

THE DINING ROOM FILLS WITH THE CLATTER OF OUR PLATES. AND THE white walls remind me of an insane asylum, the servants floating in through the doorless doorway. They all are carrying dishes from the kitchen, the delicious smell wafting around the room.

Zehra's cooking has never failed us. We're all sitting around the black dining room table, an uncomfortable silence blanketing the room. I shift in the hard wooden dining chair as I squint my eyes, the chandelier light adding to the throbbing in my skull.

Violette is on my left and Mom is on my right. Mom clenches her fists as she tries to stop them from shaking. Violette is staring at her plate, avoiding both my dad's and Nonna's glances.

Monica is next to Nonna. It's not the first time Nonna had Mon sit next to her, since she's the youngest girl and Dad targets her and Marcello the most.

"Alvize, Marcello will not be going back into the dungeons once he's out." Nonna is the one to break the silence. A stillness settles over us as we try to see how Dad might react to being ordered.

His reputation precedes him; he only got the position of Capo by dismembering the original leading family. All of them in one night. Earning him the title of the cruelest Capo in the Outfit's history.

"Mama, I have told you to stay out of the men's business." His tone is curt, speaking low enough that the servants can't hear what he's saying from their positions on the far walls.

"Alvize, for the love of God. Marcello is five. He's still a boy. You've got time before his initiation to train him," Nonna argues. Dad takes a deep breath in and lets it out slowly. He's getting pissed. If Nonna keeps pressuring him, he's going to beat someone up. Probably our Mom.

But Dad surprises us when he nods and says, "You will keep him away from his sisters. He's growing too weak. The only time he's allowed to speak to them is during breakfast, lunch, and dinner. Or if we have a social gathering."

Nonna nods and gives us all a glare.

The rest of the evening goes by quickly. They'd let Marcello out ten minutes ago, and he looked absolutely devastating. His top is ripped, the right sleeve completely torn off, and the knees of his trousers are tethered with some dry blood. A long diagonal cut on his left cheek has scabbed.

They littered his arms with bruises and cuts, but the most terrifying thing is the look in his eyes. His eyes used to be crystal blue, but now it's the look you see in a Made man's eyes, not a five-year-old child's. Violette, Monica, and I keep our distance.

The only people who are around him are Nonna and Mom. They wanted to call the family doctor, but Dad sends both a scathing look as he tells them they need to stop "babying" Marcello.

2

———

VALENTINA

I'm in my vanity room, getting ready for the party. With the soft light illuminating the large room, I watch Violette through the mirror as she sifts through my jewelry. She has six different pieces on the glass counter in the middle of the room.

Her eyes filter to mine in the mirror when I speak up. "You want to know what Nonna wanted to talk to me about?" Her face reveals nothing as she watches me before she nods. "She told me that Dad will announce in his speech that I am engaged to Nicholas Guerrero."

Violette's blonde eyebrows scrunch up and she shakes her head, as if in denial.

"Do you mean the man people refer to as the Scorpion?" she asks. My lips press together as I nod. She rounds the table and makes her way toward me.

"That can't be right. We hate the Colombian cartels. Dad was complaining that they're trying to rip the Outfit off," she argues from behind me. I grimly watch Violette as she looks at me with her eyes wide, gripping my shoulders.

"I guess they've come to an agreement." I shrug her off and get up, grabbing my clutch before heading to the door. Violette rushes after me, and we walk side by side as we make our way to the grand staircase. We can hear Nonna screaming at some of the staff down there as we head down the stairs, our heels clicking against the marble. I grip the hard wood railing, biting the inside of my cheeks. Nonna is standing at the end of the stairs with Monica, Mom, and Marcello.

"Took you girls long enough. Come on, your Dad is in the car." When we reach the final step, Nonna moves to the doors the butler opens for us, her cane loudly tapping against the floor. She mutters under her breath about our incompetence.

Dad doesn't comment on our tardiness when we slip into the limo, as he's busy typing on his phone. Our estate's gold gates open as the limo drives through, and the tinted windows stop the flashing lights of the paparazzi cameras from irritating our eyes.

"They seem to love you, girls," Mom teases, as if she doesn't already know the reason the paparazzi are obsessed with our family. I turn my face to look at her sitting across from me in the limo.

She has a soft smile on her lips, which are painted a pink nude, her blonde hair done in an elegant updo. Her green eyes stand out tonight with her wearing a sage-colored cocktail dress.

Violette leans over and whispers to her, "Mama, they're just a nuisance at this point. All they do is ask us outrageous questions to get a reaction." Mom raises one blonde eyebrow while looking in my sister's direction.

Nonna turns to look at Violette as well, her eyes narrow and her lips set into a line. Instead of saying anything, she decides to grab a glass of scotch and mutter something in Italian under her breath.

"Violette, how's school been? How's your piano lessons going?" My mom, of course, takes the opportunity to change the subject to see if she can get Violette to open up.

Violette sighs and answers with a curt, "School's fine." She doesn't like to talk about her piano progression, never does. I don't understand why, because the last time we went to one of her performances, she'd been amazing.

Mom turns her head to Monica, who's sitting next to her. "Mon, sweetie. How's school been? Are you enjoying your ballet class?" Monica stops typing on her phone to look at Mom and nods. She isn't much of a talker, ever since we were little kids, at least not after the incident.

Mom and Violette engage in some sort of conversation having to do with who's going to be coming to the engagement party, but I tune them out, instead opting to look outside. The limo is going too fast to focus on anything to admire, but when we reach a red light, I can see that it is raining, and Chicago looks magnificent in the rain. Soon enough, the limo comes to a halt in front of the grand entrance of the club. Security lines each side of the door, and the driver, Dustin, opens the limo door for Dad. I know without looking that both my hands are shaking. I inhale deeply through my nose and fist my dress. *1, 2, 3.*

As I open my eyes, the corners of my mouth pin up in a dazzling smile, and I step out of the limo. "Thank you, Dustin," I whisper, low enough for him to hear, but I don't turn to look at him. The paparazzi are here as well, all standing behind where security is holding them. There's double the amount compared to when we left our house, but I focus my vision ahead. Violette and I link our arms and the flashing of the cameras intensifies.

"Stay calm. You're the Bellissima Moretti. Remember that," Violette whispers in my ear while we both maintain the charade. *Bellissima Moretti.* Of course they'd give me such a dramatic name. What did I expect from the tabloids? The walk is short; we reach the gold-rimmed black doors in two minutes, but it would have been quicker if it wasn't for the stupid paparazzi. Nonna and the rest are walking behind Dad, and we trail after them, our heels clicking on the wet sidewalk. The guards hold the doors open for us and close them after we walk in.

Inside, a long hallway is ahead of us, with an empty round reception desk to our right. The red carpet muffles the sound of our shoes as we make our way toward the grand cream-colored doors at the end of the hallway. On the black, gold-accented walls are images of all the past Capos, all in their prime. Dad turns to us and gives us all a warning glare before walking down the hallway to the two large doors, an attendant on both sides to open them for us.

As soon as I reach the top step of the long stairs, I spot Mia in a cream dress, talking to her Dad and stepMom. I can also see my aunt and cousin standing off to the side, away from my Dad's side of the family. The floor is made of a deep brown wood and tables and chairs are scattered around the room, a cream linen fabric covering them. A large diamond chandelier in the middle of the ceiling illuminates the entire hall.

"Ugh, I don't understand what you like about her. She's quite dull, in my opinion." Violette seems to have spotted Mia as well. I laugh quietly at her absolute refusal to admit that Mia is usually the life of any party. The place falls quiet as everyone's attention turns to us.

Once we reach the last step, Dad says, "Welcome, everyone, please enjoy the festivities and have a great time."

After everyone returns to their conversations, Mia decides to head our way. She has a soft smile, which she directs at everyone who tries to stop her on her way to us. And it's quite a lot of people. I can see that Nicolette and Aunt Belinda are also making their way over. Nicolette is in a vibrant purple dress, her long brown curls up into a twisted bun, while my aunt is wearing an off-the-shoulder, long azure dress that matches her eyes.

"Val, I've missed you. It's been so long," Mia says as soon as she reaches us and pulls me into a bear hug, making me laugh into her silver bob. I inhale her musky vanilla perfume she loves to wear. "Violette, I see you've grown taller." Her eyes take in Violette, a mischievous gleam entering them. Mia is still at least two inches taller than Violette. She gives her a fake smile that Mia returns.

"And I see you're still unaware of how to greet another person." Violette loves to comment on Mia's lack of adherence to our society's rules. Mia ignores the jab and turns her attention back to me. It's all soon forgotten when Nicolette joins us.

"Hey, girls. I've missed you all so much." Nicolette pulls us all into a hug, her arm around my neck as I laugh into her soft curls.

"I've missed you more, cuz," I mumble. She pulls back, and I look around to see where my aunt has gone, when I spot her with my mom, both laughing together.

"Hey, Nikki, how have you been?" Mia asks, and I turn back to the girls. Nicolette shrugs her shoulders and scrunches her freckled nose.

"Shit. England isn't as much fun as it used to be." Nicolette and my aunt both live in England with her Jamaican dad.

"So, I'm guessing the English boys aren't as charming as I thought they would be," I tease her.

"Hell no. They all act like having their pants sagging like a diaper looks good." Nikki huffs out an amused laugh, her ocean-colored eyes twinkling.

My nose wrinkles at the image, and I can't help but say, "Don't worry, Nikki, I've seen some of the men in Chicago do the same exact thing." She pushes a curl out of her face, her tan skin lighter this time of year.

"Don't act like the little French boys you date are any better, Mia." Lottie gives Mia a blank stare before she stares at her baby pink nails. Mia's lips curl as she sends Violette a condescending smile.

"Drop the superiority act, Violette. No one fucking buys it or cares for it." Mia doesn't wait for Violette to answer her as she loops her right arm through my left one. She drags me toward the tables that are set to face the stage, where Dad will be giving a speech. Nicolette stays behind with Violette, and I try to look back to catch a glimpse of them, but make out nothing, since everyone is trying to get to their seats as my dad walks onto the stage.

Mia and I settle into our seats, when finally, both Lottie and Nikki sit opposite ours. The table only holds four people, so Monica is sat with Mom and Aunt Belinda. Dad taps the mic placed on the stage. The chandelier light dims, and the room falls into shadows as the lights on the stage remain the brightest. His face breaks out into his signature hyena smile before he begins.

"We all know why we are here today, I'm sure." Some people in the crowd clap, while some of the others whistle. "For that reason, I'll make this short and sweet. Today is not only to celebrate the thirtieth year of me being Capo of the Outfit, but today is also a very special day for one of my daughters." Everyone holds their breath, and so do I, a lead ball forming in my stomach.

I can make out some people whispering, wondering who he is talking about. "Today, we have decided to announce the engagement of my eldest daughter, Valentina, to Nicholas Guerrero, from the Guerrero clan." Dad has a broad, pleased smile as he stares at me.

Mia's hand encircles my forearm as she whispers, "What the fuck did he just say?"

Cheers and howls break out from the men, and I continue to stare ahead at my Dad, even as he surveys the cheering crowd. Bile rises and I have to push it down. Once Dad has finished the rest of his speech, he moves away from the stage and toward his business partners, Marcello trailing behind him as the lights turn back on. Mia and Nicolette both exchange looks before Mia looks at me.

"Did you know about this?" she asks, and I nod, my lips set in a grim line. "What the fuck? How could he just give you away to a man known to have killed for the first time before he could even form a memory?" She sounds exasperated. I shrug, staring at the now empty stage.

"Val! Say something. You can't seriously just accept that," Mia demands, and I turn my head sharply, facing her.

"What the fuck do you want me to do? Mia, you know I can't do anything. Dad won't tolerate disobedience," I say in a rush before I throw my clutch on the table.

"I'm going to the ladies' room," I mutter, then storm toward one of the waitstaff.

"Excuse me, do you know where the restrooms are?" I ask a young man who's in uniform, and he tells me that it's outside, in a corridor off to the receptionist's desk. I thank him before making my way up the stairs and out the doors. There is only one corridor near the receptionist's desk, and it has low lighting, creating an intimate mood. Entering the restroom, the floors were black-and-white marble and there were mirrors lining the right wall with toilets opposite. At least the restroom is well lit, unlike the corridor.

I walk up to the mirrors to look at how well my makeup has held up. It seems fine. My red lipstick is still perfectly done, and the light coral blush hasn't faded. I just need to touch up the powder around my nose and forehead. Opening my clutch, I take out the Dior powder, dabbing it all over my face. I check my hair next, still in natural waves and hasn't started frizzing. As I run both my palms down my black dress, I look like the perfect image of the woman I've curated over the years, but I feel tired. Exhausted even.

I turn to leave the restroom, but the door opens before I reach it and a large man in a suit steps inside. He's tall and fills the space with his large frame, his dark hair pushed back. My neck arches as I look up to maintain eye contact with him as he steps in farther.

"Um...sir, this is the women's restroom. The men's is down the corridor," I explain to him, but he looks at me like I am the one in the wrong place. I raise an eyebrow as his razor-sharp blue eyes assess me, cold and calculated, some malice glinting in them. When his full lips twist into a humorless smile, two dimples wink at me from his slightly stubbled cheeks. He is death personified and the devil in disguise. I'm frozen in place as his tattooed hand slips into his suit jacket, pulling out a phone before he brings it up to his ear. The dark ink swirls peek through the top of his black dress shirt, a constellation of stars donning his neck.

Swallowing past my unease, I scowl at him and say, "If you're one of my dad's bodyguards, you need to wait outside, not in here." He doesn't reply, only gives me a twisted smile.

I'm nervous, but I won't let him see that. I can see that both his hands are also littered with tattoos, an anchor on his middle finger with the chains wrapping upwards and two scorpions on both sides of a snake's head. "Target secured." His voice is like whiskey and sin. The daunting realization prickles my skin, and my chest constricts with panic. All of a sudden, the light in the restroom goes out, and dread and realization seeps into my bones. He's not one of Dad's bodyguards. He's the enemy.

CHAPTER 3
EMILIANO

We're in a meeting with four out of the ten underbosses. "I just don't see the use of paying off the cops in my ci-" My eyes narrow at Vincent Colombo, the underboss of Baltimore as I cut him off with a warning.

"It's the Camorra's city, not yours, Colombo, and paying off the fucking feds is part of it. You need to make sure they keep sniffing out of our business, or this could end badly for you and them."

"Emiliano, how are the plans for our retaliation on the Outfit going?" he asks me to try to distract from the fact that Vincent is showing blatant disrespect, due to my Pop's death.

My uncle clears his throat.

I turn to him and say, "The plans are going well. We're going to make our way to Chicago after this meeting. Our inside intel has told me that we have the building under our control." I'm being vague on purpose. This plan is between my team and me. No one else. This is my revenge. I stand and button my suit jacket.

"This meeting is over. For now," I declare as I look around at the four underbosses, then Romiro and Lucio. Colombo, being an idiot and not knowing when to shut his mouth, speaks up.

"We still haven't discussed the cocaine shipment that's meant to go through Baltimore. But, of course, you wouldn't remember that since you're still a-"

He doesn't finish his sentence and he never will. Romiro jumps up from his seat and swears under his breath as he tries to avoid getting blood on his suit, running his hand down his tie. I stride toward the door and walk into the corridor, steps echoing as I make my way to the exit.

"Jesus, what the fuck, Emiliano? He's the underboss of one of the Camorra's most important cities, you can't just shoot him like that," Romiro says with a huff as he trails behind me, Lucio at his side. I stuff my gun back into its holster.

"Was." Romiro gives me a puzzled look, so I repeat, "He *was* the underboss of one of the most important cities to the Camorra. Now he's a sack of meat and bones."

"And skin," Lucio adds with a grin. Romiro shakes his head at both of us.

"As Capo, I can do as I see fit. Understood?" I say, Romiro nods and changes the topic.

"The place is secured; our guy has the system hooked to the control panel and the men have got the place surrounded," he tells me, and I give him a curt nod.

"I want to go with you, guys," Lucio says as we get on the elevator and head to the bottom floor.

"No." I shake my head.

Lucio frowns and demands, "You're being an asshole. Come on, let me come with you, guys."

"Absolutely not. I don't care if I'm being an asshole. You're not old enough for this." But the little shit doesn't let it go.

"I am old enough," he argues and, thankfully, Romiro cuts him off.

"You're not even old enough to drink, let alone come with us. This is a very intricate plan. You, Little Lucio, aren't prepared for it."

I snort at Romiro's use of the word "little." Lucio is anything but little. At nineteen, he's already up to my neck, and I'm 6 '5". Lucio punches Romiro's left arm, which he returns with a punch of his own. They continue back and forth until we've reached our cars.

"Get Costa on the phone. I want an update on Dom's health," I tell Lucio as I get into my red Maserati.

He nods and replies, "I texted him an hour ago, but I'll tell him you're expecting a call."

I RUB MY HANDS TOGETHER AS I WATCH THE SCREEN SHOWING MORETTI and the sorry asses they call "security" walk into the Via Veneto club. My eyes stay focused on my target. Little 'Bellissima' Moretti.

That name doesn't even come close to describing her. Her long ebony hair is in soft waves down her back and her lips are painted a vampy red, making her tan more prominent. It's not a chore to pay attention to only her.

I wait for the signal from Romiro to tell me when Moretti finishes his stupid ego boosting speech so I can step in. I begin working on the logistics of our legit business. Folonari's Enterprises.

My phone rings, picking it up without taking my eyes off the screen.

"Si."

"They've arrived and are mingling with their guests now. Moretti just finished his sad excuse of a speech," Romiro informs me.

"I'm in the security room in the opposite building," I tell him.

"I'll be down in a bit." My jaw clenches when one of the tied-up security guards starts mumbling something. I pull my gun out and put the silencer on. No one will hear it from this distance and the place is full of people. His eyes widen to the size of saucers as he takes in what I am about to do and starts thrashing, trying to get free. A bullet pierces right between his eyes, and his body instantly slumps forward, blood pooling underneath him. It takes me all of five minutes to get into the building without being tracked by any of the Morettis or their security.

I stand off to the side near the receptionist's desk, which is empty waiting for the signal, but to my surprise, Little Moretti has come out of the room all by herself. She doesn't see me, as she's lost in her thoughts, turning into a corridor on the other side of the receptionist's desk.

I wait for a bit before heading after her, messaging Romiro about the changes in the plan.

ELI

Change of plans, she's gone to the restroom. I'm going to follow her. I'll call you when I secure the target.

ROM

Whatever you say, bro, but just be quick; it seems that the Moretti bastard wants to leave to go to some restaurant to discuss more business.

ELI

Tucking my phone back into my suit jacket, I run my fingers through my hair. As I push open the door, she's making her way toward it. Her brow furrows when she sees me standing in her way. God, her fucking face looks even more heavenly in person, high cheekbones, almond-shaped, honey-colored eyes.

"Um...sir, this is the women's restroom. The men's is down the corridor," she tries to explain to me, her voice sweet like summer fruit, soft like silk, almost seductive. For fuck's sake, I need to get laid if I'm getting distracted by the enemy's voice. I give her a pointed look, and in response, she raises a black eyebrow at me. Reaching into my suit jacket pocket, I pull out my phone, calling Romiro without taking my eyes off her.

"Target secured." I speak loud and clear enough for her to hear what I said as my eyes travel down her short black dress, leaving her tan legs on display. I can see her taking in my appearance as well. A scowl transforms her expression as she directs it my way, which almost makes me laugh. She resembles an angry puppy.

"If you're one of my dad's bodyguards, you need to wait outside, not in here."

I don't reply to her assumption, but I give her a twisted smile. The lights in the restroom finally go out, and if the guys did their job right, they should be out in the whole damn building. I can't see her face, but I can feel when she realizes who I really am. The enemy.

I take three silent steps to where I know she's still standing and grab her arm, pushing her into the wall. I put my left palm over her mouth before she can scream and lean over to speak near her ear.

"Be a good girl and I won't have to hurt you."

She smells of amber and sweet cinnamon. I feel her nod, so I draw myself back from her, but I don't let my grip go and my palm remains on her lips.

Dragging her out of the restroom, we hear the commotion down the hall. I pick her up and throw her over my shoulder and, as expected, she screams.

"Mom! HELP ME!"

I roll my eyes at her dramatics. What else did I expect from the Moretti girl? As I walk toward the back exit, I don't rush myself, but I feel tiny hits on my back. What. The. Fuck. Is she seriously hitting me?

"Stop it," I command, but she doesn't listen, so I smack her upper thighs just under her ass. That gets her to stop and curse at me.

"Fuck you, asshole," she seethes, and I inhale through my nostrils and pray to God for some patience. I'll need it if I want to leave with her alive.

We reach the back door and find Romiro waiting for us. His eyebrows reach the top of his hairline, and I shake my head at him, jerking my chin at the door, which he opens. The door leads us to the alleyway that's secured by my men, a car is waiting for us.

"Romiro, the cloth," I say to him as I put Valentina down. He passes me the cloth, which is doused with chloroform. She tries to push me, and Romiro and Silvio try to grab her.

"Touch her, and I'll cut off both your hands," I growl at them, and they both step back. I grab her by the waist and put the cloth over her mouth, and within seconds, she is out. Putting one arm under her head and the other under her knees, I walk over to my car with her in my arms. I turn toward Romiro when I hear multiple footsteps coming from down the walkway.

"The Morettis seem to have pulled their heads out of their asses and figured out their daughter was gone," I say before I slide into the driver's seat and promptly drive out of the other end of the alleyway, heading towards the highway. Romiro should be on his way behind me so we can board the jet at Columbus, Ohio.

I call Romiro once I'm on the highway. "Are you on the highway yet?"

"No, not yet," he says, and my eyebrows pull together.

"Why the fuck not?"

"It turned into a bloodbath. We lost two of our men and Moretti's son was shot." *What?*

"Isn't he five years old?" I ask, trying to maintain a calm voice.

"Yes," he confirms. Fuck.

"I instructed everyone to keep the fucking women and children out of the fucking shooting. Who the fuck shot a child? Is he dead?" I hit the steering wheel, nostrils flaring.

"No, he's not. He was shot in the shoulder. I'll have Beneditto, Luigi, and Tito in the cells in the OX once we're in New York. I'll deal with them," he promises.

"No. I'm dealing with them myself." I cut the call without waiting for a response. It wasn't a question; it was a command. I scratch my throat while trying to clear my mind enough to focus on the road.

***

It's been an hour since we left the city, when the Moretti brat decides it's time to open her eyes. I watch as she tries to get up in the back seat, looking confused and disoriented.

She runs her palms sluggishly over her dress, as if to check for any signs of force—as if I'd assault her. Her breathing picks up as she tries to sit up once more with effort, shifting back and forth in her seat.

I'm hoping to drive her to the brink of madness.

She'll probably be easier to control like that, and once she returns to the Outfit, they'll have lost whatever deal they had with the Colombians. Who'd want a crazy woman?

Her eyes finally drift to where I am sitting, and she speaks up.

"Where are you taking me?" Her voice comes out a bit croaky, so she clears her throat.

"That's not for you to know. Now sit back because we've got half an hour till we reach the first destination. Don't try to pull anything off. I can break you in half with one move." The threat is a lie, of course. *I would never hurt her.* I shake off that thought. She's still the enemy.

To my surprise, she obeys and sits back while maintaining eye contact with me through the rear-view mirror. Her honey-colored eyes are now a deep chocolate brown. Dark and delectable. Swallowing, I move my eyes back to the road ahead of me.

"I thought we weren't at war with you." She breaks the silence. I look back at her through the rear-view mirror and give her a crumb of information.

"Your cugino had killed some of our most loyal men." A look of calculation passes over her face before she seems to have figured out whatever puzzle she was trying to solve.

"You know." It wasn't a question, but I thought the Outfit didn't involve their women in mafia business.

She shakes her head and says, "No. We're not allowed to know, or even mention, the Outfit's business. So, I'm of no use to you."

"We're looking for an exchange for something, not information. We have all the information we need." I don't know why I told her that, but I don't look back at her the rest of the ride to the Camorra's private takeoff and landing strip. After another ten minutes of driving in silence, we finally reach Columbus Airport, and I park my car and turn my body to look her in the eyes.

"I am going to get out and open your door. No one here will help you. This is my city, my rules and my people. So, behave, and I won't have to harm you."

She rolls her eyes at me. "This is the third time you've threatened me. Don't you think it's going to lose its effect?"

I run my hand through my hair and tug a bit to get some sense of calmness.

"Who are you?" she asks, and my eyes move back to her.

"Who do you think I am?" I ask her, curious.

She shrugs. "A soldier of the Camorra, I suppose."

A mocking laugh leaves my lips, and I turn to get out, but she grasps my upper bicep. When I look at her sharply, she pulls her hand back as if I had burned her. That's what the simple touch felt like for me, at least.

"Why did you laugh at that? Who are you?" she asks again, and I open my door, but before stepping out, I say the one thing nobody wants to hear.

"Your worst nightmare."

***

ROMIRO ARRIVES AN HOUR AFTER US, LOOKING DISHEVELED WITH HIS blond curls all over the place, his bottom lip busted. He nods at me and heads straight to the mini bar near the two flight attendants who look frightened and scurry to the back. I hide a smirk with my palm, but Romiro spots it and flips me the bird. He drags his feet across the hardwood floors of the jet.

Valentina comes out of the bathroom and stops in her tracks, as if she's taken aback when she spots Romiro. Romiro ignores her as he grabs his glass of bourbon and makes his way to the seat next to me.

"What are we going to do with her when we get home?" He jerks his chin toward Valentina after taking a sip. He doesn't make an effort to lower his voice, and she flips him off and drops onto one of the seats on the other side of the jet.

I shrug my shoulders and say low enough just for him to hear,

"Get Matteo on the phone. I want him to set up the dark net link up and send it to Alvize Moretti's phone when I tell him."

Romiro groans. "Matteo's a brat. All he does is fuck about. He doesn't listen to anyone but you. Why don't you call him?"

"Because I fucking have shit to get done. Call him while I deal with her." I get out of my seat and head toward Valentina, who's trying to convince the flight attendant to help her. Yeah, she has better luck convincing the devil to repent.

"Leave," I order the flight attendant, who scurries away. Valentina glares at her back, then directs the glare to me before she faces forward. I sit in the seat next to her and lean over the armrests. She refuses to look at me, but I continue to look at the side of her face, taking in the slope of her button nose and the small jut of her chin.

Her lashes caress her cheeks every time she blinks. She finally breaks the silence. "Go away."

"No can do." Her eyes narrow slightly, but she still doesn't turn to look at me.

"You know, as much as I love this little game of yours, I don't have time to entertain a little spoiled Moretti brat," I grit out. Romiro snorts, but quickly covers it with his palm when I throw a glare his way.

Valentina's head whips around to face me, and she seethes. "You pompous ass, you-"

I cut her off with a laugh. "Did you just say pompous? Who the fuck says that?"

She turns beetroot red and shifts her face forward again. Narrowing my eyes at her, I turn her face back to me with two fingers under her chin, which she slaps away.

"Watch it, Moretti. Just because I am treating you as a gentleman should treat a woman, that doesn't mean that you're not the enemy, or that you're not the hostage in this situation. Never let yourself forget that."

Just as I'm about to get up, the sign for us to put our seat belts on to depart comes on. She sees it as well and sighs as she buckles herself in.

"Mr. Folonari, we're ready for departure if you want to leave now." The pilot's voice comes out of the sound system, and I press the button that's located at the side of the seat I'm in to indicate that we're ready.

I can see the moment Valentina realizes who I am. Her eyes widen as she turns her head to me, then quickly to the cabin door, looking lost for words. Interesting.

She knows my name, but not how I look. I'm not exactly as popular as her and her sisters with the press. My temper gets the best of me when they get in my face, and they end up with their cameras left in pieces on some sidewalk in Brooklyn.

"Glad to see you're able to put things together yourself without needing someone to spell it out for you," I remark sarcastically, which she clearly doesn't like, as she pinches my hand that's on the armrest at her side.

She fucking pinched my hand. Romiro seems to have seen the whole thing go down because he bursts out laughing.

"Shut the fuck up, Romiro." I grip her jaw in my hand. "Need I remind you why they call me the butcher of the East, or will you behave?"

She looks at me with her eyes full of defiance, defiance I want to squash. When her hand pushes mine off her jaw, I let her do it. My phone buzzes, and I see that Romiro has texted me.

ROM

So it's definitely not love at first sight? Right?

ELI

Shut the fuck up.

You're an idiot.

ROM

Oh, come on. You can't blame me, look at that face.

ELI

Romiro, for the love of everything that's holy. Shut. The. Fuck. Up.

ROM

No. Thanks.

Oh, yeah, btw you have some paperwork to
go through.

ELI

What kind of paperwork?

ROM

It's the contract for the jewelry company to
supply precious gems for other chains.

ELI

Send it over.

ROM

FolonariJewelscontract.PDF

I PRESS ON THE FILE; IT LOADS FOR A COUPLE OF SECONDS BEFORE opening. Reading through it, my eyes ache from going over the same paragraph repeatedly. *Something* doesn't feel right. I don't know what, but I have a feeling in my gut and my gut is never wrong.

I wait for the seatbelt sign to turn off before I get up and grab her arm, tugging a bit. She gets the hint and tugs out of my grip to unbuckle her seat belt.

I'm grabbing her arm again after she's done unbuckling and heading toward the back of the jet, where a room is located. Dragging her in, I slam the door behind us and hold her against it.

"Behave yourself and act like a dignified human and I won't have to tie you up. There's two hours left of this flight. You're going to stay in here and behave yourself like a good girl," I tell her. She juts her chin out and crosses her arms across her chest while narrowing her honey eyes.

"Or what?" she challenges me.

I close my eyes and take a lungful of air in, counting to five in my head.

"Or, when we get to the place we're heading, I'll hang you upside down by your pretty little feet and let you dangle like that till you learn some manners."

Her face turns red again, but this time with anger.

"Manners, yeah, because I'm the one who needs to learn fucking manners. You kidnapped me, asshole. *You* need to learn some manners." She emphasizes her point by driving one finger into my chest. A strand of hair falls over her forehead, and I reach and push it behind her ear like it's a natural reflex. My eyes widen and so do hers. Shaking it off, I grab her hand and move her out of the way, shutting the door behind me and locking it to get some peace of mind. She bangs on the door once, but then stops.

Romiro gives me a smirk, but I shake my head at him and continue toward the mini bar to grab a tumbler of whiskey, then drink it in one go. I can already see a lot of drinking in my future if I'm going to deal with that brat from hell. With a deep breath, I go back to my seat next to Romiro.

"Is the cargo ship arriving tomorrow morning at the Agnes?" I ask, Romiro turns to me and nods before elaborating.

"Yes, but there's talk about the Vipers attacking."

"From whom?" My lips curl.

"Dmitri Orlov."

That has me cracking my knuckles.

"The shipment will arrive as scheduled. If the fucking MC want to try anything, then they can, but they won't be alive by the end of the week," I reply. Romiro looks behind at the door, where I locked Valentina, and then looks back at me.

"She's going to be a handful, I suppose." He's treading on thin ice and knows it.

"Did you call Matteo?" I change the subject.

"He's not picking up," he answers after drinking the rest of his bourbon. I pull out my phone and call Matteo myself.

"Get Boris to roughen her up. I want Moretti to feel like there's a fire under his ass when he sees the live feed of his precious, sheltered daughter being treated like the garbage that he should be treated like," I tell Romiro, who nods at me. My gut clenches and something akin to guilt swirls in my gut. *She's innocent.*

But she's her Dad's daughter, and her Dad is certainly not innocent.

CHAPTER 4

VALENTINA

It's been an hour and a half since that psycho bastard locked me up in the back room of the jet. The only reason I know how long it's been is because there's an alarm clock on the bedside table.

I feel weak, so I decide to sit on the edge of the bed, my nervousness only adding to the effects of whatever he used to get me to pass out. How could I be so fucking stupid to go to the ladies' room without a guard? Unshed tears sting my eyes. I feel nauseous as I wonder what they're going to do to me. Did my parents find out I'm missing? Did anyone notice I'm gone?

The door opens, and my captor walks in. "Come on, you need to be in your seat. We're landing in twenty minutes."

I think of a way to piss him off, but decide against it. After all, he's the Capo of the Camorra. So, I get up slowly and walk toward the door, but he stops me by grabbing my upper arm. His hand is so big that it wraps around my upper arm fully and overlaps his thumb. When I look up at him, I see him glaring down at me.

"Are you going to behave yourself this time?" he asks, lifting a perfect black brow at me. I nod, refusing to speak to this brute. That seems to appease him. My eyes trail over his body, my throat drying as I take in the ink across his forearms, all the way into his rolled up black dress shirt. When my eyes make their way back up to his, I find him already looking at me. He gives me a heated stare before he turns around and opens the door, then gestures for me to walk ahead of him.

This time, he goes and sits back where his original seat was, next to Romiro—if I'd heard his name right—who is watching both of us right now as if we're on some sitcom show he enjoys in his spare time. His neck is craned in our direction, and I flash him a fake smile, which he returns, his more predatory than fake. It drops off his face as soon as it had appeared when his eyes move back to the brute next to him. Something must pass between them because he doesn't turn back around and stares ahead. I continue my way to the front of the plane, to my seat. To my surprise, Romiro gets up once I sit in my seat and heads toward me.

"So, you're the beloved Moretti of the American paparazzi." Romiro seems to have mistaken my fake smile as an invite. I turn my head to tell him to fuck off when I see an opportunity to maybe get something useful out of him.

"If you think you'd get anything out of me,"—he leans his head closer and finishes his sentence—"you're more naive than I thought you were."

My face scrunches up in disgust, more pissed that he caught on to me. "As if I'd want anything from a dirty Camorrista," I snarl. He goes to stand up, but to both our dismay, the seat belt sign lights up, and he mumbles some curses in Italian.

"What's your name?" he asks me.

"You kidnapped me and don't even know who I am?" I answer, exasperated.

He rolls his eyes. "Of course I know who you are. I was just being conversational. Why are you being so bitchy?" Oh God, I really want to slap this idiot.

"Are you honestly being purposefully oblivious, or are you just plain stupid? You fucking kidnapped me and expect me to want to talk to you. Without being bitchy."

"I'm Romiro, thanks for asking." He completely ignores my mini rant and introduces himself as if he's the most important person I'll ever meet.

"And that asshole over there"—he points his thumb back, to where the brute is sitting talking on the phone, his eyes glued to the back of our heads, and he narrows them when he sees that we've turned around to look at him—"is Emiliano Folonari."

I roll my eyes. Of course, my dad had managed to piss off the Camorra's Capo. Which in turn, gets me kidnapped. My kidnapper is known as the butcher of the East Coast. A shudder passes down my spine when Emiliano's eyes zero in on me.

I turn my attention back to Romiro, trying to appear unfazed.

"Can I at least know the reason for my abduction?" I ask, and Romiro wiggles his index finger in my face as if he's scolding a child.

"God, the tabloids said you were beautiful, but they didn't mention your dramatics," he says.

The flight attendant cuts our conversation short to tell us we've landed in New York City. My jaw clenches at how far I am from home and the fact that I'm now in the heart of the Camorra's territory. The prospect of finding a way out is slim to none. Hell will freeze over before I'm able to do that.

Romiro gets up once Emiliano reaches us, and I struggle to unbuckle my seat belt. My palms are too sweaty for this, but I need to stay calm. That's the only way for me to keep my sanity.

"Here, you need to wear this." Emiliano passes me some sort of black fabric once I'm out of my seat.

I must look confused because he elaborates. "Tie it around your eyes, unless..." I lift an eyebrow at him, and he continues. "Unless you want to be knocked out again."

I quickly shake my head and wrap the fabric around my eyes. Which causes both men to laugh. Dicks. One of them grabs my upper arm and leads me toward what I assume to be the exit.

"I'm going to pick you up," Emiliano whispers in my ear, and before I can protest, he's done just that. I am being put into a car before I know it, and the door slams, causing me to flinch.

I feel really vulnerable. I can hear everything around me, but I can't see shit. The sound of the engine purrs to life and the car begins to move, but I don't have any sense of direction so I have no clue which way we're driving.

"Don't you think this is a bit extra?" I think Romiro is the one who's speaking, but I'm not too sure.

"No, she isn't our guest." I assume that's Emiliano.

"I can hear you, guys, by the way. You know that, right?" I say to the void. Well, not the void, but it is to me.

"You're really fucking calm for someone who was taken by force." Romiro's voice comes from the right. I shrug.

"Not the first time," I tell him.

"So, we didn't get to pop your kidnapping cherry, what a shame."

I choke on air, and I hear a weird noise that sounds like a smack, followed by, "What the fuck, Eli?"

"Stop saying weird shit, Esposito, or you'll end up in the Atlantic." Emiliano's threat seems to pass over Romiro's head.

"I thought you said I couldn't become a pirate."

"Wait, Nicolo Esposito is related to you?" I cut their mini argument.

"He's not just my relative. He's my big brother," he replies.

My eyebrows reach my forehead, and I blurt out, "You have a big brother?"

"Yes, why is that surprising?" he asks.

I shrug again. "I don't know. You give off only-child vibes."

"Vibes?" he asks like a scoff, but before I can answer, Emiliano speaks up.

"The both of you are causing me a headache the size of the Middle East. Shut up."

"You're just jealous she likes to converse with me better than you," Romiro retorts.

Emiliano answers with, "Since when do you say 'converse'? You're a fucking idiot."

"I'm going to tell your Mom you're being an asshole again," Romiro threatens, as if that would work on the Capo of the Camorra, but Emiliano doesn't respond.

We drive for another thirty minutes with both Emiliano and Romiro exchanging insults. They sound like five-year-old children. Not even Marcello behaves this way. I wonder how he's doing. My poor baby brother. I wish I hugged him when he'd gotten out.

I thought it would keep him safe if we all stayed away from him, but now, I don't know when I'll see him again, or if I'll ever be able to.

We drive for another ten minutes, this time in silence, and then the car comes to a complete stop. I can hear the sound of two car doors opening and shutting, and two voices speaking, but I can't make out what they're saying.

Then the blindfold is taken off and I blink a couple of times so that my eyes can adjust to the light. Emiliano is leaning to my right with the blindfold in his hands.

He stares at me for a beat, and my face heats, which he notices. He's about to say something, but instead, he moves out the way and says, "Come on."

"You owe me ten grand now." Romiro is standing on the side of the car that I've come out of, and he smirks at Emiliano across the hood of the car.

"You bet on me?" What the actual fuck is wrong with these people? All I get is a shrug from Romiro and a grunt from Emiliano that closely sounds like "fucking Morettis losing me money."

My eyes wander around where we've stopped. It's a parking garage full of different cars. I look behind us to see an iron gate that appears to be around half a mile away, and to my surprise, there are no guards patrolling. If I thought I had a glimmer of hope to escape from the clutches of the Camorra, it's squashed now because they'll catch me before I can even step foot out the front doors. Emiliano's voice cuts through my depressing thoughts.

"You'll be leaving on my terms and my terms alone. Don't trick yourself into believing that you stand a chance of returning home without my permission. Now come on." He begins to walk toward the doors of an elevator while both I and Romiro stay behind, before I decide there is no use pissing them off.

Romiro walks beside me and whispers, "If your Dad loves you, he'll give us what we want by the end of this week." My Dad, love me? My Dad doesn't love anyone but himself, money, and walking STDs. Right now, the enemy is treating me better than he ever did. I give Romiro a weak smile, but I don't reply. Emiliano stands near the entrance of the elevator, his arms folded across his chest, making him appear even larger than he already is.

The elevator pings and the doors slide open. It has three mirrors, one on the sliding doors and two on the right and left of us. Black velvet covers the back wall.

The doors open to a large entrance area, which has six different doors. Emiliano grabs my upper arm and drags me toward the far-left door. It leads to stairs down to what I assume to be a basement. He lets me go ahead of him, which means that there is nowhere else to go, nowhere to possibly escape.

My suspicion is confirmed once we've stepped on the bottom landing and all I can see is rows of metal cells. The walls are damp. The smell of blood and other things so thick and prominent in the air that it makes bile rise in my throat, which I force back down.

"Come on," Emiliano mumbles as he walks to the first cell to the right. Opening it, he motions for me to get in. With my stomach churning, I decide it's best I do what he wants in case he goes all butcher style on me.

"I'll send down someone in a minute to give you some food," he informs me once he finishes locking me in.

The cell is empty except for a piece of fabric with a thin cushion on the floor. Probably there to be like a bed or something. I pace around the small cell, trying to figure out how I can find a way out of this place without being spotted.

I don't want to go back to Chicago. If I can escape, it'll mean I can escape the clutches of my Dad too, and he'll be none the wiser. I shake my head; I'm getting ahead of myself. First, I need to get out of here without getting caught.

My thoughts are interrupted by the sound of the cell door being opened. I look up, and to my surprise, it's a woman who's entered. A woman who doesn't seem to be that much older than me and is wearing close to nothing, which makes me blush red. She laughs softly once she sees my expression and elaborates on why she's wearing lingerie while walking around.

"Have you never seen what a working girl looks like?"

"Oh. No, sorry, I don't know what a working girl even is," I tell her, feeling my face heat up in embarrassment at my ignorance.

"A prostitute, darling. I'm a prostitute," she supplies. I grimace at her bluntness before looking around.

"What is this place, exactly?" I ask her. Her face morphs into a look of dismay, as if what she's about to answer will make me feel a certain type of way.

"You're at the Diamond." When she doesn't see anything change in my expression, she continues. "It's a whorehouse."

My eyes mist over and the room spins.

They brought me to a whorehouse. Oh my God. What the hell are they planning on doing? The woman must sense my panic rising because she comes farther into the cell and places her manicured hand on my shoulder.

"Listen, I know that you're scared and rightfully so, but don't worry. No one here will force anything on you."

I don't believe her, but it does ease the tightening in the middle of my chest. She holds a plastic plate up to me, and once I take it, she turns to leave, but I open my mouth.

"Wait..." I say. She turns around. "Uhhh...could you maybe..."

"You want me to stay with you?" she asks, and I nod in answer. I don't know why I want her to stay, but I know I don't want to be here alone.

We both head toward the sheets on the floor and sit on them.

"I'm Ruby. What's your name?" she asks after I take a bite out of a stale piece of bread.

"My name's Valentina," I tell her after I swallow the gross piece of stale bread. We both fall quiet, and the only sound is me eating my food. Every time I swallow, I feel as if she could hear it.

"Do you know what they're going to do with me?"

She shrugs and says, "Sorry, Valentina, but I have no clue. You were brought in by the Capo himself."

My head hangs a bit because I feel stupid to think that they'd tell a prostitute who works for them what they plan to do with their captive. Once I'm done with the food, she gets up and dusts off her clothes—or whatever there is of them anyways.

"I have to go now, or I'll get in trouble. The Johns here don't like waiting for long." I give her a small nod, not wanting to talk anymore. Exhaustion weighs heavily on me.

<hr />

I'D FALLEN ASLEEP. I DON'T KNOW FOR HOW LONG, BUT I JOLT UP FROM the spot I'm sleeping on. My back aches, and I feel more tired than I was before. Stretching my arms, I look around.

The place is empty, just me in here. My neck is stiff, so I try to rub it to see if that'll help, but all it does is intensify the stiffness to an uncomfortable knot. I lie back down to see if it'll help relax the muscles.

My ears perk up at the sound of footsteps coming down the stairs. I don't get up, trying to appear as if I haven't heard them. I focus my eyes on a spot on the concrete floor near the cell door.

It oddly resembles a bloodstain. I grimace at the thought that someone more than likely died here. The footsteps sound closer than they were a couple of seconds ago. A pair of black Oxford shoes are now in front of the cell door. Then whoever it is clears their throat as if to summon my attention.

I look up, only to find that psycho Capo is the one standing in front of the cell door. My nose wrinkles as my eyebrows pull together. He continues to look at me with what seems to be a mixture of disgust, curiosity, and amusement, as if I'm some circus monkey for him to be entertained by.

"What?" I bite out, unable to bear the unnerving stare of his. He runs his tongue over his teeth like a predator when they spot their prey, and the look in his eyes sends a chill down my spine as my blood cools.

"How old are you?" His question throws me off. I blink once, twice, and then a third time before I decide to reply.

"Twenty-one, why?" I retort, and he shakes his head at me, as if refusing to answer me.

"Why did your dad attack my territory three months ago?" he asks, I frown.

"I don't know. I thought you said you knew all the information you needed to."

His lips set into a line, displeased with my response. He slides his hands into his suit pants, then rolls his shoulders, as if that would ease the tension in them. As he clenches his jaws once, he sees me observing him, and I flash him the fakest smile I can muster up. He returns it with a wolfish one of his own. The smile makes two dimples appear on each of his cheeks, but they disappear as soon as they have appeared, and his face returns to its resting constipated look that seems like it's natural state. Such a shame; he would be gorgeous if he wasn't an asshole.

"How old are you?" I blurt out before I can stop myself. Christ, I need to get a grip.

"I'm twenty-seven." Oh, he's older than he looks. Even with the light stubble, he still looks around twenty-four. As if he senses my thoughts, he runs his palm over his jaw. His hands are tattooed. I can't make out what they are, but there's more ink peeking from his dress shirt, swirling all the way up his neck.

"Where's Romiro?" I ask him when the silence becomes uncomfortable. I don't know why he's here if he isn't going to speak. His light blue eyes darken as soon as the question leaves my mouth, turning the color of the ocean at night.

His brow furrows and his eyes narrow into thin slits before he barks out, "Romiro's whereabouts are none of your business, and you will not ask questions."

My face scrunches up in a scowl.

"Go fuck yourself, you brute," I shout back. He grinds his jaw, trying to control whatever he wants to say.

With that, Emiliano turns to the side and heads toward the stairs. He's leaving already? Did he come down here just to piss me off, or what? Men are actually so dramatic. Or maybe it's a Made man thing.

The lights go out five minutes later. For fuck's sake. My breathing picks up. I've always been scared to sleep in the dark. At least in our house, I could use a bedside lamp. Here, it's complete and utter darkness.

A scream leaves my lips when I think something has grabbed my arm, but it's just my imagination playing tricks on me. I lay my head on my knees and close my eyes. *1, 2, 3, 4, 5, 6...* I open one eye to see if the lights are back on, only to be met with the darkness again.

CHAPTER 5
EMILIANO

I sit behind the security cameras in the office as I watch Valentina cradle her head between her knees. I cut the power in the basement around two minutes ago to scare her straight; the only reason I can see her is because the cameras down there use infrared technology. Matteo's such a little genius for suggesting and programming them himself so we can always watch whoever we're keeping down there.

"Did you seriously cut the lights down there?" Romiro says from behind me. I ignore him as I continue to watch the brat squirm and jump away from the corner as if she's felt something grab her. It could be a rat.

"Do we have rats down there?" I ask Romiro, turning to look at him when he doesn't answer me.

He shrugs. "I don't fucking know, man, but I sure as fuck hope not. We're not here to torture the poor girl; she's just leverage so we could get that little shit Giuseppe." I narrow my eyes at him. He seems to care way too much for someone who's meant to be the enemy. Romiro holds his hands up, as a show of surrendering with a small smile playing on his lips. I know what he'll say before he even says it.

"If you feel so strongly about her, why didn't you say so? Your face is green with jealousy, and let me tell you, Eli, green isn't your color."

I flip him the bird and turn back around to look at the screen. Valentina is curled up into a tight ball that I almost miss her.

I think that's enough psychological damage for the day. I flick the button, which floods the room with light. She doesn't seem to notice for about a minute. Then when she peeks her head out of the small cocoon she'd made with her body and notices the lights are on, it looks like she releases a sigh.

"Come on. We need to go to the OX, but before that, we need to head to my place. I need a change of clothes and a shower." I tap Romiro's arm as I pass him. He follows behind me as we head toward the elevator doors.

As soon as the elevator doors slide open, my phone rings in my pocket. I slide it out to see that it's my Mom calling me.

"Hey, Ma."

"Don't 'hey Ma' me, Emiliano Folonari, where on earth are you? You've been gone for two weeks and haven't even bothered to call to check on your poor Mom," she scolds. Romiro can tell my Mom, bless her heart, has gone on a rant because he's grinning from ear to ear like the fucking Cheshire Cat, and knows that she won't be stopping till she's talked my ear off.

"Listen, Emiliano, once you get to New Hampshire, there's a sweet young lady I'd like to-"

"No, Ma, I already have enough on my plate as is. I don't want to date anyone now."

"First, don't cut me off again, or else you'll have something flying toward your head. Second, I didn't say you should date her." I wait for her to drop the other shoe because she always tries to pull this kind of shit. I'm glad she's doing better since Dad's death three months ago, but she's hyper-fixating on getting me with someone. Which irritates the fuck out of me, but she's my Mom and she's grieving. "I meant, you should marry her, figlio." Oh, for the love of everything holy. Why does she keep trying to marry me off every chance she gets?

"Listen, Ma, I have to go. I have a meeting."

By the time I'm able to hang up the phone, my Mom managed to convince me to go to New Hampshire in a couple of days. We get into my car, and Romiro can't keep his big mouth shut for a second.

"So, any thoughts on what we should do with Valentina?" he asks. I speed out of the parking garage and onto the busy streets of New York City. My jaw clenches as I remember the searing feeling that had settled in the pit of my stomach when she had asked for Romiro.

"*We* are not going to be doing anything. I will be the one to handle that Moretti brat from now on. You're being too lenient with her."

"She likes me better, doesn't she?" he asks smugly. I'm about to rebuttal his assumption, when he continues. "You know it won't hurt to be nice to her. Besides, she's easy on the eyes." I break harder than I normally would, which causes him to be slammed back into his seat. "You're just being an asshole now," he whines. I grin at him and nod at the red light we're stopped at.

"I'm not an asshole, I'm your Capo, and I demand the respect I expect from one of my soldiers."

After that, the rest of the ride is spent in comfortable silence.

It doesn't take us long to make it to the Auriga complex building. Parking my car, we both get out.

"I'll be done in about an hour. What about you?" I jut my chin at Romiro as I slam my car door shut and lock it.

"Same. If I take longer, just go ahead of me. I'll follow you to the OX," he says as we head into the elevator. He inserts his key first, then presses the floor below the top one. The top floor belongs to me and only I have access to that floor. No one else. I put my key in and scan my thumb, then when the light turns green, we begin to ascend.

"Hey, Rom, next time, dial it back on the Prince Charming act. She's the enemy, not your next conquest," I tell him once he gets off on his floor.

"No can do, Capo. Besides, Prince Charming doesn't have shit on me," he says before the doors close and the elevator ascends to my floor.

It's been an hour since both Romiro and I left for the OX. It's quite far, just on the outskirts of New York City. The parking lot is empty right now since the next fight isn't until later in the week, and the fact that it's close to nine in the morning.

We head inside and see Diego manning the front desk, scrolling through the betting system we have set up on the darknet.

"Anything I should know about?" I ask Diego, once Romiro and I stop in front of the desk.

"No, boss, except that we've made half a million on the last two fights," he says, grinning. We've doubled our profits over the past three months.

"Keep up the good work, Diego." I head toward the bar area and grab a cool beer from behind the counter, throwing one to Romiro. Catching it, he cracks it open with his teeth.

We make our way down the spiral stairs toward the basement. Down there is Beneditto, Luigi, and Tito dangling from the ceiling by their arms, naked, with tape over their mouths and a small piece of cloth each that covers their genitals. Soon, there won't be anything there worth covering. Not that there is any to begin with. I place the beer bottle down on the floor beside me.

Romiro heads to the control center to lower them till their feet are nearly touching the ground. One of the three groans, as the drug's effects seem to be wearing off. Tito's eyes twitch for a couple of seconds before they fly open and widen as he realizes the position that he is in. I can almost taste the bitter taste of his fear on my tongue. My face twists as I take in the look on each of their faces. One by one, they wake up and their expressions morph with fear and absolute defeat. I crack my knuckles while heading toward them. The chains clang together and make loud noises as they each struggle to try to get free of their chains.

"Remind me, boys, what had the instructions been when we set out for Chicago?" Romiro comes to stand next to me, tight-lipped with a grim expression. Gone is his boyish behavior; instead, a trained killer standing in his place. I keep my eyes trained on the three soldiers chained up in front of me. None of them answers my question, causing me to sigh.

"You know I expect absolute and utter respect from my men, but it seems you failed to even deliver that." I extend my hand, in which Romiro places my dagger. Dragging my forefinger and thumb across the blade, I slowly look each of them in the eye. This makes them even more restless, causing more clinging and clanging of the chains.

I step toward Tito, who, unlike the other two, seems to be less panicked. Romiro's footsteps echo in the empty basement as he steps back toward the control center and sets the controls for the other two to return dangling in the air. Tito's chains remain where they are.

"Boss, we didn-" Tito stops trying to explain once he feels the blade pierce the skin between his collarbone and drag toward the area between his pecs.

"I made specific instructions on who we were to shoot, if we needed to do so. You and the other two meatheads didn't follow through with my clear orders."

"AHHHHH!" He thrashes as he tries to move away from the blade, but it's no use. Romiro appears behind him and grabs his midsection to keep him steady, but lets it go once I shake my head at him.

"You go take care of one of the other two." I jerk my chin at him, to which he nods and heads back in the direction of the controllers. Turning back to Tito, I say, "Tito, you know what happens to soldiers who don't obey orders. I will not tolerate disobedience. But the issue isn't that you ignored direct orders from your Capo..."

I direct the blade to where his arms bend at the elbows and push the blade in while also sliding across, causing the skin to break and some blood to ooze out and slowly trickle down his arm.

"The fucking issue is the fact that you shot a child, a defenseless little child. That is something I won't forgive. I might have forgiven the disobedience to direct orders, but *that,* I will not."

His breathing picks up as I direct my blade toward his face, and when he starts to thrash, I grab his cheeks. The blade punctures his eye.

"LET ME GO, YOU SICK FUCK!" Blood hemorrhages as I continue to press my blade into his eye socket.

"KILL ME! JUST KILL ME ALREADY!" The blood sprays all over my face and clothes, but I continue to press.

"LET ME GO!" His eyes roll to the back of his head—or, well, one of his eyes does—and his shoulders slump as he passes out. I check if he has a pulse. He does, but it's weak. I continue to gouge out his left eye, and it rolls to the floor once I cut it out of its socket. The pungent smell of blood fills the air.

"Romiro, grab the drugs. Tito has passed out already," I instruct him as I walk to the bathroom in the corner of the room. I look at myself in the mirror. My face is so drenched in blood that it almost drips off my chin. My black shirt looks wet, but you can't tell what it's soaked in. Unless you smell it.

I move onto Beneditto and repeat the same thing on him, except I go for his tongue this time instead of his eye. Which doesn't make him lose consciousness, but when I drill nails into his shoulders, he froths at the mouth before passing out.

By the time we're done, both Romiro and I are soaked in blood from head to toe and the three men dangle lifeless from the ceiling, or at least what is left of them.

"Romiro, tell Eugine to clean up this mess, but to leave the men here. I want a mandatory meeting by noon tomorrow," I order as we head up the stairs.

"You want it here?" he asks.

I slant him a look as we head toward the locker room to get cleaned up and change before we head back and, without another word, he nods in understanding.

WHEN I LEAVE THE STALL AND HEAD TO MY LOCKER WHERE I KEEP A change of clothes, I see that Romiro has already finished and is probably waiting for me. I spot both he and Lucio as I step out of the changing room.

"Did Matteo set up the link?" I ask, directed at either of them, as we leave the corridor and head toward the main entrance.

"He did. When do you want to use it?" Lucio's the one to reply.

"Possibly tomorrow night." They follow me out, both Lucio's and my car the only ones in the parking lot. The sun is peeking out over the horizon, which means that it's still early hours of the morning.

"Did you call Eugine?" I question Romiro as I open my car door.

"Yes, they'll be here in five minutes. Where are we going now?"

Romiro is getting restless because he's gotten less than three hours of sleep.

I roll my eyes at him. "We're going to check on the cargo that arrived from the Japanese, then we'll head to the warehouse for a little visit. Matteo spotted some mistakes on the shipment sheets."

Romiro's face breaks out into a wide grin as he says, "You're not going all the Fourth of July massacre style on us again, are you?" I don't react to his comment about the rampage Lucio and I had gone on after our Pop's death.

"Lucio texted he's going to New Hampshire," he says. I nod at Romiro, not paying attention to what he's saying anymore.

We weave through traffic faster than we anticipated and make it to the Agnes port in twenty minutes. Mariano is waiting for us by the port's parking space. Lowering his head in greeting, he opens my car door once the car comes to a stop, and I pat his shoulder as I get out.

"Mariano, why are you here? Did I not instruct you to stay in Las Vegas?" I interrogate him as we make our way to the back of the port where our men are manning the cargo.

"Boss, shit's about to hit the fan in Vegas. Lorenzo Vitielli is dead, and his underbosses have separated. Vegas is free for the taking," he informs me, and I pause to look at him.

"Doesn't Vitielli have five legitimate sons and one bastard?" I ask.

"They were in France locked up in a boarding school, but they're gone. No one knows where the fuck they went." My eyes narrow at the revelation, jaw clenching. The eldest of the Vitielli brothers is just fourteen. Where the fuck could they have gone? I don't need more shit to worry about; I already have restlessness in my ranks since I've taken over. I don't need rumors of a fucking mafia revolution making rounds in my territory.

"Stay here. Mariano, keep your ears pierced for any disloyalty and make an example of those who dare to step out of line," I order, at which he nods and slips back to the shadows where he blends in. Romiro opens his mouth to say something, but I shake my head at him.

"Not here. Wait till we get back to my apartment."

He nods, and we continue our walk in silence. There are around twenty soldiers guarding the three cargo containers. A large man is standing in front of the cargo container, and Nicolo Esposito is speaking on the phone, but quickly ends the call and hugs his brother.

"Nicolo, how are you? How's business?" I ask him as we shake hands. His face breaks out into a smile that looks at odds with his harsh features and his emerald eyes remain vacant.

"Business is going great. How's New York been since you've taken over? My brother's not giving you a hard time, is he?" His question might seem like he's making basic conversation, but he's a snake trying to sense any weakness before there is one. Romiro might be on our side, but that doesn't mean that Nicolo is. He's a wild card.

"New York has seen worse days," Romiro answers him as he drags his older brother toward the port's parking lot.

Turning to the cargo container, I motion for the guard to open it.

"Make sure to take inventory of everything. I don't want the Japanese to think that we'll tolerate them trying to fuck us over." The men start to pile in, dragging out sacks filled with wheat. At least that's what you'll see when you rip it open and not dig around.

"Silvio texted. He thinks it'll be better to set up the camera and send the link out earlier." Romiro informs me as he jogs closer. Nicolo seems to have left. In what, I don't know, and I don't give a fuck as long as he sticks his nose somewhere other than my business.

"Ask him why. I want details. I'm not moving shit if I'm not convinced."

"I think it's because there's talk about the Vipers showing up to the whorehouse tonight," he explains.

"What the fuck do you mean, they might show up? Sort it out, Romiro. They better behave themselves if they're in my territory. I don't need a fucking headache." My jaw tightens. He pulls out his phone and dials someone's number then puts it on speaker.

"Silvio, why do you want to move up the plan?" There's the sound of paper shuffling on the line before he blows out a sigh.

"Mrs. Folonari called. Mara's snuck out last night, and she refuses to tell everyone where she went."

A scowl settles on my face. Romiro's eyes narrow as he studies me.

"What the fuck do you mean? Where were her guards? How can you allow my little sister out of your fucking sight? I trusted you as one of my best fucking men."

A deafening silence falls.

"Silvio, the Capo asked you something." Romiro urges as a hard edge takes over in his voice.

"Honestly, boss, I have no fucking clue, but Lucio is already in New Hampshire to deal with them, and Matteo is also looking through the camera footage to figure out how she was able to bypass the security."

"Find the fuck out. I expect a report on how the fuck the men under your training failed."

Romiro ends the call and slips the phone back into his pocket.

"We're going back to the Diamond," I order Romiro as I head to my car.

"I told the men to tie the Moretti girl and to make sure that she had something over her mouth," Romiro informs me as he jogs behind me. I roll my shoulders, trying to rid the tension that settles into my muscles.

"Get in. I don't fucking care what you guys did, just make sure everything is being set up." His eyebrows lift as he looks at me with his hand on the car door. "Get in, Esposito. I don't have all fucking day," I repeat. He slams the door after he gets in, making me shake my head at his childishness.

"You go monitor Silvio, Boris, and the Moretti brat while they set up the camera," I tell him as I drive out of the parking lot.

"Where are you going?"

I shoot Romiro a look to remind him that I am his Capo, not someone who answers to him. He nods, and we settle into silence as I drive through the traffic to reach the Diamond.

Once we reach the Diamond, both Romiro and I get out of the car. Romiro heads down the corridor toward the door to do as he was ordered. I shake my head at the change in his attitude. Romiro has always struggled with authority, whether it was the law or the hierarchy of the Camorra.

Opening my office door, I step into the cool room. At my desk, someone knocks on the door as I'm shuffling the accounting papers for the club.

"Come in." My voice booms after I sit in my chair. Vivian enters the room and closes the door behind her.

I stay quiet, waiting for her to tell me the reason why she is in my office so early in the day. Her blonde hair is as always, styled like she is a 70s housewife.

"Emiliano, there's a problem."

I lift my eyebrow, urging her to continue.

"Donnie Gambi still hasn't paid his debt off."

Fucking Donald Gambi. I told Stefano to keep his nephew in check.

"How much?"

She shuffles around before her eyes meet mine.

"Half a million." So, the idiot had been gambling as well.

"Is that just from the whores he's been fucking, or...?" I implore, and she shakes her head.

"He's been requesting Jasmine every night for the past six months."

What the fuck is wrong with the Gambi men and expensive whores?

I run my hand across my mouth as I try to think of a solution that won't cause a war on my turf. After all, the Gambi family is a crucial family in my operations. They supply some of my weapons.

"Tell the bouncers he's not allowed in anymore, not until he pays off his debts," I tell her. She spins around to leave, but I stop her. "And Vivian, next time, take this up with Gregory. I don't have the fucking time for child's play."

Her head bobs in a nod before she scurries out the door.

A call to Stefano is going to be necessary. I hate that fucker. Sliding my phone out of my pocket, I call Gambi's number.

He picks up after the third ring. "Folonari, to what do I owe the displeasure for receiving this phone call?"

"That would be Donnie, your nephew," I say without greeting him. He's silent for a second before he speaks again.

"What did Donald do?"

The corners of my lips tip up in a condescending smile, even though he cannot see it.

"He owes us some money, so I thought a call to you would have been more...appropriate since we have a mutual agreement." The threat isn't obvious, but Stefano will understand what I mean. Those indebted to the Camorra get one warning, his nephew gets two. This call and the bouncers telling him to fuck off.

There's shuffling of some papers before he asks, "How much?" I lean back into my seat.

"Half a million," I tell him. Some commotion seems to happen on the other end of the phone before it settles.

"The money will be in the club's account by noon tomorrow."

The line goes dead.

I get up and straighten my clothes, time for some fun.

Once I enter the room, I can see Boris eyeing Valentina while Romiro is talking to him, and my right eye twitches. Breathing through my nostrils instead of gauging out his eyeballs, I head to where Silvio is setting up the camera and microphones.

"When will it be ready?" I ask him.

"In a minute, boss," he answers without looking up from the setup.

Romiro comes toward us and says in a low voice, "I think you should dismiss Boris; he's being extra creepy with Valentina." I slant a look at him, which shuts him up. Boris knows better than to try anything that he isn't being told. If he does, he knows the price he'll pay. His life.

"All done, boss. You just have to press the large red button to start it and again to end it," Silvio announces once he straightens. I give him a nod and tell him he can leave. Once he's gone, I open Matteo's messages.

ELI

Send the link.

MATTEO

It's activated.

Romiro opens the cell door, then comes to stand beside me, behind the camera. I click the start button, which starts flashing red, and give Boris the go-ahead. He heads toward the cell door and Valentina backs away toward the concrete wall. Her wrists are tied with a white rope, and she has a gag wrapped around her mouth. She has the look of a caged animal in her eyes. Boris grabs her arm and yanks her out of the cell as agreed. He is short and stubby, but he's still taller than Valentina, which gives him an advantage.

Pulling at her hair, he smacks her. A grinding sound comes from my jaw, alerting me to the fact that I am clenching my teeth. Boris is veering off the script already. I see Romiro look at me from the corner of my eye, but I refuse to take my eyes off Valentina and Boris. At this point, Boris paws at Valentina's dress and rips one of the sleeves. Time slows down as she struggles to get out of his hold.

Valentina's head slowly turns in my direction, her face tear-stricken as she makes eye contact with me. As if to ask for my help.

Like on autopilot, I fly across the room, separating them and grabbing Boris by the throat. I throw him against the wall, my grip tightening with each word that escapes his mouth.

"Boss, you told me it's what I should do."

A red mist has taken over my self-control and my grip continues to tighten as his face grows ashier by the nanosecond. I don't stop. I don't stop when his pathetic eyes roll to the back of his head, and I don't stop when he claws at my arms. I also don't stop when I hear bones cracking and blood overflowing over my hands and over my wrists, and not when he begins to choke on his own blood as it fills his airways. Romiro has to drag me from his limp body.

My chest moves rapidly with the effort of breathing. I look back to where Valentina is and find her on the floor, her mascara running down her rosy cheeks. She looks exhausted, staring at the lifeless body, skin, and blood on the concrete floor, the bone that punctured Boris's neck and caused him to hemorrhage sticking out clear as day. The air is tainted with the tangy metal smell of the blood oozing from the sack of meat laying on the ground behind me. When she finally looks at me, she flinches, her eyes void of any emotion but fear.

"Romiro, take her to the doctor," I instruct him as I leave the room and take the stairs two at a time. I wipe my hands on my pants as I make my way to my office to get cleaned up. I don't know what happened there.

I don't think I want to know.

CHAPTER 6

VALENTINA

My chest heaves with the effort of holding in my cries.

Bile rises in my throat as the smell of blood fills my nose. The man that Emiliano had ordered to assault me is dead on the floor by the hands of the same man.

Emiliano looked like a man possessed when he slowly crushed that man's throat. It was terrifying. I caught a glimpse of the madness that the Made men talked about in gatherings, but that wasn't what had terrified me the most.

What terrified me the most was the satisfaction I had felt seeing that man slowly be crushed to death within the hands of such ruthlessness. *Cazzo.*

Romiro heads my way after Emiliano instructed him to take me to the house doctor. He reaches his hand toward me, but retreats when I flinch. He steps back to give me space so I can get up. Once I do, he tilts his head and points at the rope that's tied around my wrists. I nod since I can't speak around the gag.

As he steps closer, I take the time to appraise him. He has a jagged scar that runs from the middle of his cupid's bow to the corner of his mouth. His eyes lift to see me watching him and his lips twist into a flirty smile. It drops when I move back and yank the gag down for it to hang from my neck. I wince as I notice the redness forming on my sleeveless arm. I am going to fucking bruise.

"Come on." Romiro breaks the silence, and when I look up at him, he motions for me to follow. I take slow steps toward the stairs, feeling a little disoriented. Once we reach the corridor, I follow Romiro in silence as he guides me through the place, and then we come to a stop in front of a wooden door.

Romiro knocks and a man opens the door, filling the frame with his tall, lean stature. I lift my eyes to look at his face and, holy shit, is he good looking. His eyes are a light amber shade and his blond hair is slicked back, wearing a long white coat. So, he's the doctor. I squint my eyes at him, which makes him raise an eyebrow at me before he steps aside and lets us in. Romiro lets me walk in ahead of him before following.

"What can I help you with, Rom?" the doctor asks, as I take a look at the room. Dull cream walls and a black carpet muffles our steps. There's a desk in the far back corner of the room with a laptop and some papers. Next to the desk is a door that nearly blends with the wall perfectly if it wasn't for the black doorknob. I look to my right and see that there's an examining table.

"Eli wants you to make sure she isn't physically hurt," Romiro informs him. I face them and scoff at the way he phrases it. As if that brute doesn't want to hurt me. It makes both men turn to look at me.

"What the fuck are you two looking at?" My voice comes out soft, unlike how I intended. It makes Romiro laugh and the handsome doctor gives me a small smile. His smile might be breathtaking, but it seems cold, calculated, and almost deliberate in a sense.

"Would you get on the examining table, please?" the doctor asks me after he shoots Romiro a blank stare, who is still laughing. I send a glare Romiro's way and hop on the table with my legs dangling off the edge.

"I just want to have a look at your cheek and your arm. They seem to be the ones that need immediate attention. After that, I'm going to check if your eyes are fine." The doctor walks me through the examination, being careful not to make me uncomfortable. He grips my chin, turning my face from side to side before tapping my cheek. I wince, and he gives me an apologetic smile.

"I'll give you an ice pack for this; it seems like it will be swelling soon. Do you have a headache?" My temples throb, and I feel a bit sick in my stomach.

"Yes," I tell him as he examines my bruised arm.

"Could you tell me how it feels? Is it pulsing? Is it on only one side or both sides?"

"It feels like there's something pressing on both sides of my head," I explain.

He hums but doesn't say anything, then walks off after he's done examining my arm. When he comes back, he has an ice pack in his hand and two pills.

"Here's some paracetamol for that headache and here's your ice pack. Other than that, you seem to be fine, but I do recommend that you keep monitoring her and make sure she's drinking enough water." He says the last part to Romiro before he moves to the desk in the far corner and sits behind it to write something. I look at Romiro, who shrugs at me before asking the doctor.

"So, she's fine?"

"Yes, that's what I said, Romiro. There isn't anything wrong." He replies as he continues to write. Romiro scratches his head.

"Then what the fuck are you writing?" he asks.

"I am writing a report for you to give to the boss." Well, he's definitely straight to the point. The room settles into a silence, the only sounds the shuffling of paper and the scratch of the pen.

After a couple of minutes, the doctor gets up and walks toward Romiro. He extends his arm and hands Romiro the sheet of paper. I decide to get off the examining table and head to the door.

"Wait a second." It's the doctor who stops me. I turn to look at him, but I'm met with his retreating back as he steps over to a large metal cabinet. Opening it, he picks something up and comes back my way. Once he reaches me, he extends his hand out. I look down at what he's giving me and to say that I am shocked is the least of it.

Clothes... He's giving me clean clothes. I reach my hand out tentatively and take them.

"Thank you..." I say slowly.

"Doctor Callahan," he supplies. My eyebrows shoot up. He's Irish. Romiro is the one to inform me as to why an Irishman is within the establishment of the Camorra, when neither the Irish Mob nor the Italian Mob like each other.

"He works for the Camorra. He doesn't have any affiliation to the Irish Mob."

Doctor Callahan continues to look unbothered as Romiro scans the paper before sighing and folding it to fit into his jeans pocket.

"See that door. In there, you'll find a shower, some toiletries, and other things you might need. Take your time." Doctor Callahan points at the door near his desk. I nod and mutter a thank you as I pass him.

Romiro and Doctor Callahan remain quiet until I close the door of the washroom. I can't exactly make out what they are saying through the door. It also doesn't help that they're speaking in hushed voices. I, instead, decide to look around the washroom. Pale green walls, black marble tiles, and a black-accented shower.

There is also a toilet on the far end of the room. Next to the shower, there are two brown cabinets. After searching both cabinets, I find that there isn't anything but nine bottles, three shampoos, three conditioners, and three body washes. All vanilla scented. In the second cabinet, I find towels, also in threes. I'm starting to think that the doctor has a thing for the number three.

I DIDN'T REALIZE HOW DIRTY I HAD FELT, NOT UNTIL I FINALLY showered and changed into some clean clothes. I try to dry my hair as best as I can with the towel, but it's still damp by the time I walk out the door. Romiro's pacing the room while speaking on the phone about something that doesn't make sense, while doctor Callahan is sitting behind his desk, typing on his laptop.

Neither of them looks in my direction. But Romiro is quick to end the call. He runs his hand through his hair and slips his phone into his pocket.

"Come on, we need to leave." He heads to the door and holds it open for me. I huff a breath of frustration and do as he ordered. Romiro lets me walk ahead of him, but not for long. I stop at the end of the long corridor, confused as to where I should go. There are two doors. Romiro comes to a stop next to me.

"So what's the plan, boss?" His tone is teasing, as if he's talking to a friend, but his friendly exterior doesn't fool me. I know that behind that exterior lies a man willing to maim, kill, and absolutely destroy those who pose a threat to the Camorra.

"Not taking the bait, I see. Smart girl. Come on, this way." He huffs out a breath at my refusal to speak to him and moves with the gracefulness of a panther to the door ahead of us.

We go through multiple corridors before we find our way to the one that had the cells, but instead, he heads to the elevator doors and presses the button. The doors slide open with a silent hiss. Romiro looks back at me and raises one eyebrow. It makes me aware that I have stopped a few steps away from him.

"Don't make me grab you. I am rather fond of my hands." He mutters the last part. I don't know what he means.

He also doesn't explain it to me when I give him a look of confusion. We step onto the elevator, and he presses the top button, a screen near it glowing red. It scans his thumb print when he presses the screen, then it flashes green and the elevator ascends.

Romiro doesn't look back at me, just straight ahead as if he's lost in his thoughts. The elevator doesn't take long as the doors slide open to a sleek modern office with colors of gold, black, and some hints of dark green.

The Capo of the Camorra is sitting behind a large glass desk, leaning back in his office chair. I guess even the devil looks magnificent in hell. He seems to be on the phone, answering whoever is on the other end with grunts muttered words.

Romiro and I step off the elevator, but I maintain eye contact with his boss. His eyes burn as they take me in. I guess he has a problem with the joggers and hoodie I'm wearing.

I narrow my eyes at him, which makes the left corner of his lips lift in a smug smirk. Ass. His gaze then flickers to Romiro, who sits in one of the two chairs positioned near the desk, but they quickly move back to me.

"Listen, Carmine. As much as I would love to come to help you to rein in your wild son, I have more pressing matters at hand." His tone suggests anything but what he just said, but his eyes don't move from mine. The smirk on Emilino's full lips doesn't disappear, even as he continues to take in the scowl on my face. He throws his phone on his desk after ending the call, not waiting for a response.

"Can you two stop eye-fucking each other? It's making me uncomfortable. If you want, Eli, I could leave."

My head snaps in Romiro's direction. His attention moves from me to Emiliano to get a better look at our faces, grinning from ear to ear.

"You know, I'm starting to believe you're just a clown for the Camorra's Capo."

Romiro's expression doesn't change at the insult I hurled his way, but he leans back into his seat. Amusement dancing with something else in his eyes.

"She's funny, I like her. Can we keep her?" He turns his head to Emiliano. Does this asshole think I'm a doll or some shit? Emiliano shakes his head at him and turns my way.

"Sit." His command comes out the way you'd expect it to from a Capo. Authoritative, domineering, and assertive. Leaving no room for argument.

"Should I bark as well?" He doesn't answer, his expression bored as he stares at me. My mouth lifts in a sneer as I stomp my way to the chair opposite Romiro, who's sitting there, now trying to hide his grin behind his palm. I cross my arms over my chest and sit down, staring at the wall behind Romiro.

"Well, what's the plan, Eli?" Romiro's the one to speak up after a beat of silence.

"We'll be leaving for New Hampshire soon. I just need to sort some shit out first," he replies. The sound of papers shuffling fills the room, but it stops when a noise erupts from my stomach. Oh my fucking God. I can feel my face turning red as the heat travels up my neck. Someone clears their throat.

"Romiro, go grab her some food. I can't exchange a dead body for someone alive. She'd be useless dead."

Of course, it would inconvenience them if I were to die. I roll my eyes and decide to pick at my nails instead.

A chair scraping against the floor and footsteps heading in the opposite direction should sound alarm bells in my mind. But they don't. I continue to pick at my nail bed until a small bead of blood forms on the surface.

I can feel a pair of eyes on the side of my face, but I refuse to look up. Emiliano clears his throat, and with a sigh, I finally look at him.

The asshole has one thing working for him, for sure—his looks. Other than being Capo, of course. I raise an eyebrow, prompting him to say what he wants, but he just continues to stare.

"What?" I blurt out, unnerved by the way he's looking at me. He just shakes his head and runs his hand through his hair, leaning back in his seat.

"I have a question." God, could I sound any more demanding than I do right now. His gaze comes back to me, and the corners of his eyes tighten.

"What is it?" He doesn't seem to be happy about my sudden curiosity.

When will you let me go? Is what I want to ask, but instead, I ask, "Why are you going to New Hampshire?" I just want to go back to my family. I want to see my sisters and hug them. Kiss my mom and Nonna and tell Marco that I love him. Eat my mochi ice cream in peace while reading my cheesy Matteonce books.

"We," he says. *What?* I frown as I look at him. "We are going to New Hampshire. You're coming with us," he elaborates.

No. Despair claws at my throat as the tears fight to build up, but I just push away the feeling.

"I want to go back to Chicago," I say, and he gives me a blank stare, his fingers tapping against his desk.

"Let me make myself clear, I don't give a fuck what you want." My jaw clenches when he condescendingly adds, "Princess."

I narrow my eyes, fists balling in my lap.

"I didn't do anything!" I argue. The corner of his lips tilts up into a harsh smirk as he leans over the desk.

"I don't think you understand. I don't give a fuck what your involvement is in your Dad's business. You are guilty in my eyes by association." His eyes are cruel, a snarl morphing his handsome face. I dig my nails into my thighs, my throat closing up.

When I go to protest, the elevator doors open and Romiro stalks in, pushing a cart with food and drinks, snapping the tension in the room. The smell of warm bread fills the space. Notes of sweetness and saltiness intertwine and reach us.

He comes to a stop in front of us with the cart positioned in front of me. There is an array of three different kinds of bread, some caviar, and pule cheese. There are also three different desserts, water, and some sort of juice.

"Let's eat," is all he says before he begins to transfer the plates onto Emiliano's desk. We eat in silence, but I can't concentrate on anything other than the questions brewing.

***

WE'VE BEEN ON THE ROAD FOR THE PAST HOUR AND A HALF. I DON'T know where we're headed, but Romiro keeps bugging Emiliano to stop at a gas station. We see a huge sign pointing to a gas station that's coming up in a few miles, and Emiliano steers the car into the lane to head into the gas station.

"How come you don't have a driver?" I ask before I can stop myself.

He shrugs. "I do, but I prefer driving myself." His eyes stray back to the road before Emiliano looks at me sternly through the rear-view mirror and adds, "Don't think about pulling any kind of shit. No one will help you."

I roll my eyes, already tired of his repetition. The man has nothing to say to me other than threats. And like I previously thought, it's kind of losing its edge.

As the car comes to a stop outside of the gas station, Romiro gets out, muttering something about his poor bladder, while Emiliano stays in the car. He rolls down his window and takes out a cigarette pack.

Extending his arm back to me, he offers me a cigarette, at which my nose wrinkles and I shake my head at him.

I watch him put the cigarette between his lips and pull out a lighter in the shape of a dagger. He lights the cigarette and takes a couple of puffs before blowing the smoke out of the window.

"Why did you take me instead of just attacking, since you could come and go from Chicago as you please?" My question comes off selfish. I don't want him to attack and hurt my family. I would die for my family.

His eyes meet mine in the rear-view mirror once more. They look colder than they did a couple of seconds ago. They narrow as he blows out another puff of smoke.

"If I'd just attacked the Outfit just like you suggested, then I wouldn't be getting what I want." He seems so set on getting revenge on the Outfit, but for what? I don't know.

"And what is it that you want?" It's a risky question to ask since his mood seems to run hot one second and cold the next. Silence chases the question away, and we sit there, him watching me and me watching him. Something passes through his eyes, and he opens his mouth to say something, but then clams his lips shut. Tension settles into each crevice of the car, making it almost unbearable. Until the car door opens and breaks the moment.

"Man, gas station toilets are the fucking worse," Romiro grumbles, his frustration and disgust clear as he runs a hand through his hair.

"Are you done?" Emiliano asks him as he puts the butt of the cigarette in the console. Romiro simply nods.

"Watch her, I need to grab something." Without another glance our way, Emiliano opens the car door and heads toward the gas station doors.

"Did you kids behave yourselves while I was gone?" Romiro twists himself slightly to face me, his voice light and teasing. I chew on the inside of my mouth to stop myself from smiling.

"Are you always this...weird?"

He almost looks exasperated by the question as he places a hand on his chest as if wounded.

"Are you always this catty?" he rebuttals. I shake my head at his childishness.

"Only to people who kidnap me and try to punish me for the mistakes of others." My tone is sharp. I tilt my head, trying to get a better sense of what he might be thinking. But Romiro isn't the easy kind to read. His friendly exterior might somewhat deceive those who aren't looking deep enough, but behind it, there is an emptiness in his eyes. No, not empty, but almost haunted.

"Well, in our world, there are bound to be those who fall in the middle of conflict. You, unfortunately, are the one to fall in this situation." He is so dramatic; I'm surprised he didn't think a stage actor was a more suited job. I roll my eyes at him and lean back into my seat.

"Where are we headed?" I ask while looking out the window. The gas station's parking lot is deserted. The sign reads 'Rob's gas station.' But the only letters that are actually working are the *r*, one of the *a*'s and one of the *t*'s. *Rat.*

"We're headed to the airport," he responds, just as his phone rings and he picks up.

"Yes, Lucio, we're on our way." He pauses for a minute.

"What the fuck do you mean?" Romiro's voice is tense, his shoulders brunching up as if ready to fight.

"Right, just wait till Eli and I get there. Don't make any decisions." Ending the call, he rubs a hand down his face.

I can see Emiliano leaving the gas station. He has his phone up to his ear, clearly talking to someone. His face is all harsh lines, brow furrowed. He ends the call when he reaches his car door and slides in with the gracefulness of an arctic wolf.

Neither of them speak or even make a sound. Emiliano just starts the car and drives out of the gas station's parking lot. It doesn't take long for us to reach the airport. The car doesn't take the same route as the other cars and heads into a separate lot. I give a tight smile to the man who opens my door.

I can see the change in Romiro's expression. Becoming more serious, his smile disappearing. Emiliano doesn't change at all. Unlike Romiro, he doesn't hide in sheep's clothing. He carries himself with the knowledge that he is well deserving of his position.

"Is the jet ready?" Romiro's voice is void of any emotion. It causes a cold shiver to skitter down my spine. A tall woman is the one to answer as we approach the jet.

"Yes, everything is ready for flight." Emiliano walks toward the stairs that lead up to the jet and Romiro nods. He looks at me and motions for me to walk ahead of him.

I'm reluctant to do so, as my Mom has always told me to not give my back to a predator. Especially one I don't know what they're capable of. He takes a couple of steps toward me, just enough so he's able to whisper.

"I would never hurt you and, this might surprise you, but neither will Eli." His tone is gentle, and he sounds so convincing, but he's the enemy. I can't trust someone who wants to use me as leverage.

I swallow down my fear and move toward the stairs, making sure to grab the railing as I take the steps. There are two flight attendants standing near the door of the aircraft.

Both are smiling and each have their hair in a slick bun. I give them a small smile as I head past them into the jet. The carpet is a soft magenta, and the chairs are a cream leather with brown wood armrests.

Emiliano is already sitting in one of the chairs, typing something on his phone. I decide to go to the chairs farthest away from him.

Romiro looks between the two of us and seems to decide he wants to sit next to me. He flashes a smile as he plops into the seat opposite mine.

"Go away." I really want to be left alone. I'd rather sit by myself than sit with the clown of the Camorra, but he doesn't seem to mind my disdain.

"No, I think I'd like to stay."

The corners of my eyes tighten as I narrow them at him.

"How old are you?" I ask.

"Twenty-seven, you?" he replies. Great, I am surrounded by two men in their late twenties. One who has the emotional intelligence of a rock and the other has the mental age of a twelve-year-old.

"I'm twenty-one."

He nods and turns to look at one of the flight attendants.

"Emilia, I'd like a Cosmo. Please," he orders.

My eyes bulge out of their sockets. Romiro laughs when he sees the look on my face after he turns back around.

"I like fruity drinks." He shrugs when his laughter dies down a bit. The rest of the flight, I don't speak to either of them. Not that I want to. The exhaustion must have caught up with me, because the last thing I remember is closing my eyes and feeling a warm blanket covering me.

CHAPTER 7
EMILIANO

We landed in New Hampshire about ten minutes ago. Valentina slept the entire flight. Romiro walks toward her, but I stop him and shake my head. I pick her up, making sure that I support her head.

She's easier to manage when she's asleep. I head to the jet's exit, and when the flight attendants see me, their eyes widen in shock, but they don't say anything. They are under strict instructions not to involve themselves unless asked.

I slowly take the steps to make sure that I don't wake the little hellion in my arms. The gravel crunches under my shoes, the sound of a plane taking off in the distance as the soft fall breeze blows a strand of Valentina's long black hair onto her face.

Izaak opens the door of the car once I reach the ground. I thank him and lower Valentina onto the seats, removing the strand off her face. Adjusting her blanket, I make sure she's covered.

Romiro follows closely behind us and sits in the front seat. That leaves me with the seat next to Valentina. I slide in, making sure to keep some distance between us. The car seats are uncomfortable to lay on, so I reluctantly move her head onto my thigh. With her hair splayed all over my lap, I feel an urge to wrap it around my fist. Pulling me from that thought, Izaak moves into the driver's seat and starts the car.

"Lucio called when you were in the gas station," Romiro informs me. I meet his gaze in the rear-view mirror.

My fingers toy with the ends of Valentina's soft black waves as I ask, "What did he say?" Romiro must have stayed quiet because he didn't want to speak in front of Valentina when we were in the car.

"Dom is on the verge of waking up," he tells me, but I know that's not the only thing Romiro has to say so I wait for him to finish talking. "He also mentioned that girls are dropping dead one after the other, and all of them have had sex with Lucio recently. Absolutely skinned." *What the fuck.* Who would target girls Lucio just fucked for the fun of it?

"Get Costa on it. I want to know who the fuck is pulling this kind of shit in my territory," I say as I rake my fingers through the soft curls attached to Satan's spawn. I wonder what noise she'd make if I tugged on her hair as I fucked her. Clenching my jaw, I shake my head, pissed my mind keeps going in that direction.

"Will she stay at Tartarus?" he asks, tilting his head in Valentina's direction. I shake my head at him. Rom nods once before opening his mouth, but our conversation is cut short when a little groan comes from the brat laying on my thigh. I yank my hand back to my side as she stirs before she slowly sits upright.

She looks around, a bit dazed, her wavy hair getting in her face. When I reach forward and push it back, her face morphs into a scowl.

"Don't touch me," she spits out before turning toward the window. I grit my teeth, fighting the urge to grab her by the throat and teach her how to speak to me. But I opt to ignore her.

It doesn't take long for us to reach the house. The iron gates open inwards, and we drive in until we stop in front of the fountain. Opening the door, I step out, giving Valentina my hand, but she opens the door on the other side instead.

I run my hand through my hair and pull a bit, trying to release some frustration. We head up the stairs, toward the entrance doors.

Romiro reaches the security pad that's embedded in the wall and enters the security details. A beeping noise alerts us that the doors are now unlocked.

The door opens to the entrance hallway, the floors made of marble and the walls a soft celadon. I can hear the voices of Lucio, Mara, and Matteo speaking as they make their way out of the living room and into the hallway.

"Of course not, Lucio. You can't expect me to be happy about you going after my friends."

Mara probably had to give Lucio another lecture about backing off her friends. It never works. Lucio opens his mouth to argue, but they spot us and head our way. Lucio and Matteo come closer, but Mara stays behind. her eyes darting around the room.

"You finally made it. What took you guys so long?" Lucio seems to have the answer to his question as soon as his eyes land on Valentina.

"Oh, uhhh...Hi. I'm Lucio." He rubs the back of his head as he introduces himself to her. She gives him a small smile.

"Hi, I'm Valentina."

Matteo doesn't seem like he's going to introduce himself to her any time soon.

So, Mara decides to take a tentative small step forward and says, "Hi, I'm Mara, and this is Matteo." Valentina gives her a bigger smile than she gave Lucio. Something bitter swirls in my mouth as I watch them interact.

"That's enough, she's not a guest. Mara, I want to have a word with you soon." I cut their little get-together short and grab Valentina's arm.

As I quickly walk ahead, our steps ring out against the marble floors. I turn to the left door to the side of the living room entrance and let the scanner scan my face. After entering the code, the door opens with a click into the dim hallway, which has six different doors. Each door leads into four cells. The white marble turns into dark granite and the walls become a deep forest green. I open the door to the far right and motion for Valentina to get in. She does, but only after sending a scowl my way.

"How creative, I'll be staying in a cell. Again." Her voice drips with sarcasm, but I can hear a hint of fear in her voice. Ignoring her, I walk to the nearest cell and unlock it.

"Get in," I order. Valentina crosses her arms over her chest.

"No."

"No?" My mouth twists into a snarl as I repeat what she said back to her. She doesn't seem fazed by the look on my face as she tips her chin up again in that fucking holier-than-thou way.

"Yes, *no*, I will not go into that cell just because you want me to."

"Listen here, you little brat, getting in the cell isn't an option. Now get in there, or I will drag you kicking and screaming." I pause for half a minute to see if she'll walk in by herself, or I'll have to pick her up.

To no one's fucking surprise, she doesn't listen and glares at me. I throw her over my shoulder for the second time in the span of forty-eight hours, which she insults me for.

"Put me down, you imbecile."

"Deal with it. You brat!" I throw back. It takes me two seconds to get her into the cell and to set her down onto the concrete floor.

"You son of a b-" I cut her off before she even thinks of insulting me and my Mom.

"I'm warning you, if you call my Mom a bitch, I will gut you like a fish. Behave yourself, you're not a guest in this house."

She recoils at my tone and goes to sit on the slab of concrete with a sheet over it that she'll call a bed tonight.

"I didn't do anything. I have nothing to do with the Outfit's business," she says once I reach the cell door. Her voice is meek and small.

I don't turn, but tell her, "You may have nothing to do with the Outfit's business, but your Dad is the Capo of the Outfit."

"So that is enough to deem me guilty. Tradition says to not involve women and children in the wars."

"I don't give a flying fuck about tradition. The Outfit violated my territory and killed my men. For that, someone has to pay." I don't wait for her reply. I lock her cell door and leave.

Romiro is waiting just outside. He's leaning on the wall, as if he's on the cover of some magazine.

"How'd it go? I heard you guys shouting at each other."

I don't answer him, so he follows me into the living room. I head toward the glass doors, which lead into our back garden and the pool area.

The house is eerily quiet since it is close to two-thirty in the morning. Everyone is asleep and the bite of the mid-October wind nips at the tips of my fingers. I run my palm down my face. Exhaustion will definitely play a hand in my decisions tomorrow morning.

I don't know what the fuck I'm going to do with a brat like that. I thought that she'd be docile, but instead I got a bitch specially carved and raised by Satan himself.

"Hey. You should probably rest," Romiro says, standing in the doorway. I nod and tell him he should head home as well. Which he does, after a moment of hesitation. I decide it's time I get out of my suit and head toward my wing.

Taking two steps at a time, I find myself standing in the hallway of my wing, which has different pictures of me and Ma from when we were younger. There are also other pictures of me with other family members. I don't understand why Ma insists on hanging these pictures in my hallway.

I finally reach the double doors at the end of the hallway, which open into a personal living room. I loosen my gray tie and throw it on the couch facing the fireplace, heading to the mini bar near the far wall, but then decide against it and step back over to the couch.

I grab the water pitcher and down the warm water as I sit down. Wiping my mouth, I grab the remote that controls the fireplace and turn it on. Then I reach for my gun holster and plop it down onto the coffee table in front of me. I turn the TV on next and go to the news channel. The corners of my mouth lift as I listen to the news anchor speak.

"The daughter of businessman, Alvize Moretti, has been kidnapped. It is unknown who the kidnappers are, but the young Miss Valentina Moretti had been last seen at the Chicago City

Country Club in Chicago for the celebration of Moretti Industries."
Businessman, my ass. I roll my shoulders and put both my arms on
the back of the couch, but my hands hang off the edge. I need to get a
bigger couch.

I decide to go change and have a shower. Flicking the light switch
on, I wince at the state of my room. Papers are all over the room, my
bed sheets dangling off my California-king bed, and clothes are
spewed all over the place.

I need to tell Ginevra to clean up my room soon. For now, I step
over the chaos and head to the doors that lead into my bathroom.
The bathroom's state isn't any better than the bedroom, but it's less of
a mess that I'm able to shower and dry off.

I open a cupboard which I keep extra clothes in and pick a set of
gray sweats and a wife beater. Leaving my hair wet, I go to my home
office to get some work done. The clock on my office wall reads four-
thirty now, which means I have a couple of hours before everyone is
awake.

It's already eight in the morning and over forty-nine hours
since we successfully kidnapped Valentina Moretti.

Before going downstairs for breakfast, I open the system that's
hooked to the cameras in the cells. Valentina is pacing the cell like a
trapped wild animal, and I suppose she is, in some sense.

With a sigh, I close the tab and head out of my office and toward
the dining room, but the noise from outside indicates that my family
is outside eating breakfast since the mornings in New Hampshire
have a nice cool breeze. Before I reach the glass doors, I can hear the
voices of Romiro and Lucio behind me.

"Sup, Eli. I called Costa like you wanted. He'll be here around
eleven for the thing you asked," Romiro informs me once he sees me.
Lucio looks confused at what I might want from Costa that he can't
know. I nod at Romiro and open the glass sliding door and step
outside, both of them trailing behind me.

I spot Ma and Aunt Clarissa both sitting at the garden table, talking. They enjoy sitting outside in the mornings and evenings year-round. I guess they enjoy the scenery. Our garden is still lush, even though it is the middle of October.

My Mom spots me as I head in their direction, and her face breaks out into a wide smile, her blonde hair in a braid on her shoulder.

"Mio figlio, where have you been? I miss you." I bend down and kiss my Mom's forehead.

"I had some business to deal with, Ma."

"You always have business to deal with. Spend some time with your poor Mom." She's trying to guilt trip me because I've been gone for two weeks since their vacation started, but I ignore the little remark and sit across from her next to my aunt.

"Hello, Aunt Clarissa," I greet her and lift her left hand to place a kiss on her knuckles.

"Always a charmer, Emiliano," she says as she places her right hand on her cheek.

"Boys, why don't you join us?" my aunt asks both Lucio and Romiro. They both look at each other, then look at my aunt and Mom, then shrug and sit in the two chairs between my Mom and me.

"How's Dante been?" I direct the question at my aunt, since I know my Mom will try to sugarcoat the situation.

"He's been improving, but the issue is, he keeps trying to move his arm and do heavy lifting around the house. The doctor said he's not allowed to do that. He risks opening his stitches and causing more internal bleeding."

I shake my head. Dante Folonari has always been a stubborn man.

Mara and Matteo both stand near the glass doors, staring at us for a second before deciding to join us. Mara stops near Ma, but Matteo goes and sits near Lucio.

"So, why is that girl in our house?" Mara knows who Valentina is, but she's acting coy. She's trying to inform our ma and aunt indirectly.

My Mom looks at me with a raised eyebrow and asks, "What girl?"

"No one important," I say at the same time Mara also says, "Valentina Moretti."

Ma's eyes widen at the mention of the eldest daughter of the Moretti's. I shake my head and send a glare at Mara.

"Why is she in the house, Eli, and what will you do with the girl?" Ma's question comes quickly with a hint of warning.

"She's staying in one of the cells in the house instead of the Tartarus. She's what we'll use for an exchange with the Outfit for her cousin," I answer.

"We don't use women as bait, Emiliano. Women and children are innocent in the wars between the Camorra and the Outfit. Honorable Made men don't use women to punish the men in their families," my aunt says, and I can see my Mom agrees with her as she nods.

"I don't care what honorable Made men do. I am the Capo of the Camorra, nothing less and nothing more. And I will do all that I can to protect my territory, my people, and avenge those who died in the name of the Camorra. If I need to use a woman to extract my revenge on the Outfit, then so be it." My voice holds no room for argument.

"Romiro, we're leaving," I tell him as I get up out of my seat.

I head inside and make my way into the kitchen, where the staff are making food.

"Lydia, please make me a plate of food," I tell our head kitchen maid. Everyone continues their work, but Lydia and Ginevra stop what they're doing. Lydia, to do what I have asked of her, but Ginevra comes toward Romiro and I and bats her lashes at me while giving me a coy smile. Ignoring her, I don't return the smile.

"Emiliano, when did you get back?" she asks me.

"Ginevra, go back to your work, and next time you don't ask me questions that don't concern your job." My voice is icy. Ginevra needs to understand that just because I slept with her once doesn't mean we're an item. It's been three months and she's married. Not that I cared in the first place, but still.

Lydia heads our way after she's done putting together a small plate of two eggs, some goat cheese, turkey bacon, and two pieces of toast. I grab the plate and kiss her cheek. Lydia has worked for the family before I was even born, for my pops before he married Ma. As I head toward the left hallway, Romiro follows me.

"Are you going to follow me around like a lost puppy?" I mumble once we reach the door that leads to Valentina's cell.

"Whoa, just say you want some alone time with the beauty you have in one of the cells and I'll leave. Besides, you asked me to follow you." He wiggles his eyebrows at me when I turn to glare at him.

"Go, make sure that the cameras are working around the house. I want to know how that little shit Mara was able to leave the property without anyone noticing," I order him. He shrugs and heads out of the hallway. Opening the door, I walk in to see her still pacing around the small cell she's in. Her heels have been ditched in the corner of the cell, her hair frizzy and all over the place. She doesn't seem to notice me until I'm unlocking her cell door.

"I brought some food for you. Eat." I lift the plate to emphasize my point and take a couple of steps toward her. She was short when she was in heels, but now she's even smaller.

"Would you like me to get on my knees and beg for mercy?" she asks me, my stomach tightens at the image. I ignore her and hand her the plate, which she takes and turns to sit on the concrete slab. I'm still standing in the same spot when she looks up at me.

"Are you just going to watch me eat?" she asks condescendingly. One day, I'm going to teach this brat a lesson. Swallowing roughly, I turn and head back to her cell door.

After locking it and leaving, I head to my office to make some calls. To no one's absolute surprise, the Outfit has spread their soldiers on the borders of their territory. Waiting to strike back.

My phone rings around an hour after I've gone back to my office. It's a Chicago number. I guess the Morettis are tired of waiting.

"Capo of the honorable Outfit is calling me himself, that's a surprise." Each word drips with sarcasm after I pick up the phone call.

"You fucking bastard. Give me back my daughter, or you'll pay the price." His threat doesn't faze me. In fact, it bores me. I was expecting better than this. What a shame.

"Now, now, no need to throw a temper tantrum. You are a grown man and Capo of the prideful Outfit. I'm hoping you enjoyed our little show. I sure did." I end the call, but before I do, I make out some cursing and a woman crying in the background.

A knock sounds at my door.

"Enter." My command is loud and clear. I don't look up to know who has entered my office. Ginevra. Her lavender scent fills the room. She rounds my desk and comes to stand before me.

I push my chair back, and she bends her right knee, resting it between my legs as she hovers with her face inches from mine. She sinks her teeth into her bottom lip, trying to appear seductive, but she looks anything but. Wrapping my hand around her throat, I give it a small squeeze, at which she moans. Her breath skitters over my lips, and she tries to close the distance, but I don't let her, holding her in place by her neck.

"You want this?" I ask her to make sure she knows what she's getting into. She nods eagerly.

"Use your words, Ginevra, or I'll throw you out." Her eyes widen at the threat.

"Yes."

"Yes what?" I ask.

"Yes, I want you to fuck me," she breathes.

"So vulgar." I tsk before pulling her to me. Our mouths fuse together and my tongue darts out to run over her bottom lip, which I tug at. I swallow each moan that leaves her mouth, but something doesn't feel right. Reaching for my sweats, I shove her hands off me. I don't know what I'm doing until I've dragged Ginevra halfway across my office and have the door open with her over the threshold, and me slamming the door in her shocked face.

Romiro calls me, and I pick up with a groan.

"Costa is here," he says.

"Send him to my office, and I want you here as well. Also, tell Silvio to set up the camera and sound system near the front and back entrances."

CHAPTER 8

EMILIANO

"What the fuck do you mean, you couldn't track down who's doing all the killing in my fucking territory?"

Costa's report is just a bunch of bullshit about the techniques and the links between all the girls who were killed. I didn't want that. I wanted the fucking person who's littering my city with dead fucking bodies and the only link is Lucio.

Costa leans back in his chair with a bored expression, unbothered.

"I don't know what to tell you, Folonari. Whoever the fuck is doing all of this, isn't someone easy to track. I don't think anyone can track them. It looks like they don't want to be found."

I clench my jaw to stop myself from punching this asshole for pointing out the fucking obvious. Throwing the file on my desk, I run my hand through my hair.

"Why don't you ask Matteo? He might be able to track whoever this is."

Romiro might be right, but Matteo isn't going to do this without knowing fully what he's looking for. I don't want Lucio to know that we're looking for whoever is doing this, and so far, have come up with nothing.

"No, no, that won't work. Matteo will only do the work if he knows everything. I don't want this to get back to Lucio. He'll tear the city bit by bit if he knows we can't find the person. And whoever the fuck is doing this clearly doesn't give a fuck about pissing off the Camorra."

I lean back in my seat as I try to make sense of this mess.

"Costa, you can leave, but keep on the lookout. I want updates every once in a while."

He nods and gets up, buttoning up his suit. Romiro follows to escort him out of the house. Who the fuck wants to get rid of girls Lucio is fucking? The boy is fucking nineteen. Everyone who might hold a grudge for the little massacre we'd gone on is long dead. And if anyone wanted revenge, why target the girls he's sleeping with and not him? My phone rings on my desk, interrupting my thoughts.

"Yes, Silvio, what is it?" I put the phone on speaker as I sift through the file again.

"The camera and sound system are up and running. They're both connected to the same camera system as the infra-red ones."

"Good. Have you figured out what happened to the footage from the night Mara snuck out?" I ask. He pauses, trying to figure out how to answer my question.

"Honestly, boss, I have no clue. The most likely explanation is that Mara and Matteo were in on this together. Matteo is the only one who's capable of pulling this kind of thing."

He's not wrong, but my men not being able to watch my two teenage siblings is quite pathetic. The twins are only eighteen, yet they still manage to fuck over every Made man in the Camorra.

"Figure it out," I tell him before ending the call. A knock echoes in the silence of my office.

"Come in." Lucio walks in, his posture tense and shoulders stiff. His blue eyes dart around the room as he runs his hand through his dirty blond hair. A nervous tick of his.

I narrow my eyes on him. He presses his lips into a thin line before he blows out a breath. Leaning back in my office chair, I continue to watch him for minute changes in his posture.

He opens his mouth, but then slams it shut before opening it again, imitating a fish. I know Lucio; he'll spit out whatever he has to say in a matter of seconds. He's always been easy to read.

"Valentina broke the plate that you gave her and she's threatening everyone who comes near her," he blurts out, and I stand abruptly, which causes Lucio to stagger backwards.

"What the fuck do you mean?" My chest heaves with the effort to control the absolute rage building in my chest.

"Did I, or did I not, order everyone one of you fuckers to stay out of that place and no one to approach her?" I ask. Lucio rubs his temple, trying to find an excuse for the blatant disregard of my orders.

I don't wait for him to come up with one as I storm past him and out the door. Romiro is making his way up the stairs. His eyes widen as I pass him, taking the stairs two at a time.

"What on God's given earth is going on?" I can hear him ask Lucio as they both trail behind me. I reach the landing and make it to the door within seconds.

"Eli, man, calm down," he says. I don't calm down, nor do I stop. I fling the door open to find one of my idiotic soldiers standing in front of Valentina with his hands up in a surrender position.

She stands in a defensive stance with a shard of the plate in her hand, pointing it toward him. Near them are some broken plate pieces. She doesn't seem to notice that she is too close to the shards.

Engrossed in fending off the man, her face contorted in a snarl, she doesn't see us, too focused on the idiot in front of her. At least not until I stand behind him, and her eyes fill with pure venom.

I growl at the soldier as he backs into my chest, "Out. Lucio, I want him alive."

Lucio drags the soldier out and leaves, leaving Romiro, Valentina, and I in the room. She's still holding on to the piece of shard, in a defensive stance. When I take a step toward her, she doesn't cower.

Instead, she stands her ground, but when I go to grab her hand, she whirls around and faces the other direction to try to get away. I grab her around the waist before she can take another step. She struggles, thrashing around and nearly causing me to lose balance, but I don't let her go.

"Eli." Romiro's voice is close, his steps echoing in the room as he comes closer.

"Don't, stay back, I can handle this," I say, my voice strained. The only reason there's a struggle is because I don't want to injure her.

I manage to grab onto her fist to pry the shard out of it. Instead, she digs the shard into her palm, breaking her skin. The shard presses into my palm too after loosening my grip, deep enough that my blood slowly seeps out of the cut in my palm and drips to the floor.

Romiro grasps her arms by the elbow swiftly, and I take the opportunity to snatch the shard from her. She thrashes around, trying to get free but, ultimately, she fails.

"Take her to see Alessia. Make sure that she doesn't get an infected wound," I order him as I head toward the door. My cousin, Alessia, should be able to fix her up.

"What about you? You're bleeding," Romiro counters.

"Go and take that brat to Alessia. I'll deal with my own cut." My voice is sharp, leaving no room for arguments. I make my way to the kitchen, where we keep an extra kit of first aid.

The kitchen is empty, the silence welcoming. Releasing a breath, I grab the first aid kit and get to cleaning up the cut. I don't know whether to be impressed or to be pissed at the brat's resilience. I wrap up my hand in some gauze after cleaning it up.

"Oh my God, what happened, Eli?" Ma's worried voice fills the kitchen. She rushes to my side and takes my hand in hers. Her eyes narrow as she examines my hand. I go to pull it away, but she just tightens her grip on my wrist.

"Who did this?"

Ma has always been protective of us, and it only got worse after she lost Dad.

I shake my head as I say, "Ma, I'm fine, it's just a little cut." Her eyes become slits as she narrows them at me. I breathe through my nose, trying to figure out how I'll explain it to her.

"It was Moretti's daughter. She had a piece of a plate she broke and she refused to give it up without putting up a fight," I tell her. Ma's face becomes blank as she assesses how to deal with what I told her. Face twisting, she gently drops my hand.

"Was she hurt, too?" she asks. I nod, and her lips set into a grim line. She runs a hand over her face as her eyes search mine.

"I'd like to talk to her. What she did wasn't okay, but in retrospect of everything that she's gone through, I can sympathize with why she'd felt the need to do it."

"Fine, but I'll go with you."

She shakes her head.

"No, Emiliano, I want to speak to her alone. You being there will only set her on edge."

I grit my teeth, not liking the idea of my Mom alone with Satan's spawn.

"As you wish, Ma. It's your choice." I sigh. Her face glows as the corners of her mouth lift.

"But I want Alessia to stay in the room with both of you."

She nods and says, "Lead the way."

I shake my head as I make my way out of the kitchen, already regretting my decision. It doesn't take us long to get to Alessia's office. The door is open, and we can hear them talking. Romiro is leaning on the wall, his eyes on Alessia with a small smile on his lips.

"Yes, I know. I had to tell him to mind his business." Alessia is talking animatedly with Valentina, who's nodding with a small smile.

Alessia and Satan's spawn turn their heads when they hear Ma say, "I see you ladies are getting along." Valentina's eyes narrow as she sends a glare my way. I return it with a sarcastic smile.

I take a couple of steps toward Romiro and lean next to him on the cream-colored wall, and Ma steps closer to Valentina and Alessia.

"What did Alessia say?" I ask him as we both watch the three women talk in hushed voices.

"The cut wasn't too deep; she didn't need any stitching."

I nod, still watching them as they throw glances our way.

"What are you guys talking about?" Romiro asks after they look at us for the third time.

Ma waves her hand at Romiro before saying, "None of your business, Romiro. Now you boys leave us alone. We want to talk about things that don't concern you."

Both Romiro and I get off the wall and head out the door, but I stop.

"Behave yourself and remember that you're not a guest," I warn Valentina. Ma looks at me, her eyebrows raised and eyes wide while Valentina gives me a blank stare.

"Emiliano Folonari, I did not raise you to behave like this," Ma scolds me as I leave the room and close the door behind me. Romiro gives me a suspicious look that I choose to ignore.

"Anything I should know about?" I ask him as we make our way into the living room. Romiro doesn't reply until we're sitting on one of the couches.

"The doctors said that Dominico might be waking up sooner than they thought."

"Any news on Thalia?"

Dominico's wife has been in critical condition for the past two months, and it doesn't look like she's improving any time soon. She was already stressed about Dominico's coma when she herself was shot by the Terranovas.

"No, man, I really hope she gets better, or Dominic will wipe out the entire Terranova clan," he tells me.

I blow out a breath, trying to find a way to get us out of this mess. The Terranova clan ruled over a large part of New York before the Camorra swiftly disposed of most of them. They still control some important routes that we occasionally use, and we've been in a silent truce for the past seventy years, but Thalia had been in unchartered territory when she was injured. This is going to be a problem if we want to maintain control without stretching our resources.

Romiro continues, "We can't afford two wars on our turf. We need to make our demand clear with the Morettis so we can get our revenge."

Our revenge. God, it feels like everything is finally falling into place. I nod and place my elbows on my knees.

"Mara wants to go back to New York. She said she can't keep doing online school," Romiro says, and my nostrils flare. The reason I moved them to New Hampshire is to keep them safe. After my pop's death, New York had gone through so much to the point it became unsafe for them to even be in our territories.

"Fuck no, not yet. We still need to establish power over New York. Everyone thinks they can fuck with us because my dad is gone," I say. Romiro leans back and sighs.

"Listen, Eli, I understand your apprehension, but life goes on. And if they want to attack, let them, and we'll fucking show them who the Camorra is. Besides, I'm sure everyone isn't too keen on getting your attention, not after that day," he says, running his hand through his hair. I grind my teeth as I let what he said seep in. Romiro rarely mentions the Fourth of July massacre. So, the fact that he's mentioned it twice is suspicious.

"Is something going on? This is the second time you've mentioned the massacre in two days." My voice comes out casual, but Romiro knows better than to think that.

"You seem on edge. You have that wild fucking look every time you talk to Valen-"

I lift my hand up to cut him off.

"Don't mention her. Her name being said is enough to make my fucking blood boil," I say harshly. Romiro's face is a mask of cool indifference.

"See, you've got that look again. Listen, I'm just saying, the faster we can get what we want from the Morettis, the better for us."

We're interrupted when my ma, Valentina, and Alessia walk into the living room, still talking.

"Who said she can leave the fucking office?" I stand up, my voice full of rage.

"I did, so stop your bitching. I didn't raise you like this." Ma's voice is sharp as she makes her intentions clear.

"I don't want Valentina to go back to the cell." She crosses her arms over her chest.

"Ma, you can't seriously suggest she doesn't go back to the room she was in."

Ma narrows her eyes. "That 'room,' as you like to refer to it, isn't a room. It was a cell. You know it, I know it, Romiro knows it. Everyone knows it. She'll be staying in Mara's wing." Hell will freeze over before I let the enemy sleep in my house comfortably, let alone my sister's wing.

"No. She will not." My refusal makes Ma harden her expression, "If you insist she doesn't go back to the cell, then she'll stay in my wing. No one else's."

Ma looks appalled by the suggestion, Valentina looks like she's plotting a painful death for me, and Alessia is wide-eyed as she stares at the three of us.

"She cannot stay there. She isn't related to you, and she isn't married to you either. Tradition doesn't allow for that, Emiliano. Besides, she's engaged," Ma argues. I shrug my shoulders at her.

"I don't give two fucks what tradition says. If you don't want her to go back to the cell, that's the only option." I can see she doesn't like anything that I have just said, her mouth set it a line.

"Fine. I want the lock on her door to stay," Ma concedes. My eyes widen at her agreement.

"What?" I breathe out. I feel cheated. She wasn't meant to agree.

Ma gives me a smug smile. "You thought that I wouldn't agree and you'd get your way. Emiliano, don't forget I was married to the Capo, your Pop. Whatever he taught you, I have seen. Don't take me for a gullible woman."

Great, I'm stuck with Satan's child in my wing, and she's plotting the best way to kill me. I'm so fucked.

"Don't I get a choice?" Valentina speaks up.

"No," I say as Ma also says, "Of course, you do."

Ma sends me a glare, and then smiles gently at Valentina.

"I don't want to stay in his wing. I'd rather go back to the cell."

My ma's smile falls as she tries to understand why Valentina is reluctant to stay in a comfortable bed and room.

"Valentina, are you sure?" Ma tentatively reaches her hand and grabs Valentina's. Valentina looks at me, but then quickly averts her eyes to look at my ma again.

"Yes, I'm sure." Her voice is soft and low. Where was this attitude when she's with me?

"She'll stay in my wing, then." Ma's head snaps in my direction as she declares her solution. I shake my head again, amused at her insistence to get Valentina out of the cells.

"She will not." My tone makes my decision clear, and my Mom's face crumbles, her eyes appearing glassy as she sniffles. Great, I've upset my Mom. I rub my temple, feeling a migraine coming on.

"Fine, but there will be a guard staying in front of her door. And if she tries anything, she'll be hanging in the cells by her feet." I say the last part while looking into Valentina's eyes. She just wrinkles her nose and sends a scowl my way.

Ma rushes in my direction and wraps her arms around my midsection. I return her hug while sending a glare at Valentina over Ma's head.

"Thank you, Eli."

"Anything for you, Ma, anything," I mutter into her hair.

I have a feeling I'll be regretting this decision.

CHAPTER 9
VALENTINA

Emiliano sends a final warning glare my way before he and Romiro leave the living room. Their steps ring out down the hallway, and once we can no longer hear them, Mariana, Emiliano's Mom, heads to one of the couches.

"I can't believe that boy had the heart to tell me no to begin with." Mariana sighs as she sits on one of the Persian couches. The living room is spacious and has various art pieces on the walls. One of the walls is just a floor-to-ceiling window with a glass door that leads to what I assume is the garden.

"I don't understand your insistence on me being out of the cell. Don't you want revenge for whatever my family did?" I voice my confusion at Mariana's behavior, and her face turns solemn as she looks at me.

"No, I don't want revenge on your family through you. You're innocent and had nothing to do with the Outfit's plans. But I can't do a lot. My son is Capo, and I cannot undermine his plans."

I sink my teeth into my bottom lip as I mull over her words.

"Sit down, girls. We have a couple of things to talk about," she says. I let out a breath and take a seat on the opposite couch while Alessia takes a seat on the armchair.

"Alessia, tell me, how is medical school going?" Mariana must have seen the apprehension on my face at the thought of her asking me to share anything first. Alessia leans back into her seat and releases a sigh.

"Honestly, Aunt Mari, I hate it. I'm exhausted with the amount of work we have to do. Between the rotations and studying, I barely have any time to myself. I went into medicine because I love it, but this is all very stressful." Alessia rubs her temple. I wanted to go to college and get a degree, but Dad said I could only do a course from home. I had to choose between a psychology or a beauty program.

"I mean, you did it because you love it, but do you regret it?" I ask her. She gives me a small smile and shakes her head.

"I still love it, but I don't love the mental load it has put on me, you know. And to top it off, I have to deal with balancing my schoolwork and family functions."

I nod, understanding the pressure of being a woman in the mafia world.

"What about you, Valentina, did you study anything?" Mariana asks me.

I shake my head and tell her, "No, I wasn't allowed to go to college. Dad wanted us to stay home after we finished with our high school studies."

Her eyes widen, a look of bewilderment on her face.

"Were you hoping to go to college?" she asks. I look down at my hands before looking back at them.

"Yes. I did, but I was only allowed to enroll in online classes."

Alessia asks me, "And did you enroll in the course you wanted?" My eyes sting as a feeling of helplessness bleeds into my veins.

"Uh...no, not really. I wanted to learn more about coding since I liked it in high school and was good at it, but I was only able to get into a psychology course," I explain. Their eyes fill with pity, and I hate it. I don't want their pity. I don't need their pity, because one day, I'll be able to leave all of this behind and do whatever I want. One day.

"God. I don't know what I would do if my dad didn't let me study. Sorry, Valentina, but your dad is kind of an asshole."

I laugh softly at Alessia's irritation.

"I got used to it. You know, in our world, we don't really have much choice." Our world, the mafia world. Where killing, stealing, maiming, oppressing, and bribing is the norm and anything else is abnormal.

"The world used to be like that. Valentina, it's changing, and with it, everyone else will change." Mariana's conviction almost convinces me. Almost.

"Not the Outfit. We're bound by the traditions and honor of our predecessors," I say.

"Of course, we're the ones to be tied by some traditions made up by some weird old dudes." Alessia scoffs and moves a piece of hair that falls in front of her eye.

"Alessia! You know better to respect our ancestors after what they'd gone through," Mariana admonishes after stifling a small laugh. Alessia shrugs her shoulders and continues.

"Come on, Aunt Mari, not even the most traditional person I know is like that."

"Anyways, I have a plan for tomorrow evening. My sister and I want to have a picnic in the garden. Alessia, are you free to join us?" Mariana asks.

Alessia's shoulders slump as she answers Mariana, "Unfortunately not. I have another round of rotations that don't finish till the early morning hours. But have fun."

"Valentina, would you like to come? Honestly, the more the merrier. I don't want it to just be Mara, Clarissa, and me again," Mariana asks me, sounding hopeful. I feel awful for saying no. Since she's been nothing but nice to me.

"I don't want to intrude and, besides, your son might not want me roaming around your house or anywhere near with the rest of you." It's probably true, but I don't really like the idea of mingling with the enemy either.

She waves her hand. "Nonsense, we'd love to have more girls.

Don't worry, I'll handle Eli. Now that's settled. I'll make sure to have a cute dress for the picnic set out in your room." She's just as stubborn as my Mom. It makes me smile and my eyes sting from thinking about her. She must be hysterical. My cheeks suddenly feel wet, and something drops on my palm. I reach my hand up and try to wipe the tears away.

"Valentina, sweetie. I might not understand how it feels to be taken from your family at such a fragile age, but it'll get better. I'm hoping you'll be able to go back soon," Mariana says as she makes her way to me and grabs my hands in hers.

"Oh God, this is mortifying. I'm sorry." I sound strange even to my ears. Lips quivering, I try to breathe in to help stop me from crying more.

"Can't you speak with him? Please," I plead with her, my voice taking a desperate edge to it.

"No." A sharp voice cuts Mariana off before she can answer. Emiliano stalks toward us and stands behind the couch, looking down like an angry devil.

"No, she will not talk to me. You need to understand that your family's name has consequences. And whether you think that you don't or do deserve this is irrelevant. You're nothing more than a pawn in a game bigger than you." He pauses, making sure that his last words seep in before continuing. "Whether it be your dad or your future husband or me who gives out orders, it doesn't change the fact that you are a piece on a chess board." He leans over the couch, his face close to mine. I can make out a faint scar on his left eyebrow. "So no, Miss Valentina Moretti, my Mom will not speak to me about letting you go back to your family. You will not manipulate my Mom into doing your bidding. Do not try to take advantage of her kindness."

I steel my expression. "You think that just because you are Capo, that makes you some sort of God, but all you are is an animal who would step over anyone just to get his way." I clench my jaw, my teeth grinding together. "I hope fate fucks you over just how you fucked up my life for whatever sick mind game you're playing."

He gives me a twisted smile. "Fate. You believe in something as fickle as fate."

I narrow my eyes at his mocking tone and his face becomes an unreadable mask.

"That's enough, the both of you." Mariana's demand is final. But neither of us break eye contact. A slow smile forms on his face and amusement dances in his eyes. I break eye contact and look back at Mariana, who gives me a small smile.

"Come on, you're going to your room." Emiliano speaks up as he makes his way out of the living room.

I get up after Mariana and Alessia hug me. Both of them wish me luck. I have to stifle a giggle. I know I'm in enemy territory, but I'm not going to war. We walk in silence as we head to one of the stairs near the entrance. It leads into a long hallway, and I can see that at the end of it is another set of stairs.

"You can go to the picnic." Emiliano breaks the silence as we make our way to the second set of stairs.

"What?" I breathe out in disbelief. He looks at me, then back straight ahead.

"Do you need to get your ears checked or something?" he asks. My lips pull back in a scowl and my eyebrows scrunch up. He laughs when he turns to look at me again and repeats, "I said that you could go to the picnic."

"The one your Mom invited me to?" I ask him.

"Is there another picnic you're invited to, other than my ma's?" he asks, lifting one of his eyebrows.

"No. But I thought that you'd want to keep me locked up?" I'm so confused. Maybe he's trying to get information on the Outfit. Information I don't have.

"No point in isolating you if everyone in my family refuses to stay the fuck away from you. I'd prefer it be done on my terms. The only time you'll be locked in the room is when I'm away on business," he clarifies, but it rings hollow.

I shrug off the feeling that he's up to something and continue walking. When we reach the top of the stairs, there are six doors. Two on the left, three on the right, and one at the end of the carpeted hall-way. He heads toward the one closest to the stairs and farthest from the one at the end of the hallway. Stopping in front of the door, he turns to me and steps closer. My skin tingles with anticipation and my face heats. His eyes narrow as he takes in my flushed face.

"Why is your face as red as the bell peppers I grow outside?" he asks. And just like that, he pisses me off. There's no way I find him even remotely attractive.

"You love being an asshole, don't you?" I counter. His fingers reach for my face, tracing the slope of my nose. I wrinkle it, trying to shake off the way my skin pebbles with goosebumps. He gives me a somber look before stepping back, and I let out a breath. Flinging the door open, Emiliano steps in, moving aside to let me in.

Inside is a beautiful light cream carpet, the walls a sage green, and the bed has blush pink pillows and covers. Emiliano walks toward a glass door and stands next to it.

"Don't try to leave out of this door. You're on the third floor of the house and will die if you try. I won't lock it because you might be stubborn, but you're not stupid," he warns, as if I'd try to get down from a second-floor window, let alone a third-floor balcony. I must look insane for him to even think that. "Got it?" he asks once I don't give any indication that I'll listen. When I nod, he heads past me and to the door, taking out the key.

"You can lock it using the key. If anyone tries to break the door, an alert will sound on my phone and I'll know. The only other person who has a key is me. I won't use it unless you make me."

I just give him another nod. He doesn't say anything, but I can tell it annoys him. He walks toward another door near the head of the bed, opening it and flicking a light.

"This is the shower and toilet. Don't try to lock yourself in here. I'll break down the door. And if I break down the door, it won't be going back up."

"Are you done with the threats? I don't want to talk to you more than need be."

He gives me a 'are you stupid' face and strides closer. Stopping three feet from me, he slides his hands into his pants pockets.

"Listen. If your dad cooperates, then it won't be long before you're sent back to your family."

"Oh, how kind of you to remind me that I'm only here till you get your way," I say sarcastically. He steps close to me, backing me against the wall, making my breath catch. My eyes widen when he reaches for my arm, squeezing it tightly. My throat dries up as I try to ignore the tingles that spread across my body.

"Keep up with your snarky little remarks, and I'll have you dangling from your feet over a vat of acid. Such a waste, a pretty face, but a rotten soul." His words are harsh, but his touch is intoxicating. As he reaches out a hand, I hold my breath. I stay completely still as he tucks a piece of my hair behind my ear. My skin breaks out in more unwanted goosebumps, his eyes searching mine. I spot an anchor tattooed on his middle finger when he retreats his hand. Then he leans in and whispers, "Wishing you the most horrific nightmares."

I recoil, and he huffs a laugh before moving back and heading to the door. I clench my jaw, my teeth grinding against each other. He shakes his head, as if he's amused, and leaves without another word. I walk quickly toward it and turn the lock.

I don't know how my life went from uneventful to a shitstorm within two days.

CHAPTER 10
EMILIANO

I lean against the door and hear the faint click of the lock turning. A small smile dances on my face before I wipe it away and call Romiro.

"Get the jet ready. We're leaving soon," I tell him as I take the stairs two at a time.

"Where are we going now?" he whines.

"Back to New York City, or did you forget that I called for a mandatory meeting back at the OX?" It wouldn't be the first time Romiro had forgotten our little sessions. I guess he likes to block them from his memory.

He sighs and replies, "Bro, Eli, my friend, and boss. I would like to take a holiday."

I laugh at his tone.

"You knew what you were getting into," I tell him lightly. Being a Capo isn't the easiest job in the world and you need to have some people you trust around you. It is what it is.

"So, is that a yes?" he asks with a fake high-pitched voice. It irritates my ear to the point that I have to move my phone away for a second.

"Fuck no. See you outside." I end the call and slip my phone in my pocket.

I spot Mara sitting on one of the armchairs in the library on the second floor as I walk past it. I can tell she's seen me, but she doesn't turn her head to look at me.

"Mara, are you-"

She cuts me off before I can finish.

"I know, Eli. I know I messed up and there will be consequences when you get the time. I don't need a reminder. I'm eighteen, but I can barely breathe without someone telling you." Her face is set in a scowl, her voice full of frustration.

Taking a breath, I sit on the edge of the mahogany table a few feet from where she's sat.

"Listen. Mara, I know that all the attention from Matteo, Lucio, Ma, and me is quite a lot, but we're only doing it to make sure you stay safe. Our enemies will try anything to hurt us. They think the way to do that is you and Ma," I tell her, and her shoulders sag a little. I reach my hand to rub her arm.

"Wasn't Dad enough?" she asks. I close my eyes as my chest starts to ache.

"Carissima, when power and corruption go hand in hand, death is the only price that is enough, but Dad's death didn't eliminate the Camorra and they won't stop until they do. I understand that Dad's death hit you very hard, but that doesn't mean I'll stand by and watch you endanger yourself."

"I want to go back to New York. I have schoolwork to finish, and I miss my friends. New York is our home. We've spent too much time in New Hampshire, and for what?"

I shake my head when she finally looks up at me.

"No, I can't have you in New York. Not yet. And you know we've been in New Hampshire for the family's safety."

"But it's been three months. You can't expect us to hide in fear for the rest of our lives," she argues. The corners of my eyes tighten, and I tip her chin up with two fingers.

"Mara, I may be your brother, but I am still Capo, and what I do is for the family and for the Camorra." I stand up, signaling the end of the conversation.

"You know, Eli, I remember when we were younger, and you used to say that you'd never want to be like Dad, but here you are, doing whatever you see as right without taking other people into consideration," Mara mumbles to my back. I freeze, my muscles tense. But I roll my shoulders, not turning around.

"Dad wasn't wrong in the things he did; it was all to protect the family," I finally say.

"No. Dad did whatever he could to protect the Camorra. He chose the Camorra over Ma, over us. I just hope you don't do the same." Her rebuttal is harsh. The sound of a book page being turned fills the space. My cue to leave.

When my feet touch the gravel of the courtyard, I spot Romiro talking to Matteo near my car.

"The next fight needs to be soon, or else the bidders will pull out." I catch the end of Matteo's sentence when I'm close enough. My eyebrows pull together as I come to a halt between them.

"We have a fight tonight. Why would the bidders pull out?" I direct the question at Romiro, whose face is set in a frown.

"Both of our two big fighters have backed out and so did the other four," he explains. I run my tongue across my teeth.

"Have they been dealt with?" I ask him, and Romiro nods.

"Find replacements for the five. I'll fill in for one of them," I tell Matteo. He keeps his lips tight and nods once before he heads back to the house.

Romiro, on the other hand, of course, has something to say. "Eli, come on. You can't fight tonight." I don't reply to him until we're both in the car and are driving toward the large gates at the end of the property.

"Rom, I don't need you to tell me what I can and can't do." Everyone thinks they can tell me what the fuck I can do. Fuck, I have enough of it from my ma and now everyone else is on my ass like it's a fucking trend. I pull out the cigarette packet from my suit pocket and flip the lid open.

"I thought you quit smoking," Romiro comments. I wait until I pull a cigarette out of the packet with my lips before deciding to reply.

"I had a couple after Alberto's death." Pops isn't Pops when I'm with Rom. He knows why. We both do. He failed to protect the family more than once, even if he tried his best. He put the Camorra first.

I keep one hand on the steering wheel as I light the cigarette and slip the lighter into the cup holder. Romiro takes the cigarette from my hand after I have a couple of puffs and takes a drag himself.

"I thought you didn't smoke?" My voice is teasing as I snatch the cigarette back from him. A small smile tugs on his lips as he rests his head on the headrest behind him.

"Yeah. I didn't for a couple of years. Remember when I told you about Nicolo walking in on me smoking, and he was so mad that he took the packet and just didn't speak to me for two days. The dude just iced me out," he recounts with his eyes closed. A laugh leaves his mouth as he sits back up.

"Yeah, you were so pissed that you couldn't get a reaction out of him, that you thought it was a good idea to stay out late. I can still remember the way he was looking at you when he came to get you from our house," I say, as Romiro takes the cigarette from my hand and takes the last puff before lowering his window to throw it out.

"I nearly pissed myself from how scared I was," he says. Nicolo had never laid his hands on Romiro, and he wouldn't do that even when Romiro acted up. Their parents had done enough damage.

"So, how's it going with you and beauty?"

My lips curl at the idea that anything could be going on between me and that brat.

"Nothing's going on. Tell me, has Costa sent an update on the murders?" I try to change the subject, and Romiro gives me a knowing look, telling me that he knows what I'm doing.

"Nah, he's been radio silent since he'd come to meet you," Romiro says. I nod, and we fall into a comfortable silence.

It doesn't take us long to get to the private airport, where the jet is usually parked. Romiro winks at one of the flight attendants as we pass them to go to our seats. He gives me a cocky grin before he heads toward the back of the jet, where two rooms are located. My nose scrunches up in disgust, and I turn on some music to blast through the jet's speaker system when the flight attendant follows him. I can hear his laugh when the music plays.

Romiro comes out of the room, looking like a freshly fucked king before we're due to land in ten minutes, and sits in his seat, giving me a smug smile. I shake my head at him.

"You use protec-" I ask, but he cuts me off.

"Do I look stupid?" he asks. I cock my head to the side and feel the corners of my mouth lift.

"Is that meant to be a trick question? And yes, you do look stupid enough to forget about a condom."

He flips me off and takes out his phone as he leans back.

"You know what they say birds of a feather are the same." He shrugs.

My face scrunches at the half wrong proverb. "It's birds of a feather flock together, you fucking asshole."

"You got what I meant, so that's all that matters."

"Are you saying that your Capo is stupid?" My voice holds no edge to it. He's my brother and I'm his. Whether I'm Capo or not is irrelevant. He yawns and stretches one of his arms before looking at me.

"Bro, do you hear how stupid some of the shit that comes out of your mouth is? Sometimes I think I might actually piss myself laughing."

"Fuck off and stop trying to be a clown," I tell him. He pulls a face, which takes me a second to realize that he's trying to look upset.

"Do you think I can still make it into clown college?" Romiro asks. For fuck's sake, this dude is meant to be my advisor, and he's joking about going to fucking clown college.

"There's a thing such as clown college? What the fuck would they even learn?"

Romiro's face turns serious as he starts his own description of a clown school.

"On day one, it'd probably be makeup. You know, it's important to nail down the pasty white shade for the base, the way to properly draw the lips of a professional clown and, of course, to perfect the arches of the clown. I suppose they would also teach them how to make people laugh without saying a word." He continues to look at me with a serious expression. We both start laughing, my sides cramping. We're able to compose ourselves before the seat belt light turns on and the pilot asks for permission to land in New York.

By the time we are off the jet, our faces turn to stone. We are the Capo and his advisor now. Benedicto is by the car to discuss the shipments. The drive back to the OX is spent discussing new routes for our new shipment.

"No. I want them to be distributed through six different routes. Alberto wasn't careful in the eighties and that got one of our cousins twenty years. So, they'll be distributed through the six different routes at different times," I tell Benny.

"I'll contact the guys and tell them to set up the six different trucks. They won't be loaded until an hour before they are due to leave the property," Benny says as he nods.

Romiro speaks up. "We don't want another near run-in with that fucker Damian again."

A bitter taste fills my mouth. Damian Barak, the bane of my fucking existence and the pain in every made man's ass. The Momfucker has been trying to steal our suppliers for years now.

Our car comes to a halt outside the OX and we get out of the car. The parking lot is packed with more than a dozen cars. I straighten my suit jacket as Romiro comes around to stand beside me. A hush falls over the place when we walk through the door. My men are scattered around the bar, each of them either holding a drink or smoking.

All eyes are on us. On me.

"Basement. Now!" I shout, my voice loud enough to echo. We

watch them as they all scatter to go down the spiral staircase. Everyone follows the order, and Romiro laughs as he shakes his head.

"It never ceases to amaze me how they all scram like fucking rats, but always have shit to say behind the family's back."

CHAPTER 11

VALENTINA

I'm lying on the bed, trying to summon an ounce of sleep. I toss to my left and then to my right. Huffing, I roll onto my back. My chest constricts as I think of Mom, Violette, Marcello, and Monica. I really hope Dad hasn't taken out his anger on them. My eyes begin to sting, and I rub them with the heel of my palms. Sighing, I sit up and throw the covers off. I've showered, changed the clothes I had on from Doctor Callahan, and I still can't sleep.

I look over to the balcony window, debating whether I should go out there. My curiosity gets the best of me, and I slide the balcony glass doors open. A cool breeze drifts in, cooling my hot cheeks. It smells like rain, but it hasn't rained today, which means the clouds are brimming with rain droplets. I step out onto the cool surface of the glass balcony. I can see that the garden is an array of lush oranges, browns, and reds, even in the middle of fall, when everything is dying and nothing seems to be as beautiful. Resting my elbows on the rod of the balcony, I wonder if I'll ever get this sense of peace ever again. Even if I am in enemy territory.

My hand snaps to my cheek as I feel a singular wet droplet land on my cheek. I'm not crying again, am I? I feel my other cheek to see if I have started to cry without realizing it, but my cheek feels dry. I look up, and once I do, it begins to drizzle light rain. I don't go back inside. I stay out on the balcony and let the sensation of feeling rain cascade down my body. The smell of grass in my lungs and my hair sticks to the sides of my face. Rain begins to pound on the ground harder, soaking the garden, and slowly a mist forms in the air. I take that as my cue to go back inside. A shiver slithers down my back and goosebumps pepper my arms. I rub my palms over them, trying to make them go away. When it doesn't work, I decide to go take another shower. Afterwards, I slip back into the bed, the bed creaking as I readjust for the third time, but sleep continues to evade me even as I close my eyes and count to three hundred. I give up, trying to fall asleep when I notice the first rays of sunshine peeking through the balcony doors. Looking at the bedside table that has an alarm clock on it, it reads six-thirty in the morning.

Sitting up, I rub my palms over my face and groan loudly. Frustration doesn't even cover the level of pissed off I am. I quietly tread toward the door and flip the lock open. The door is silent as I carefully lower the door handle and open it an inch. "Go back inside, miss." Fuck. That asshole was serious when he said he'll put a security guard outside. Shutting the door with a thud, I turn the lock. I lean against it before walking to the small armchair and coffee table in the corner.

It's not until around seven-thirty that there is a knock on the door.

"Hey, Valentina, it's me, Mariana. I'm here to check on you and to see if you'd like to come down for breakfast," Mariana says. I hesitate to open the door when I reach it, but my hesitation quickly dissolves when my stomach growls and I feel a dull pain in my lower abdomen. Mariana stands a couple of steps away from the door with a small smile gracing her face.

"Morning, how did you sleep?" she asks, and I plaster on a smile.

"Well, thank you." The lie comes out smoothly, and a flicker of guilt nags me before I douse it. I can see the bodyguard at my door, standing in the far corner of the hallway with his eyes on us, unwavering. It sends an uneasy feeling settling into the pit of my stomach.

I shake it off when an arm loops through my own and drags me toward the staircase.

"I didn't know what kind of food you like to eat for breakfast, so I had the chef make some pancakes, eggs, sausage, a fruit salad, and some other things." She waves her hand around as she tells me what to expect at breakfast. Mara, and another woman, and two other young men are sitting at the dining table. They seem to be engaged in a conversation.

"No, I don't think that's fair because you guys can do whatever you want, and when I try to go out with my friends, you guys flip your shit." Mara spears her pancakes after she finishes her statement. Mariana clears her throat.

"This is Valentina. Valentina, that's my sister, Clarissa, and those two are Matteo and Lucio, my sons. You've already met Mara, I suppose." She points at the woman on the right of Mara and the two boys who sit on the opposite side of the table.

I nod at everyone and mutter, "Hello." Mariana all but drags me toward the two empty seats beside Mara. She motions for me to take the seat between her and Mara.

There is a beat of silence before it is broken by the voice of one of the boys.

"So, are you going to be a part of the family?"

I look up with my eyes darting between them. Only one of them is looking at me, and he's the one with the long lashes and strong jaw. His eyes are eager and teasing. I deflate a little when I see that he's just messing with me.

"No, I'd rather be burned alive than join the Camorra." I bite my tongue as soon as I realize how ungrateful I sound to the women around me. When my eyes dart to Mariana, I find that she's just giving me a sad smile. I open my mouth to apologize, but she just shakes her head.

"No, I understand why you said what you just did. You have a right. My son hasn't exactly brought you here out of your own will."

I nod and give her a grim smile. The air feels so thick I can cut it with a knife.

The woman, Clarissa, speaks up, "I heard you'll be able to come to the picnic today. Do you have any allergies we should be aware of?" A small smile graces her lips.

"No, I don't, but thank you for asking."

The rest of the morning is spent finishing breakfast and avoiding talk that might tread near sensitive topics.

———

MY HANDS SHAKE AS I DEBATE WHETHER TO GO OUTSIDE AND SEE THE garden. Instead of doing the right thing and heading back upstairs, I slide the glass doors open and step outside. A light fall breeze drifts over me and the sound of leaves rustling fills my ears. I tuck a loose strand of hair behind my ear as I make my way toward the huge greenhouse. It's made up of glass and foliage snaking the sides of the building, adding a beautiful edge to it. I peek my head in through the open door, the inside just as breathtaking as the outside. The floor is a mosaic of greens, blues, yellows, and oranges. When I step inside, the humidity feels like a layer on my skin and the earthy smell of the dirt fills my lungs. In the middle of the room, a water fountain with a marble bench, and a spiral staircase to the far back of the greenhouse.

"What are you doing in here?" a deep voice asks. I press my lips together, wincing before I turn around to face an infuriated Emiliano. "I asked you a question, Valentina. I expect an answer." He's standing by the door, watching through narrowed eyes, his fist clenched around what looks like gloves. He's wearing some joggers and a wife beater; it's kind of weird to see him in casual clothes.

"I...I just wanted to get some air." I almost wince at the stupid explanation. Of course, I shouldn't be exploring. This isn't some friend's house. Emiliano cocks his head to the right as he regards me before he sighs and makes his way past me to the spiral staircase. He stops at the foot of the stairs and turns to look at me.

"Are you just going to stand there like an idiot, or are you going to follow me?" he asks condescendingly. I give him the finger before making my way toward him. He takes the stairs two at a time, and I have to bend my head as I make my way up because of the dangling lavender flowerpots. Emiliano is standing near the top of the stairs with his arms crossed over his chest when I finally approach.

"Here." He extends his arm, gloves in his hand. Looking down, I get a better look at them to know that they're gardening gloves.

"You garden?" That's such a stupid question. Of course, he gardens. His answer is a raised eyebrow.

"Take the damn gloves, Valentina."

I grab them as I look around the second floor. There's a lot of greenery in here, but there's also the colors from the vibrant flowers that are planted around. The greenhouse is huge, big enough that it has a row of olive trees. When I look back at Emiliano, I find him still looking at me, this time with something akin to curiosity. He shakes his head and moves toward the cape bushes, dropping to his haunches. I follow behind him and watch him pull out dead leaves before he feels the soil.

"Aren't you going to wear gloves?" I ask. He doesn't turn around to answer me, so I walk closer till I'm close enough to see the side of his face.

"No," he says as I pull the gloves on.

"Why not?" I pry. Emiliano sighs before looking at me from his position.

"Because I gave you the only pair I have." Something in my chest warms at the fact he gave me the only gardening gloves he has.

"What about your hands?"

"You worry about yourself, and I'll take care of myself. Any more questions, Miss Moretti?" His question is sarcastic, but it doesn't do anything to diminish the gratefulness I feel for his kind gesture.

"No." I shake my head, fighting off a small smile.

"Good. Now, would you like to plant something? Or would you like to cater to the plants that are already here?" Planting? That piques my interest. I don't know why I've never thought of picking up gardening as a hobby.

"What can I plant, exactly?" I ask him. He stands up, which causes me to step back since he's around a foot taller than me, maybe even more, and I'm just under 5'5".

"There's violet, cape bush, and bougainvillea seeds. There's also thyme and some lavender seeds left over, if I'm not mistaken. I also have some zinnia seeds." He counts off. I follow him as he makes his way toward a small cabinet near the olive oil trees.

"What do you suggest?" I ask. It's a bit overwhelming, especially since I've never actually planted anything.

"The zinnia seeds are known to be one of the easier flowers to grow. So, I suggest those, unless you want to choose something else." He turns his head to look at me, and I shake my head at him.

"Right, then zinnia seeds, it is." He opens the top drawer of the cabinet and pulls out a medium-sized pot, placing it on the table that's positioned near the cabinet, before turning back around to grab a small bag and a shovel. He sets them on the table as well. Emiliano opens the bottom drawer, which is bigger than the top, then pulls out a large bag of soil and puts it on the table. There's a small spray bottle on the table as well, which is halfway full.

"You don't actually need to have the gloves on for this specific process, but if they make you more comfortable, then keep them on."

The gloves are huge, so I opt to take them off; they'd only be an obstacle instead of helping. He watches me take them off before he turns toward the table.

"You'll need around three quarters of the pot to be filled with soil."

I grab the shovel, and when I try to move the soil bag close to me, it only moves a couple of inches before Emiliano pushes it with the palm of his hand till the bag is closer to me.

"Thank you," I mutter as I shovel the soil into the pot until it's three-quarters full.

"The soil needs to be tamped, but not to the point that the water runs out from the bottom of the pot." He grabs the small spray bottle and spritzes the soil three times, then reaches his hand and feels the soil. Emiliano sprays it again once before putting the bottle down.

"Can I ask you a question?" I ask as I grab the small bag of seeds and pour out three small seeds.

"That's a question in itself," he points out, before sighing, "Only if I can ask you questions."

"Fine. Why do you guys live in New Hampshire if the heart of the Camorra is New York?" I ask. Emiliano grabs the shovel again and puts some more soil in the pot, covering the seeds.

"New York is our home, and it was where we lived before the attack in Ohio, but after my Pop's death, it became too dangerous to keep my ma and sister down there. We didn't know who was an enemy and who was an ally."

"But why did New York become too dangerous if the attack was in Ohio?"

His eyes make their way to my face before an amused gleam enters them.

"It's my turn to ask. Why are you trying to get close to my family?" he asks. I turn my head back to the pot, grabbing the small spray bottle.

"I'm not. Not in an intentional or malicious way, at least. They're very kind and have been strangely warm toward me," I tell him as I spritz the soil.

"To answer your other question, my Pop died in Ohio because he had gone down there to cut off the Outfit's deals with the Russians there. It seems like your little cousin had wanted to become a hero in the eyes of other Made men and decided to attack our territory."

Emiliano seems to be apathetic towards his dad's death.

"Were you guys close? You and your dad?"

His fists clench as he shakes his head.

"When I was younger, maybe. But once I became a Made man, he...changed." He grabs the pot and feels the soil. "What about you? Are you close to your Pops?"

I slightly cringe at his question, and my body goes still. He notices the change in my mood and turns his face to look at me.

"No. No, my dad and I have never been close... It's complicated, my family is complicated." I sigh as I try to avoid talking about my dad's abusive nature. Emiliano looks like he wants to probe some more, but instead, he simply nods.

"Why do you like to garden?" His veiny hands flex as he tends to the soil, and it strangely looks sexual. Jesus, I need help.

"I don't know if you noticed, but we're practically surrounded by death and destruction. Bringing life to something, even something as small as a plant, makes me less inclined to believe that there is only evil in this world. It also relaxes me. I don't have to think while I do this." Emiliano doesn't give me much time to process what he just said because he moves on to the next question.

"What's your favorite color?" I give him a look. It's my turn to ask the question, but I let him have this one. He's trying to change the topic, which I'm grateful for. I ponder for a couple of seconds.

"It doesn't take that long to know what your favorite color is."

"Shut up, I'm thinking."

"Don't think too hard, you might pop a vein," he teases, and I wrinkle my nose. He's awfully impatient for someone who should be making important decisions.

"Red. Yours?" I counter.

"Mine? I don't know if you've noticed a theme, but green. Green is my favorite color. Favorite movie?"

I don't have to think about that one.

"*Pride and Prejudice*. Yours?"

"Really, *Pride and Prejudice*?"

"Yes, really, what's wrong with *Pride and Prejudice*?" I ask. He shrugs his shoulders.

"Nothing, but that seems a bit generic."

"I'm not trying to be different, asshole. In fact, I prefer blending right in."

"You can never blend in."

My cheeks heat at the tone of his voice. If he had said it any differently, I would've thought he was insulting me.

I swallow down any nervousness and ask him, "What's your favorite movie?"

"I'm warning you, it's generic as well."

I roll my eyes. Of course it is.

"What is it?"

"*Men in Black.*"

"Have you read the comics?" I ask him as he grabs the pot and takes it near the violets. He bends on his knees and digs in the empty spot in the soil near the violets.

"No, I was never able to get into them. You need to go back inside." He stands up and dusts the dirt off his hands before he turns back to me.

"Right, well, thanks for letting me plant something," I say. He nods once, before we silently make our way back inside the house.

EMILIANO HAD TAKEN ME BACK UP TO THE ROOM I'M STAYING IN. HE silently passed me a copy of *Pride and Prejudice* before he walked out. I sit by the coffee table, reading, when a knock at the door startles me. Mara stands on the other side. Her eyes widen as she bites her lip, trying to brush her side bangs out of her eyes.

"Uh...hi. I'm Mara," she says. I puff out a small sigh before I smile.

"I know, you told me already."

A blush creeps up her neck and she looks like she wants to book it out of here. I speak up again before she does, "Do you want to come in?" I widen the door to show that I'm being sincere, but she shakes her head.

"No, thank you. Um...I was actually here to see if you'd like to come help me bake some cookies?" she asks. My eyebrows reach my hairline. I must look reluctant because she quickly adds, "If you want to, of course. I'm not like my brothers, who think that they can order around everyone."

I press my lips together to hold in a laugh.

"Sure, I'd love to help you, but are you sure that it's okay?" I ask.

She hesitates for only a second. "Yep, it's fine, I asked my mom about it, and she agreed."

Her hesitation makes me wonder if she's just doing this to spite her brothers. I shrug it off and shut the door behind me. My shoulders bunch up when I feel the gaze of the guard burn into the side of my face, but I don't look at him. I ignore the uneasiness that has taken root in the pit of my stomach.

Mara loops her arm through mine and tugs me slightly toward the stairs. We walk in silence until we reach the second floor.

"Have you ever been in love?" Her question catches me off guard, and I nearly miss a step, stumbling.

"No. No, I don't think so."

She purses her lips together before turning to look at me, her gray eyes darkening into molten black.

"But you're so pretty. Have you never had a guy ask you out?"

I nearly laugh at how ridiculous her question sounds, but then I remember that she knows nothing about what my Dad does if we don't behave.

"No, I went to an all-girls school and my dad would probably chop a man into the smallest pieces possible before disposing of him in the ocean, if any man in the vicinity showed an interest," I explain, and her lips form an O.

"Have you ever been in love?" I turn the question onto her.

"Yes, at least, I think so, but he's so much older than me and doesn't really see me like that."

I narrow my eyes at the way she insinuates that he is someone she isn't meant to look at, let alone have a crush on.

"How much older exactly?" I ask as we enter the kitchen.

She sighs dreamily before she replies, "He's twenty-five years older."

Jesus. I'm not saying that their age gap is a problem, but the fact that she's barely legal is. I'm thankful he has no interest in her. I look around the kitchen; the walls are painted an eggshell white and the floors are a black marble with swirls of gold in them. Mara stands near the granite kitchen counters, fixing her hair.

"Mara, you know it's a good thing he isn't interested in you. You're really young and you're still developing as a young woman."

Her eyebrows pull together before she waves me off.

"I know, I know. I just wish he wouldn't treat me like I'm a piece of gum stuck beneath his shoes." Her shoulders deflate as she moves around the kitchen, tying an apron around her waist before handing a navy-blue one to me with eggshells on them.

"Do you have a hair tie I can borrow?" I ask, and she pulls the one around her wrist off and hands it to me, before heading toward the cupboards to take out the ingredients we'll need.

"We're making cookie s'mores." Her moves are graceful as she moves the flour, sugar, and other dry ingredients onto the counter.

"What can I help with?" I feel kind of useless just standing in the middle of the kitchen.

"In there, you'll find milk and eggs." She tilts her head at the two large fridges near a closed door. I look around, debating whether to try to escape. Once I reach the fridges, I decide against it, because Mara will be blamed and she's just being nice. And the possibility of no guards being at the door is slim to none. So instead, I open one of the fridge doors and grab the milk and place it on the counter, before heading back and grabbing the egg carton. Mara eyes me, but she doesn't say anything. I go and stand beside her and start pouring the dry ingredients into the bowl. I can see from the corner of my eye that she has moved to the edge of the counter and is pressing something.

A song comes on. I quickly recognize it. It's "Fly Me to the Moon" by Frank Sinatra. She wiggles her eyebrows at me as she sways from side to side. I laugh and shake my head at her and turn back to the bowl. The music floats around the kitchen, making my skin tingle and my stomach fill with butterflies. I whisk the dry and wet ingredients together as Mara continues to dance around while whisking a second batch. She spills some of the mixture on the floor, but she just steps over it and continues to dance.

By the time we're done and have the cookies in the oven, we're covered from head to toe in cocoa powder and Mara has some chocolate mix on the tip of her nose. We sit on the counters after we've wiped them down and mopped the floors. Our legs dangle as we talk about how different New York and Chicago are, when the absolute bane of my existence walks into the kitchen with his nose buried in his phone, his eyebrows pulled together so close he looks like he's about to have an aneurysm. Oh God, I really fucking hope he does.

An idea crosses my mind and I turn my head to look at Mara to see if she's thinking what I'm thinking. The corners of my mouth lift in a twisted smile as we both nod and get off the counters with a thump. Emiliano's head snaps up and his eyes narrow into slits once they land on me. I return his glare with my middle finger, at which he scowls before slipping his phone into his pocket.

Mara and I each grab a handful of flour when he comes close enough. He realizes his mistake too late and growls as he lunges at us, now covered in flour. Me and Mara scream as we try to get away, but only Mara manages to escape out of the kitchen with her giggles drifting behind her. I try to move to the end of the counter nearest to the door, but he blocks me by going to the other side as well. I move left, he follows. I move right, he follows. I huff out a breath when we continue this little dance a couple more times.

"This isn't fair, you let her go," I argue. He raises an eyebrow at me.

"What isn't fair, ragazza mocciosa, is the fact that I'm covered in fucking flour," he growls.

I shrug my shoulders. "Come on, it's not that bad. Don't be dramatic. At most, you're just dusted with flour."

He clearly doesn't like what I said because he lunges forward and is able to catch me off guard. Grabbing my wrist, he twists it behind my back, effectively trapping me between his body and the counter. I see his hand reach for the flour and scoop a handful of it. Oh my God.

I try to wiggle to get out of his grasp, but it's no use. His laugh echoes in the kitchen, making my cheeks heat in the process as I watch his face break out in a breathtaking smile. Dimples digging into his cheeks make my breath catch in my throat. His usual dark and cold eyes are light and warm as he regards me with humor, and my chest constricts, an ache settling in between my breasts. Fucking hell. I'm not blind; he *is* an attractive man, but I cannot actually be attracted *to* him. A mischievous gleam enters his gaze and the corners of my eyes pinch as they narrow at him. He returns it with a smirk.

His hot breath is in my ear. "I wouldn't call you dramatic if you were covered in flour by someone you barely tolerate, Valentina." My name rolls off his tongue like a caress, and I like that way too much. I can feel his smirk as he presses his lips over my ear.

"Now, should I cover you in flour as well?" he purrs, and I shake my head feverishly. He lets out a breathless laugh and whispers, "I'm afraid that isn't good enough. I need you to use your words."

"No."

"No, what?" he asks, and I grind my teeth.

"No, please, don't cover me in flour."

He sharply inhales a lungful of air.

"Why would I do that?" he asks, his hard body pressing into mine.

"Because you want to be nice?" I wince at the stupidity of my words. He huffs out another laugh. I try to get out again by wiggling, but he whispers harshly.

"Try that again, and I'll drench you in flour and eggs, and then fry you in oil."

I freeze, his flippant tone gone.

"This isn't fair. I wasn't the only one to cover you in flour." I'm resorting to whining, and if that gets me out, then I don't care about anything else.

An idea comes to me so prominently that I grasp it and act it out before thinking. I use my free arm to elbow him in the stomach, but all that does is result in him huffing out a breath. Before I know it, I'm twisted around and pressed up against his front, my chest heaving. I search his face for any hint of an explanation, but I'm rudely disrupted when he wipes the full hand of flour down the side of my face. My eyes widen, and he bursts out into laughter at my expression.

"This isn't funny, asshole," I admonish, but he just laughs harder.

He wipes the corner of his eye as he says between laughs, "No, it really is."

His laughter dies down, his eyes searching my face, scrutinizing, before they dip to my mouth. A shallow breath escapes from my lips and his throat bobs, his eyes still fixated on them. My stomach tightens as I feel his fingertips dance across my back.

"You know that your fiancé must be devastated by you being kidnapped." As his breath fans over my lips, I swallow, feeling my throat dry. He leans into me farther, and I involuntarily arch my back to be closer to him. Heat radiates off his body in waves.

"I don't have a fiancé," I breathe. With his lips hovering centimeters over mine, they slightly graze as I say each word.

"Not yet," is all he says before his lips meet mine. My skin heats and my cheeks burn as my brain feels fuzzy. The kiss is savage, all I could ever want. I loop my arm around his neck as his hands roam over my body, every touch lighting me up inside. A gasp escapes from my mouth when he sinks his teeth into my bottom lip, before swiping his tongue to soothe, making my thighs clench. Cheeks flushing, he swallows my moan as his hand rolls over my hard nipple. I press myself into him, wanting more, *needing* more. He releases a groan when I grind into him, not breaking the kiss. God, if he could kiss like this, then how would—

Is someone clapping?

"Well, this definitely wasn't what I had expected to see when I walked into the kitchen."

Someone's voice causes us to rip away from each other. Emiliano's chest heaves as he avoids looking at me. Breathless and heart racing, I look behind me to see Romiro smirking, his arms crossed over his chest.

CHAPTER 12
EMILIANO

There are only a couple of times I've fucked up and regretted it. Kissing Valentina Moretti is definitely not one of them. I scowl at Romiro, who's still standing in the kitchen, smirking at us like he's caught us with our hands in the cookie jar. Valentina's gaze is set on the marble tiles, refusing to meet my gaze. I sigh and walk past her, stopping with my back to her.

"Go to your room," I whisper, low enough for Romiro not to hear, and then continue toward him.

"Come on." I drag him by his elbow out of the kitchen. I ignore the looks he keeps throwing at me as we make our way through the hallways.

"I told you, you had a thing for the Moretti girl," he teases. I continue to ignore him until we've reached my office.

"I thought I told you to go check on Dom." I stand behind my desk with my hands in my pockets.

Romiro shuts the office door before speaking up. "I know, but something happened that needed your urgent attention." Alarm bells ring in my head as I take a seat in my office chair.

"What is it?"

"They found another dead girl. This time, a socialite from the Hoffmann family."

Fuck. I groan as I rub my hands over my face, trying to make sense of who could be killing these girls.

"Has Ernie contacted us yet?" I ask.

Romiro shakes his head.

That means he's either scheming or grieving. There wasn't an in-between for the Hoffmans.

Placing my elbows on my desk, I rest my chin on my fists.

"Rom, I need you to call up the Vipers and see if they've had any dead girls in their territory. Also, check on Dom before coming to see me."

He nods before turning to head out.

"Eli, don't think I forgot what I saw in the kitchen, and when I come back, I want to know what's going on," he says, his hand on the door knob. I blow out a breath.

"As my friend, or as the Capo's advisor?" I ask.

His shoulders stiffen before he replies, "Both." The door closes with a click and the office settles.

I lean back into my chair and run my thumb across my jaw. Pink pouty lips, flushed cheeks, and wide doe eyes. *No!* I can't let this happen again. She is the fucking enemy. I groan into my hands. I can't believe I fucking kissed her, and if Romiro hadn't walked in that second, I know for sure that I wouldn't have stopped.

I really need to get laid. This whole thing is so messed up. Her inexperience was clear as day, but that didn't give me pause. It only makes me want to corrupt her, completely ruin her for anyone else. A twist of possessiveness buries itself into my chest at the thought of anyone else having her.

The sound of laughter drifts into my office from the open window. As I rise from my chair, another laugh makes me stop in my tracks. It's soft and airy, as if the person laughing doesn't have a worry in the world, but I know that it isn't true. I stand by the window and watch my brothers, Mara, Ma, and Aunt Clarissa, and Valentina, all sitting by one of the trees on a wooden bench.

I can tell by their body language that they are enjoying them-selves. I can only make out the faintest words of their conversation as it floats in my direction.

I leave my office and head to my bedroom, needing a shower to clear my thoughts. The room has been tidied up and all my papers are stacked on my coffee table in front of my fireplace. I yank off my suit and throw it over the couch, unbuttoning my black dress shirt as I head toward the bathroom and fling it on the floor. When I'm finally in the bathroom, I'm left in my slacks and socks. I quickly discard them and set the shower to the highest temperature.

The scolding water drums down my back as I step under the showerhead. I squeeze my eyes shut and the image of Valentina's lips flash in my head, another of her on my bed making my stomach flip, and my cock hardens. I breathe harshly through my nose, gritting my teeth. *Just this once*, I think to myself as I grab the base of my hard cock and begin to slowly stroke it. Soon, my groans fill the steamy bathroom, and I speed up my movements as I squeeze my eyes shut. I see myself between her legs, taking my sweet damn time with her. Gritting my teeth, I feel the control slip from between my fingers. My hips thrust forward, trying to create more friction, while my hand continues its frantic stroking. As I imagine Valentina between my legs, waiting for my cum, my breaths come out harsh and I'm unraveling.

My chest heaves with the effort of trying to gulp as much air as possible, dick now limp as cum drips off the head and swirls in the drain. I watch it, feeling worse than I did at the beginning, before I decided to fucking masturbate to a fantasy that will never fucking happen. I calm my breathing down, then proceed to finish washing my hair and body before wrapping a towel around my midriff.

I need to get away before I do something that will completely ruin my plans. I can't let some girl stand in the way of avenging my Pop, no matter how much I desire her.

With frustration burning through my chest, I comb my hair as I dry it and throw on some comfortable clothes.

Grabbing my papers off the coffee table and dropping onto my couch, I sift through them. I lean back and try to focus on what's in front of me, but all I can think of is Valentina. Gritting my teeth, I throw the stack of papers back onto the coffee table and run my hands through my hair. My phone rings from the inside pocket of the suit jacket that I'd placed on the couch next to me.

A smirk threatens to break out on my face as I see that a Chicago number is calling.

"I didn't expect a call this early after our last one," I taunt as I answer after the third ring.

"This is Diletta Moretti. I want to speak to my daughter."

My lips curl at the idiocy of Alvize Moretti to have his wife beg for him. I thought the Outfit prided themselves for their so-called honor.

"No," I reply sharply.

"I beg of you, my husband doesn't know I called you. I just want to speak to my daughter. I don't want to have called you all for nothing."

Desperation reeks from her voice. And the fact that she has called me behind her husband's back is definitely interesting.

"You only will speak with her for a minute, no less and definitely no more."

"Yes, yes, thank you." She's whispering now, which probably means that someone might be near.

I tell her to wait a moment as I head down the stairs. My Mom, my aunt, Valentina, and my sister are still sitting on the bench outside. Making my way across the garden, passing the pool, Valentina is the one to first spot me, but then my Mom does and so does the rest. Matteo and Lucio are nowhere to be found, hopefully not doing something they shouldn't be. I stop beside the bench.

"You, up." Without saying another word, I turn back toward the house. The sound of footsteps echo as she walks across the tiled area of the pool to follow me. Once we reach the living room, I turn around abruptly, which causes her to bump into my chest. I grab her elbow to steady her, and she tilts her head up to look at me. I grit my teeth and let go of her, taking a couple of steps back.

"Here." I extend my arm for her to grab the phone, but she just stares at me, eyes wide. Snapping my finger in front of her face, she scowls at me before snatching the phone.

"Hello?" Her voice is soft and full of confusion, but her eyes throw daggers at me. I raise an eyebrow at her, but she isn't looking at me anymore.

"Mom, how have you been? I miss you. No, I'm fine, as fine as a person held against their will can be." Her voice has taken a different edge to it.

"Has Dad…" She pauses, looking at me.

"Mom, I'm not in New York anymo-" I snatch the phone out of her hand before she can finish her sentence and end the call.

Her eyes narrow at me. "I wasn't done," she says, as my face remains closed off.

"I don't give a fuck if you weren't done. Your dear Mom was only promised a minute. That's all you get."

She stares at me, jaw locked and eyes narrowed. I should leave before I do something I really shouldn't.

Before I do the correct thing and leave, I make the fucking mistake of letting my eyes trail down her petite frame. Fuck me thirty ways till Sunday. She is something to behold. She's wearing a red maxi dress with a black cardigan on top to keep her warm and her dark hair is swooped to the side, reaching her hip. When my eyes make their way back up, I can see that she is so flushed she nearly resembles the beetroots I grow every year.

"Why are you such an asshole?" Her lips curl as she tries to land an insult.

"Is that the best you could do? How disappointing." My eyes narrow as she steps closer.

"I suggest you sleep with one eye open because a man like you must piss off a lot of people."

Her bright eyes and pink cheeks make me wonder how she would look if I fuck her.

I clench my jaw and do what I should have done after I ended that call and walk away. On my way to my room, I decide to call the family pilot and tell him to get ready because I'm flying back to New

York. I need to leave; this whole thing is fucking with my head. Besides, I have a meeting with that asshole Stefano.

Once I reach my room, I grab the papers off my coffee table and stuff them into one of my bags. I collect anything else that I'll need in New York for the week before calling Romiro.

"I'm going to kill you if you're calling me to go to the airport," he says, and I release a sigh.

"I'm not asking you to come along. I'm calling you to tell you that I'll be in New York for the week and need you to make sure our little prisoner doesn't do something she'll regret."

There's a pause on the line before he gasps.

"Emiliano, Capo of the Camorra, runs from the daughter of the enemy because he can't handle his sexual feelings," he says in a dramatic voice. I grit my teeth and tell him to shut up and to call me if there is an emergency before ending the call.

I don't run into anyone on the way down to my car, thankfully. Looking back at the house through the rear-view mirror, I wonder if I'm running away just because I'm in denial. I shake my head before turning my attention back on the road as I drive out of the open gates.

THE JET LANDS IN NEW YORK JUST BEFORE SEVEN IN THE EVENING. I SEE that Ma has texted me back.

ELI

Hey, Ma, I'm staying in New York for the week. Call me if you need anything.

MA

You couldn't tell me before you left? I barely see you anymore. Stay safe.

ELI

Sorry, I was in a rush.

Slipping my phone back into my pocket, I slide into the car, thanking my driver for opening the door. We reach my apartment half an hour later, and I take the golden elevators to the top.

* * *

The lobby of Folonari Enterprise is full of employees, guests, and reporters, all waiting to snap a photo or a small nugget of information on us. My shoes click against the black quartz lobby floor, walking past the reception desk. Silvio follows me, the sound of the papers he's shuffling filling my ears.

"Mr. Folonari, would you like to make a comment on the disappearance of your family from the social gatherings at the Hoffmans this year?" I fight the urge to snap that stupid mic the reporter has in my face. Instead, I keep walking ahead, ignoring them.

"Security needs to get them the fuck out of my building, or else I'll be fucking up each and every one of their lives," I order Silvio. He pulls out his phone, typing on it before sliding it back into his suit jacket.

"Stefano is waiting upstairs in conference room 451B," Silvio tells me as we make our way to the elevators reserved for the three top floors. The elevator doors distort our reflections as we stop in front of them. A twinge of satisfaction finds its way into my chest at the thought that Stefani Gambi is waiting for me to meet with him.

"How long?" My voice doesn't betray my emotions as we step into the elevator.

"Around half an hour; he's been quite antsy."

I run my tongue across my top teeth as the elevator slides up.

"Have the lawyers gone through all the paperwork we need for this meeting?" Pulling on my tie to loosen it, I tab through my emails, and messages.

"Yeah, they have, and they've found a couple of things we could probably bargain more for."

Interesting. I guess I shouldn't be surprised that Gambi is trying to fuck us over in every aspect of our business partnership. The elevator doors open with a hiss, which grates on my nerves.

"Get the mechanic to look at those elevator doors. They shouldn't be making any kind of noise."

Silvio nods before he slips away. The walls are gray, with accents of blood red. The black carpet mutes my steps as I make my way toward the conference room. I don't knock, swinging the door open and walking in. I'm stopped dead in my tracks when I spot Stefano sitting in my seat, behind the glass meeting table. My lips twist into a disgusted snarl.

"Get the fuck out of my seat, Gambi." Instead of doing what I told him to, he leans back into the seat, flashing me a grin.

"Good to see you too, Folonari." Stefano taps his hands on the table before getting up and making his way to me. "You know, the Morettis have tried to uh...how do I say this? They've contacted us to ask an interesting favor."

Clenching my teeth, I move around him and walk toward my seat.

Keeping my voice casual, I ask, "And pray tell what that fucking favor was?"

He twists to me, an amused grin on his stupid face.

"You have their daughter. Valentina, is it?" Stefano moves to the seat opposite mine like the serpent he is. I fight the urge to cut him to pieces with my ancestors' dagger, just for uttering her name. Clenching my jaw, I press the button for the blinds to go down on the floor-to-ceiling windows, blocking the sunlight.

"Just fucking say it, Stefano, I don't have the fucking time for your bullshit," I snap.

He clicks his tongue as he leans forward, placing his elbows on the table, an amused grin stretching his lips, but it doesn't reach his mismatched eyes.

"You're no fun. They wanted us to help them get Valentina back to Chicago in exchange for a hefty load of cocaine."

Cracking my knuckles before I lean back in my seat, I give Stefano a humorless smile.

"And I suppose you have a proposition for me?" I ask.

His grin falters for just a second, and I lean forward before I continue.

"Stefano, you know you're in my territory and that you need me. Not the other way around."

Stefano narrows his eyes, and he's about to respond, but he's cut off when his lawyer and mine walk into the conference room.

SOMETHING FEELS OFF, BUT I DON'T KNOW WHAT IT IS. MAKING MY WAY toward my kitchen, my feet against the dark mahogany floors is the only sound echoing in the space. I place my phone on the island before I move around the table to the green cupboards, looking for my coffee mix. Finding it in the third cupboard, I take it out and put two tablespoons into the Arabic coffee pot, just as my phone pings.

New message from Rom.

My brow furrows, confused as to what could be so important that Romiro is messaging me at five in the morning.

ROM

Hey, asshole, just thought you should know
that Valentina has been sick for the past
couple of days.

ELI

What the fuck do you mean? Sick how?

ROM

I don't know if the atmosphere in New York
affects your comprehension abilities, but she
has been out for the past two days with a
high fever.

ELI

Why the fuck haven't I heard about this
before today?

ROM

I thought you didn't care.

ELI

Don't make random assumptions, you fucking idiot.

ROM

Hate the message not the messenger.

ELI

You're an idiot. I'll be in New Hampshire in a couple of hours.

The sound of my coffee overflowing onto the stove fills the kitchen, and I wince when I turn and see the mess it's created. Dumping the pot into the sink, I make my way back to my room, throwing on a random blue suit before leaving the apartment.

BY THE TIME THE JET LANDS IN NEW HAMPSHIRE, I HAVE A SPLITTING headache that I have to power through to get to our house. Heading up the grand staircase toward the front door, Romiro meets me near them, a smug look on his face.

"Wipe that smug fucking look off your face before I wipe you off this planet."

He shrugs at my threat as I head straight to the room I placed Val in, Romiro hot on my trail.

"What did the doctor say?" I pause at the top of the stairs when I don't get a response and turn to look at Romiro. "Tell me you got a doctor to see her," I demand. Romiro rubs his hand over the back of his neck.

"Alessia was checking on her every day…"

I can't leave these fucking idiots for two days without them needing me to tell them what they should be doing.

"You're more of a fucking idiot than I thought you would be." Turning back around, my steps pound as I make my way into Valentina's room. Mara, Alessia, and Ma are all sitting in chairs around a sleeping Valentina. But she doesn't just look like she's sleeping, she looks like she's dying. Her normally tan face is a pale greenish color, and when I step closer, her pillow looks like it's been drenched with a gallon of water.

"Oh my God, you're finally back. Please tell me you'll call a doctor for the poor girl." I barely register what my Ma says as I feel a lead ball of guilt settle in the pit of my stomach.

"Yeah, Romiro, go call Callahan. Tell him I'll triple his salary if he can get here in the next hour." Placing the back of my hand on her forehead, I check her temperature. She's burning up.

"How did she get sick?" I ask no one in particular.

Mara is the one who answers. "We found her in the bathroom passed out in her clothes under the shower, her clothes drenched."

My throat constricts, and I swallow, trying to elevate the pressure building.

"Alessia, do you know why she's sick?" I ask as I turn to my cousin, who looks at Valentina and back at me.

"She most likely has a weak immune system. I'm not entirely too sure, but she probably had a virus," she says.

I turn and face Ma and Mara before announcing, "She's not staying in this room. I'm moving her to my room," I say to them. Ma opens her mouth to protest, but I beat her to it. "Ma, come on, you can't seriously expect me to let her stay here. None of you have even taken proper care of her." That makes her clam her mouth shut, turning around to face Valentina. I slip my arms under her and lift her off the bed. Valentina stirs around and makes a deep groan at the back of her throat when I'm half-way down the stairs.

"What...no. I don't want to." She thrashes, and I have to tighten my grip on her so she doesn't fall.

I lean down until I'm close enough to whisper, "Shhh. You're fine. Go back to sleep." Standing still, I wait for her to go back to sleep before moving off the stairs and toward my own wing.

CALLAHAN ARRIVED A COUPLE OF HOURS AGO, CHECKED ON VALENTINA, and prescribed some medicine for the fever, which I sent Romiro to pick up. Now, it's around midnight and everyone has retired to their rooms. She hasn't opened her eyes again since she woke up while we were on the stairs. I'd dragged the armchair into my room next to the bed to make sure her temperature didn't rise. A groan that slips from between her lips makes me throw my book down on the bedside table.

"W...water. I'd like some water...pl...please," she groans.

Reaching out, I pour her a cup of water and help her to sit, holding the cup to her lips. I don't let the cup go, even when she grabs it with both hands, shaking like a leaf. Valentina's eyes only open ever-so-slightly before they shutter closed once again as she drinks. I pull it back when she coughs and nearly chokes.

"Slow down, tiger, the water isn't going anywhere. I promise." Every muscle in my body pulls taut when she rests her head on my shoulder. I have to force myself to relax because she's sick.

"You're so nice." Her voice is barely an audible whisper.

"I'm really not that nice." I don't know why I'm whispering, but I don't want to startle her.

"No, maybe not by normal people's standards, but in our world, you are, at least compared to my Pop."

My jaw clenches as I fight off the urge to bulldoze into asking her about what she means. Instead, I settle for, "I doubt that very much."

"You seem to be doubting a lot of things. You know, I think I like all the green in your room. I used to think green was an ugly color, but I've grown quite fond of it."

The little nugget of information she has given me feels more like a gold bar than anything else, but I don't ask for more. As I open my mouth to reply, a snore interrupts me, and when I look down at her, I find her sleeping. Taking in her relaxed state, I lay her back down on the pillow. Her temperature has gone down, but it's still quite high.

"I think I'm becoming quite fond of something I unfortunately cannot keep or replace."

Brushing some strands out of her face, I swallow roughly and take a deep breath. With one more look, I turn back around and place the cup back on the bedside table, grabbing my book. Then I lean back into my seat, waiting for her.

CHAPTER 13
VALENTINA

A week ago

To say I have whiplash would be an understatement. I head back to the three women in a daze.

"What did Eli want?" They all turn and look at me as Mariana asks, "If you don't mind me asking."

"My mom wanted to talk to me." I still feel out of sorts, as if my head is floating above my body. They're silent for a moment before sensing I'm not in the mood to talk about my family, so they change the topic. I don't really pay attention to the conversation, still confused. After we finish the food and the sky has become an array of orange and red, the women decide it is time to retire to our rooms.

I'm sitting by the balcony door in the room I'm trapped in. I'd managed to drag the armchair close enough to see outside, and the mid-fall breeze cools the room.

The sky has become pitch black, and I could make out some stars in the distance. In Chicago, we could never make out anything other than the black sky. I close my eyes and try to imagine what it would be like to be back home.

In my Mom's arms, and to have Violette making snide remarks

toward Mia when she'd come over. What it would be like to braid Monica's hair, and to play with Marcello and the dogs. To hear Nonna tut at us for being unladylike.

The smell of Zehra cooking her infamous Adana kebab wafts around the kitchen and the four of us are all sitting around the kitchen island, waiting to taste it.

She places the plate of hot kebabs and slaps Marcello's hand when he reaches for them, causing us to giggle. But the memory slowly disappears, leaving me with just the darkness.

I still can't believe that Dad is taking this long to negotiate with the Camorra. I already know he doesn't care about us as his family, but it's as if he doesn't care about the deal he'd made with the Colombians.

Unless he's going to use one of my other sisters. I shake my head; no, Nonna would never allow it. Even if she doesn't have much hand in Dad's decision, she still has my uncles on her side. Besides, Violette is nineteen and Monica has just turned fourteen.

I bring up my legs and set the soles of my feet on the edge of the armchair, resting my head on my knees. I still can't believe what the hell has happened in the kitchen today. Lifting my fingertips, I graze my lips.

Mortification drums through my veins persistently at how easily I kissed him back. God, this whole situation is so fucked up. What the hell does it even mean? Why did he kiss me? And why did I like it? I'm so confused, and it doesn't help that he's the literal enemy and the person who kidnapped me. I wish I was just a normal person, a normal twenty-one-year-old.

I really hope he doesn't use that against the Outfit, because if he tries that, Dad will take it out on Mom and my sisters, or even Marcello since I'm out of reach. If only Dad cared about us as much as the fucking Outfit and his pride, maybe we wouldn't be in this situation.

I lean my head back onto the back of the chair and keep my eyes shut. They begin to sting, and I know what will be coming, but I just keep my eyes closed tight.

Hot, wet tears roll down the sides of my face and my body shakes with the effort of containing my sobs. I breathe heavily through my nose, trying to calm myself, but I just continue to cry silently.

I cry until there's no more tears left and my cheeks have dried. The soft breeze soothes my heated face, and even though my eyes are already closed, my eyelids feel heavy.

Exhaustion weighs heavily on me. I cover my mouth with the back of my palm as a yawn breaks out. Even though goosebumps litter my arms, and the light pajamas Mara gave me aren't keeping me warm, I still don't get up from the armchair. Shivers break out across my entire body and the darkness swoops in to take me away.

"Valentina, you're finally back." Mom stands in the middle of my room with her arms wide open. I run to her, feeling my tears leave wet trails down my cheeks. "I've missed you too, Mia cara," she says as she buries her face into my hair.

I pull back, my eyes scanning her from head to toe. A gasp leaves my lips as I spot the fading bruise under her right eye, and she winces when I graze her forearm. I grit my teeth to stop myself from confronting my dad for being a coward and thinking that putting his hands on us makes him a man.

Mom shakes her head at me. "Cara, I know how you feel, and I understand. I agree with you and support you, but a man like your Dad cannot be dealt with. At least not by us." She squeezes my shoulders firmly.

I shake my head right back as I tell her, "We can do something, Mama." Her eyes widen at my suggestion.

"I know we can't escape the Outfit. But Dad will get his karma. Someday, someone will give him his due." I tilt my chin, refusing to cower anymore. My Dad's tyranny may work on his soldiers, but not us. Not anymore. Mom's eyes soften as she scans my face.

"You have grown into such a strong and smart young woman. I am so proud of you, beyond what words can convey." Mom's eyes glaze over, and she sniffles a bit before turning her head to the side.

"I've had an amazing role model, after all." I smile. Mom bites her lip and shakes her head, her long blonde hair falling around her shoulders.

"No. I'm not strong. I wish I was, but I couldn't even do my children

justice and protect them from a vile man." The poison in her voice is clear as day, but behind it, her sadness is palpable.

"No, Mama, you are strong. Never think that just because you couldn't leave or protect us, that it's your fault. None of it is your fault." I grab her palms, trying to emphasize my point.

"How adorable, a Mom and daughter reunion."

My eyes fall shut at the grating voice of Nonna from behind me. I breathe in deeply before opening my eyes and turning around to face her. Her salt and pepper hair is twisted into her classic bun, and she is wearing a knee-length burgundy dress. Sporting her permanent scowl, her brows furrows.

"Hi, Nonna." I give her a tight-lipped smile, which she scoffs at and mutters something in Italian before hitting her cane on the hardwood floors twice.

"You came out exactly like your Mom, a pathetic good-for-nothing wench, you have ruined yourself and the family name in the process." She continues after I give her a puzzled look. "You thought the Folonari bastard wouldn't tell us, mock us for stealing a kiss, and in doing so, stealing your virtue."

My throat becomes so dry that my tongue sticks to the roof of my mouth. Chest heaving for breaths, I sway, but Mom's hands steady me from behind. My stomach dips and the bile rises, burning my esophagus in the process. God, I think I'm going to be sick.

Nonna points her wrinkly finger at Mom and I as she says, "For that, your Mom will pay the price, since she didn't know how to raise her daughters to be honorable Italian girls. Angelo and Giovanni, take Diletta." The two soldiers come from behind Nonna and head in Mom and I's direction. I step in their way to stop them, but Nonna steps closer and slaps me, causing me to fall to the ground.

Mom struggles in the soldier's grasp, but she is ultimately dragged away. When I try to get up and follow Mom, Nonna blocks me.

Stomping her cane close to where my hand is, a clear threat. My eyes sting, and I hate myself for how weak I feel. Nonna bends down, her eyes harsh and cold. Almost dead more than alive, and with the little life in them, it's full of hate and cruelty. She grabs the lower half of my face and squeezes, causing pain to shoot through my jaw, but I keep a straight face as she sneers.

"I knew your Mom was a no-good rat when your nonno had introduced her as your Dad's future wife. I tried to warn him, but a woman in our world is nothing more than a glorified 'cum dump,' as you young people say."

I physically recoil at the words she uses, but she keeps her hand firm on my face. She seems unfazed by my absolute disgust as she continues. "I knew your Mom was a whore the day I met her. After all, the Gallo women were known for falling for lower-ranking men. Your youngest aunt ran away with a mere soldier, yet we still accepted your Mom into our family and agreed to marry her to our son. But a defective family such as hers should have never been considered." My nose wrinkles at the way she degrades all my Mom's side of the family, and her eyes narrow before throwing me back and standing up.

"You'd do well to remember yourself, Valentina. You are nothing more than an asset to further your family, your Dad, and the Outfit."

The room shifts into a dingy basement and the sound of something dripping onto the floor echoes. I frantically turn around, trying to see where Nonna has gone. My body becomes taut with terror as I see Mom's, Violette's, Monica's, and Marcello's bodies hanging limply from the ceiling by their arms, their eyes torn out and their mouths agape.

"Valentina, why?" Their moans echo around the basement.

My eyes fly open as my chest constricts, my knuckles turning white as I have the chair's armrests in a death grip. A fine sheen of sweat covers my body. Even as my hands grip the armrests, they shake with the effort of not collapsing back into the chair.

Stomach churning, I stumble before getting to my feet to make it to the bathroom door. The door hits the wall with the effort of me opening it. I struggle to lift the toilet bowl lid before I vomit.

The acid burns my throat, and the smell etches itself into my nose. My body trembles with sobs as I continue to throw up until my stomach is empty. I lean back as I dry heave, small pieces of my hair sticking to my face.

I slowly make my way onto my feet and head to the sink. I lift my shaking arms to rest them on the counter, but looking in the mirror makes me grimace. My cheeks are flushed, my hair resembles someone who's gotten struck by lightning, and my shoulders are shaking even as my hands grip the sink.

Goosebumps litter my arms as the cold sweat dries. I manage to drag myself toward the shower and sluggishly turn the knobs till the bathroom fills with steam, and the scorching water pummels on top of my head, soaking me. I don't bother with taking the pajamas off, exhaustion winning over.

I lean back onto the wall behind me, just listening as the water hits the tiles. The smell of vomit is still strong, and it makes me retch a couple of times before I decide that I should probably get out of the shower.

But instead, my knees buckle, and I feel my body descend till my butt hits the floor. My eyes feel heavy, and even the shivering doesn't stop me from falling asleep again. The darkness takes the place of the bathroom walls.

I GROAN AS I TRY TO PUSH BACK THE BLANKET OFF MY OVERHEATED body, but a hand slaps my hands, and someone scolds me.

"No, don't try to move the blanket. You have a cold and you need to stay warm."

My eyes flutter open, but I shut them as soon as I had opened them, the light blinding me and causing my head to throb.

I feel the bile rising as my stomach swooshes, and I rush to get up to get to the bathroom. When I finally manage to stumble inside, I spill my guts into the toilet bowl.

A large, warm hand rubs my back, and I can vaguely make out a soothing voice encouraging me to breathe. I groan as I squeeze my eyes, feeling so tired and disoriented. As I lean back into the warmth, I feel a sense of security and safety I've never felt before, even as fatigue leaves me disoriented.

After emptying my guts and dry heaving a couple more times, I let the person guide me back to the bed and cover me with the blanket. A shiver rolls through me, and I snuggle into the bed, bringing the blankets up to my chin.

I struggle with the exhaustion once more, and before I fall asleep, I mutter a thank you, but I can't make out a response I'm sleeping once again.

I CAN HEAR FAINT VOICES FLOAT AROUND ME, AND FOR A SECOND, I think it's my family, but then the memories of what had happened over the past couple of days come rushing back to me.

I keep my eyes closed and try to listen to what they're saying, but the pounding in my head doesn't help.

The room goes silent for a minute, and multiple footsteps sound around the room, coming closer, then stopping before someone says, "I know you're awake."

I sigh and open my eyes to see Emiliano, Mariana, Alessia, Mara, and Romiro all standing around the bed. My head throbs as the light irritates my retinas, and I wince but keep them open.

"Wh-" My voice comes out hoarse, so I try clearing my throat. Emiliano pours me a cup of water and hands it to me. I accept it, grateful for the gesture. The cold water soothes the dryness in my throat. "What happened?" I finally manage to ask. No one answers for a couple of beats, and my eyes filter around to look at their faces.

"Mara came to your room the next morning after the picnic, but you weren't answering, so she thought you were still asleep, but when you didn't come out at all, and then you also weren't answering the door, Mom and Mara decided to ask Romiro to break the door to see what happened." Emiliano pauses for a second as he clenches his jaw.

"They found you passed out on the bathroom floor with the shower on and the room was practically full of steam," he finishes saying. Oh. I don't remember any of that.

I notice that I'm not in the same room I was in. The walls are a muted sage with light brown accents, the bed covers a light green with white leaf patterns.

"Where am I?"

"My room." Emiliano's the one to tell me, and confusion spears through me. I give him a quizzical look, which he chooses to ignore. My eyes fall to the bed sheets as I try to comprehend what the hell is going on.

"How many hours have I been out?" I ask, looking back up at them. Mariana, Mara, and Alessia all wince as if they don't know how to answer that, and both Romiro's and Emiliano's faces are set in unreadable masks.

"You've been out for close to a week now." No... A week, as in, *seven days*. I try to get up, but the room spins, and a palm presses into my shoulder, pushing me back down. A hysterical sob rises in my throat, but I swallow it and look at Alessia.

"Why was I out for that long?" The panic, clear as day in my voice, seems to incite sympathy from her as she gives me a weak smile.

"You were technically out completely for three days, but then you became hysterical and wouldn't lie down, so we had to give you some medicine to calm you. You were also in a lot of pain."

My throat suddenly feels dry and the pounding in my head seems to be getting worse. I close my eyes, pushing my head farther into the pillow. She's not wrong about the pain; I can still feel the aches and tiredness lingering in my limbs.

I'm drained, my eyes heavy. Everyone seems to see that, and Emiliano nods and says, "Get some rest, we'll be nearby." I wish I had the energy to say something back, but the room fades as my eyes fall shut.

CHAPTER 14
EMILIANO

I pace my room while Valentina sleeps off whatever she has.

"I don't understand why you didn't tell me earlier," I tell Romiro.

He shrugs. "I didn't think it was that important to you. You barely know her. I mean, yes, you've had a few moments together and all, but we truly didn't think it was that serious."

I run my hand through my hair, pulling at the root, trying to figure out why it bothers me that she was sick for three days before I knew about it. And why the fuck I felt the need to fly back the New Hampshire the same day to come see for myself.

"I have to go, but make sure she has plenty of fluids. She's been vomiting a lot and needs to stay hydrated," Alessia says as she walks by to head to the door of my personal living room. I nod grimly.

"I'll take you home," Romiro offers. Alessia gives him a shy smile. My eyes narrow as I watch them leave the room, but I brush off the suspicious feeling that something might be going on between my cousin and best friend. Ma closes the bedroom door behind her, leaving Mara in the room with Valentina.

"She feels guilty for not saying something earlier. She blames herself that Valentina is this sick." Ma sighs as she plops down on one of the armchairs. I shake my head.

"She shouldn't be feeling guilty at all. It's not her fault." I don't say what everyone is thinking, but the insinuation hangs in the air.

"No, Emiliano, it isn't your fault either. At least not her becoming this sick. You didn't want her to get sick, but you do want to use her as leverage against her family, which isn't something I like or agree with."

"Ma, I don't know what you want me to do. The only way for us to get our revenge is by dangling Moretti's daughter in front of him," I tell her. Ma's shoulders drop, and exhaustion bleeds into her face. She leans back into the armchair and carefully watches me.

"You know, when I married your Dad, I was scared. I thought he was going to be cruel and try to break me." She shrugs one shoulder before continuing. "At least that's what everyone tried to tell me, and the rumors certainly didn't help. Our families had been enemies up to the peace agreement and the wedding. He didn't speak much during our engagement, but after the wedding, when I slowly got to know him, I liked what I learned. He was kind in his own way, and he never thought of me as any less when the…incident happened."

I grind my teeth as I try to calm the wave of rage that has taken over at the mention of the past.

"Let's not, Ma. The past is the past, and talking about Dad isn't helping." My voice is strained and my entire body tenses as I run my thumb over the small scar on the side of my neck.

"Why not? You're Capo, but lately all you seem to be doing is running from the problems instead of trying to solve them."

The sound of the bedroom door falling shut reaches us, and Mara steps closer.

"Watch your tone, Mara. I will not tolerate disrespect," I warn, and she glowers at me before sighing and heading toward the doors to leave.

"Where are you going?" Ma asks her.

"To get Valentina some hot soup, since someone refuses to stop throwing his weight around." She gives me a pointed look, at which I laugh and shake my head.

"I'll come help you." Ma quickly rushes after Mara, and the room settles into silence after the door closes with a click.

I look at my bedroom door, debating whether to go in there. I decide against it, grab a glass of water, and sit on the couch facing the fireplace. The TV is on, but it's muted. My brow furrows as I read the headline. *"Freda's Jewelry, one of the most well-known Jewelry stores in the country, has been robbed in their New York city location in the jewelry district. The company is yet to make a statement."*

My glass shatters as it hits the wall next to the TV. For fuck's sake, I can't leave for a couple of days without things going to absolute shit. Just as I reach for my phone to call Romiro, it rings.

"I want to know who the fuck attacked one of our stores," I demand, leaning back.

"It was the fucking Outfit. The fucking little shits thought they could attack without being caught," he tells me with a sigh. My eyebrows reach my hairline as my jaw clenches.

"What the fuck do you mean by that? Are you saying that they stepped foot in my territory?"

"Yes, some soldiers were in the area and were able to get them." *Fuck yes.*

"Is the little bastard with them?" I really fucking hope so, so I can send the little Moretti headache back to her family and be rid of her. To my disappointment, Romiro answers with exactly what I don't want to hear.

"No."

"I want you to take care of them, and take both Lucio and Matteo with you. It's about time they got their hands back in the game."

"Are you not coming as well?" he asks, but I don't answer, not wanting to look too deep into why I'm not going.

"I have things to take care of. You make sure that everything goes smoothly."

"Yes, I'll also keep you updated."

I end the call and place my phone back on the coffee table. I still need to contact the Morettis to ask for what we want for the return of their daughter. A thud comes from my room, instantly concerning me. I get up and rush to the door to check if Valentina is okay.

When I slightly crack the door open, I find Valentina gripping one of the bedside tables. I rush toward her and grab her by her upper arm, and she glares when she looks up at me.

"Why are you getting up? You need to be resting."

She tries to swat my arm away, but stops when I don't budge.

"Let me go. I want to go back to the other room," she demands. I narrow my eyes as I observe her, setting her back on the bed.

"Why are you being stubborn?"

"Why are you being a busybody? It's annoying."

I ignore her and place my palm on her forehead to check her temperature. It seems to have gone down since last night. She pushes my arm away with an eye roll, and I let her.

"Why am I in your room?" she asks. I turn around and walk to some of my drawers.

"Because the room you were staying in isn't suitable anymore, and I don't trust you to place you anywhere near my family, so you're stuck here," I say as I pull out a pair of green pajamas from when I was younger, hoping that they'll fit her, even though they still look a couple of sizes too big.

"Where the hell have you been sleeping, then?"

When I turn to look at her with the pjs in my hand, I see that she's still glaring at me. I shake my head and step toward her.

"Don't get all worked up over nothing. I slept out there on one of the couches." That's a lie' I barely slept, because she was so sick that she was burning up most of the night, just like the other past five days I have been here. But she doesn't need to know that. I place the clothes next to her on the bed.

She crosses her arms and tilts her chin up before asking with narrowed eyes, "How do I know that you're not lying?"

Her question amuses me more than it should, and I feel my lips lifting into a smug smile. "Maybe I am lying, and I slept right next to you in *my bed*," I tease. She wrinkles her nose in a way that makes her look younger than she is. Her face is now less pale with some color bleeding back into her cheeks.

"I'm just fucking with you. The shower is through that door if you want to use it. I'll be out there, so if you need anything, don't hesitate to ask me."

With that, I walk out the door and into my living room and plop back onto the couch. I don't do anything but listen to any sound that indicates that she has decided to use the shower. When I hear a door slamming from inside my bedroom, I turn up the volume of the TV and sit back with my hands behind my head.

After thirty minutes, both Mara and Ma walk into my living room with two trays. One full of fruits and light snacks and the other has a soup bowl with two cups of smoothies. They place both trays on the coffee table in front of me. I give them a grin as I sit up.

"Ma and my precious sister prepared appetizing snacks for me, how sweet?" They don't look impressed by my fake enthusiasm, and Ma slaps my hand away when I reach for some blueberries.

"Stop it, Emiliano," she reprimands, and when she spots the shattered glass on the floor, she raises an eyebrow but doesn't say anything.

I open my mouth to ask her about when she wants to go back to New York, but my bedroom door opening snags our attention. Valentina walks out with her hair wet from the shower. The clothes are big on her, making her look comical. But seeing her in my clothes makes me want to own her body and soul. It's a jarring feeling to ignore. Ma and Mara both shoot me a look like they can read my mind before heading to her. I can tell they're fussing over her, but I can't make out anything.

They keep throwing glances my way before Ma turns on her heel and faces me. "Emiliano, go to your office or somewhere else."

"Fuck no. This is my room."

"Oh my God, just get out. You're being annoying," Mara whines. With a huff, I give her the finger and get up, grabbing my phone off the table and slipping it into my black jogger pants.

"Try anything, Moretti, and I will not hesitate to skin you alive," I warn before leaving out the door. Instead of going to my office, I head to the garden, stopping on my way to grab my gardening tools. The weather is surprisingly warm for October as I head out to the backyard.

The wisteria plants cling to the side of the glass door and around the glass windows, snaking up to the second floor of the greenhouse. Unlocking the door, I'm met with the earthy smell of the plants.

The humidity sticks to my skin and my shoes are muffled as I step on the grass from the mosaic pavement. I place the gardening tools on the stone bench next to the fountain, turning the fountain on before surveying the greenhouse, making out the distinct smell of rosemary.

I check on the rosemary shrubs before moving to the thyme and oregano on the right of the fountain, then head up the spiral stairs.

I bend my head as I pass some of the low-hanging lavender flowers. I tend to the wild olive trees, making sure that there aren't any moths, ants or bacteria eating at the plant. After watering them, I begrudgingly move to the cape bushes, violets, and the bougainvilleas planted on the other side of the greenhouse, opposite of the trees. I water them, ripping out any dry leaves and making sure that I don't overwater any of the flowers.

By the time I'm done, I sweat drips down my forehead and off my brow. My joggers are dirty at the knees and some dirt has managed to get on my shirt. The sound of footsteps up the metal spiral staircase alert me to the presence of someone else. I don't turn around, instead taking off one of my gardening gloves to check on the flower petals of the cape bushes.

"You barely go in here after Dad died," Matteo comments. I grit my teeth.

"I know, Matteo, I don't need you to remind me." I get up, turning to face him. "Why aren't you with Lucio and Romiro?" I ask as I take off my other glove, holding both in my hand as we head to the stairs.

"I didn't want to go. I needed to get some codes done before going down to New York."

I let him go ahead of me.

"Right, well, you need to go down there by this evening, or tomorrow, at the latest."

He doesn't reply but nods, walking past the fountain and pausing near the door. Crossing his arms over his chest, his eyes are emotionless as usual. I pick up my phone and the gardening tools I had left and move closer to the house.

"I've set up the codes and ran the tests. They'll surpass any security the Russians might have." He gives me a look before continuing. "I'm going to see Mara and Ma before heading to New York."

"Don't drag it out, Matteo. Make sure to call me when you get to New York."

He nods and we break off at the stairs. I head to the guest wing to take a shower and change into another set of clean clothes.

The room is smaller than mine and has cream walls and a black carpet. With the curtains drawn, the room is shrouded in shadows. I flick the light on and head into the bathroom, quickly washing my hair and moving on to lathering my body until every inch is covered. After rinsing, I dry myself with a towel, realizing I forgot to grab some new clothes. I wrap another towel around my midsection and shoot Victor a text to grab me a change of clothes from my room.

I comb through my hair as I dry it, running my fingers through it every couple of minutes to check if it's dry enough. As I'm shaving my stubble, I see the bathroom door open and Ginevra slips in, wearing a red robe.

I ignore her and continue to shave my face, washing the blade before moving to the other side. Ginevra and I make eye contact through the mirror. She winks at me, and I narrow my eyes at her.

She takes it as a sign to glide her hands down the robe and untie the knot holding it closed. When the robe opens wide enough, I can see that she isn't wearing anything underneath. Her pink nipples harden as she toys with them, still watching me.

"You better not have been walking around my house naked under that while my family is here," I warn. She struts to me and wraps a hand around my bicep.

"Jealous?" she asks. I bark out a laugh at the absurdity and accidentally cut my cheek in the process. A small bead of blood forms before slowly dripping down my face till it hits my chin and drops into the sink. Ginevra gasps before trying to turn me around. I shrug her off and continue to shave.

"Go away, Ginevra. I'm not going to fuck you."

She bats her lashes, pouting at me through the mirror.

"Maybe I just want to spend some quality time with the best boss ever."

I break eye contact and focus on my jaw. After wiping the blade, I wash my face and pat it dry.

"I will boil you alive, fry your skin, and feed you to my dogs if you don't get the fuck out," I threaten. She scurries off, but not before quickly grabbing her robe off the ground. I grip the sink, dropping my head between my shoulders.

Today is the day I need to call Moretti to demand what we want. I'm done playing the long game. I thought making him feel like he was being forced into a corner, waiting for us to make up our minds, would have been a sweet revenge. But all it has been is torture, torture that whatever I have with Valentina will eventually come to an end. Before it even truly begins.

I need Valentina out before she fucks with my head any longer. I run my tongue across my bottom lip, remembering how she was so fucking responsive. I splash my face with cold water and walk out of the bathroom to an empty room. I spot some clothes on the floor and guess that they are what Ginevra was wearing before coming into the bathroom.

Instead of going back to my room, where I know the little Moretti vixen is, I head to my office and call Costa.

"If you're going to ask about any updates of our murderer, then don't. There aren't any. Also, the Vasilievs want to set up a meeting when they're back from Moscow." He jumps right in after picking up the phone. I lean back into my office chair and release a sigh of annoyance.

"Tell Romanov Vasiliev that I'm not talking to his hag of a father. He can wait until he drops dead, and then we'll talk," I tell him.

"You really hate that man." Costa chuckles.

"Let's just say that if he'd tripped and landed on a knife, I wouldn't be sad about it." I pick up my pen, clicking it a couple of times before placing it back on my desk. "How are you and your little wife?" I ask him.

Costa clips, "Fine." Costa and his wife, Chiara, have been married for just over two years. The union was arranged by their parents to finally put their businesses together. Both families have been trying to put the other out of business for at least three decades. Guess even if you marry the enemy and live together, you'll still hate each other.

Ending the call, I flip open my laptop and browse through our bets on our latest fight. Aurelio's last fight was another to the death. The madman of the Famiglia has been fighting in our clubs for a while. My gut tells me that it's not because he can't fight in Vegas.

I shoot Romiro a text, telling him to see what the fucker from Vegas is up to.

Stretching, I get up from my chair. I've been working for the past couple of hours on the legitimate side of our business. Smoothing out things with our lawyers. I crack my fingers and roll my shoulders before heading to the door.

I have never minded the silence; it is always welcomed. Especially in a family as big as mine, they can become a headache very quickly.

I'm surprised to see that my living room is vacant and no one is in there. My eyes narrow slightly, as Valentina should still be here. My sister and Ma might not agree with the things I do as Capo, but they wouldn't act out and go against my instructions.

I make my way to my bedroom and relax when I hear the tap running in my bathroom. I settle on one of the brown armchairs in the corner of my room. Slipping my phone out, I scroll till I reach Moretti's number.

My thumb hovers over it, but my eyes snap to the bathroom door when I hear soft humming. She's humming? Whoever is marrying her is definitely getting a handful. An amused smile touches my face. It quickly turns into a smug smirk as she steps out of the bathroom. She jumps a little, her small palm clenching her chest.

"What the fuck! You scared me," she yelps. I remain seated and rest my elbows on my knees, watching her.

"Such a filthy mouth for a supposed honorable Italian woman. Besides, how can I scare you when I'm just sitting in my room?" I tut, amused. Valentina glares at me and flips me off before heading to the door.

"Where are you going?" I ask. She pauses and looks back at me.

"To hell. Actually, never mind, that's your actual home."

I bark out a laugh and her cheeks seem to heat in response.

"Come here," I order, at which she shakes her head. "Come here, Valentina, or so help me God, I will fucking spank you for being disobedient."

Her eyes widen before she darts toward the chair farthest away from me. Once she settles, she looks at me with a strange expression, but it's gone before I'm able to decipher it.

"Thank you," she says softly. My jaw clenches, and I shake my head.

"What for?" I murmur.

"For taking care of me while I was sick." She fiddles with her hands.

"It wasn't for your benefit. You're no use to me dead," I say, and she flinches. A flicker of guilt settles in my chest, but I quickly put it out. I grind my teeth to stop myself from retracting what I said. She's the fucking enemy, no matter what she makes me feel. I clear my throat before speaking.

"What do you know about your cousin?" I ask her. She tilts her head. It's subtle enough that it's barely noticeable, but I notice it.

"Which one?"

"Giuseppe."

She stiffens for a second before trying to appear relaxed. I narrow my eyes.

"Not much, except that he was initiated a couple of weeks ago."

The lie rolls off her tongue so well, if I didn't know better, I would've believed her. I stand abruptly and stalk toward her.

"Don't fucking lie to me, Valentina. You don't want to fuck with me," I warn. Her face twists in disgust.

She sneers, "You don't scare me, Emiliano Folonari. Especially a man who can't even look at a woman after kissing her."

I trap her in her seat with my hands on the sides of the armchair. My face is inches from hers. I take in her eyes, flushed cheeks, shaky breaths, my gaze stopping on her lips.

"You want to bet that I can't look a woman in the face after kissing her?" I challenge. She clenches her jaw, not answering me. "Answer me, ragazza mocciosa," I purr in her ear.

A shiver racks her body. Without a thought, my tongue darts out and sucks her earlobe into my mouth. I tug on it lightly before letting it go. As my nose trails down the side of her slender neck, she makes a strangled noise in the back of her throat, but she doesn't move. I pause, stepping back abruptly, running my fingers through my hair. She stares up at me, confused and unsure. I should leave the room before I do something that I'll regret...or worse yet, not regret at all.

"I'm leaving," I mutter.

CHAPTER 15

VALENTINA

My nails dig into my palms as I try to think clearly, but my thoughts remain a foggy mess. I debate whether to stop him or not. He's the enemy, the man who took me from my family and disrupted my entire life. But it's not like I had any choice in what I was going to have to do in that godforsaken house.

Fuck it, this is the only chance I have at any semblance of control over my life. With a jolt, I get up my steps, unsure Do I really want to risk everything just to have my first time under my own conditions? Yes, yes, I do. I bite my lip, taking hurried steps after Emiliano.

Once he's an arm's length away, I reach my hand out and tug on his shirt. He stiffens with his hand on the doorknob, but doesn't turn around.

"I don't think you know what you're doing," he rasps.

"I want this," I whisper to his back. He's quick. He turns around and grabs me by the throat, pinning me to the wall next to the door. His eyes are dark, assessing me. My throat flexes under his grip, and he squeezes tighter.

He brings his face next to my ear, whispering, "What is it that you want, exactly?"

"You're really going to make me say it?" I run my tongue across my lips.

"You either say it, or I'm walking away," he threatens.

I place my hand on his abdomen, and he tenses for half a second before pressing up against me.

"I want you," I murmur.

"You want me to do what?" He runs his nose along the side of my face, making me shiver.

"I want you to..." My cheeks heat as I trail off, breaths stuttering. He releases a breathy chuckle against me.

"You want me to fuck you?" he asks, and I nod. Has his voice always been this husky? My hands shake as I try to understand what's going on when he squeezes my throat again.

"It's a yes or no question. I need you to use your words."

A tingle travels down my spine and lands between my legs as his voice caresses my neck.

"Yes, I want you to fuck me. Please."

"So fucking sweet and polite when you want something. Huh," he teases, and I gasp when he tugs on my earlobe again. His hand on my throat drops, then both of his hands rest on my waist.

"I'm not fucking you, not today, but I will teach you something else," he tells me, and I instantly feel the need to question him.

"Why not?" I ask, brow furrowed as I look up at him. His grip on my waist tightens.

"Because I want you desperate and needy when I fuck you." He removes his hands before caging my wrists in his grip, placing them on the wall beside my head. His face slowly inches toward mine, his eyes on my lips.

They darken when my tongue peeks out to run across my bottom lip. Brushing his lips against mine, he finally kisses me. He bites my bottom lip before gliding his tongue over it. Darting my tongue out a little, I flick his.

A groan sounds deep in his throat as he swirls his tongue around mine. I press myself deeper into the wall, my knees buckling for a second at the sensation. When a whimper escapes me, Emiliano breaks off the kiss. He rests his forehead on mine, our breaths mingling as both our chests heave.

"Get on the bed." He moves to the side to let me walk by, and I swallow, feeling uneasy with my back to him. As if he'd bounce on me any second, but he doesn't. As I sit on the edge of the bed, Emiliano is watching me from where he's standing. He juts his chin toward me.

"Take off your clothes," he orders me. I'm not wearing anything under the joggers and hoodie. My fingers tremble as I reach for the bottom of the hoodie, adrenaline pumping through my body.

The hoodie lands with a whoosh on the ground, and Emiliano sucks in a breath as his eyes leave a hot trail down my body. My nipples pucker from the cold air, and I reach to cover my chest. Emiliano shakes his head before growling, "Take the rest off."

We don't break eye contact as I reach for the joggers, my hands shaking like leaves on a branch in the wind. The joggers join the hoodie on the floor.

He stays where he's standing, his body almost too still. My heart pounds so hard against my ribs that I think he might hear it. Is he going to leave?

"I want you to lay on the bed and spread your thighs."

My thighs involuntarily clench together, causing his eyes to follow the movement. I quickly follow his instructions before he decides otherwise.

A flicker of disappointment runs through me when he heads to the door. It dies as soon as it appears because he just flicks the lock. The cold air makes the goosebumps covering my skin even more prominent as it licks at the warmth of my body.

Once I rest my head on the pillow, I can't see Emiliano from where he is standing, but then his steps thud on the wooden floors. Slow and steady. Confident and patient. He stops at the foot of the bed, hands in his pockets, watching me. His eyes drink me in, and my body warms under his stare. "So fucking beautiful. I wonder what I fucking did to deserve both torture and pleasure in one package," he says, but before I can think of a reply, he continues. "I'm going to drag you to the edge of the bed. Is that okay with you?" His voice is dark, causing another shiver to run through me. I nod, unsure of what I should do.

"Yes," I breathe when he quirks an eyebrow. His hands clasp my ankles, and they slowly pull me to the edge of the bed. I suck in another breath as the sheets drag along my sensitive flesh.

He gets on his knees, his hands trailing up my legs before he moves them to his shoulders. Emiliano's face is so close to my pussy that when he blows a breath out, it reaches my wet folds.

I grip the sheets lightly, waiting. His eyes stay on my face as his tongue darts out, swirling around my clit before thrusting inside. A moan tears from my lips, and I clamp my hand over my mouth. He shakes his head.

"I want to hear you when my fucking face is between your thighs. Don't try to hold back anything. Your moans are mine as much as every orgasm I'm taking from you," he growls. I remove my hand off my mouth, and he begins to lap up the wetness dripping down.

Becoming more demanding, his tongue thrusts inside me more powerfully, a hot molten ball building up inside me, in the pit of my stomach as I clutch onto the sheets. Everything he's doing feels so good, so different. My hands shake, palms becoming slick with sweat as he flicks my clit with his thumb. Another loud moan rings out, causing him to flick a couple more times. With a groan, Emiliano parts my pussy lips before lapping at entrance.

"So fucking wet and sweet," he murmurs against my pussy before inserting one of his thick, long fingers inside me. It goes in easily because of how wet I am. The feeling is uncomfortable for a bit before he begins to massage my inner muscles.

"Oh God," I breathe out. My moans turn into pleas when he thrusts deeper and inserts a second finger, curling them while his tongue circles my clit. My stomach tightens, and my back arches slightly, grinding lightly against his face. As his tongue swirls around my clit, the sensation only has me more sensitive. His fingers pump viciously inside me, curling between thrusts.

"That's right, baby, I am your God, but I'm the one doing the worshiping," he growls as he speeds up. Emiliano's movements become savage, almost blinding, my vision blurring, and I find it hard to maintain eye contact as my core clenches.

"Be a good girl and come for me, *ragazza mocciosa*."

At his coaxing, I throw my head back, eyes rolling as white-hot pleasure spears through me and I clench around his fingers. Running my hand through his hair, I tug at the roots and cry out.

Emiliano doesn't stop lapping at my center, only slowing his pace as my walls ease pulsing around his fingers. When he eventually removes his fingers from inside me, they come out with a pop.

We stare at each other, my chest heaving as I try to catch my breath, and he brings his fingers to his mouth before sucking my arousal off. "Divine," he says as he winks. If I wasn't already flushed, I would become as red as a tomato.

My skin is slick with my sweat, and I stare at him with droopy eyes. Throat constricting, something weighs down in my chest. I shake off the shame, not wanting to feel the way I do after my first orgasm. My entire body's sore, and my limbs feel heavy as I try to get up.

"What about you?" I ask, pointing to his erection when I notice it as he stands back up.

"Not today. This is enough for now. Get some rest." He takes one of the pillows off the bed and heads to a drawer in the corner of the bedroom.

"Where are you going?" I ask.

He doesn't turn to look at me as he digs through the drawer.

"I'm sleeping in the living room," he tells me. My eyebrows pull together in confusion.

"Why?" I probe. He pauses and looks back at me.

"So you can sleep in here."

"I'm sure it's fine after what just happened," I point out. He narrows his eyes as his face closes off.

"I don't sleep in the same room, let alone the same bed, with a woman."

Ouch. Okay, I guess I'm just being lumped in with every other woman he's had a sexual encounter with. If he notices that what he said hurt me, he doesn't comment as he pulls a blanket from the drawer.

He places the pillow under his arm and the blanket over his shoulder as he heads to the door. But before he leaves, he pauses in front of it with his hand on the lock, as if debating whether to stay. Shaking his head, he unlocks the door and opens it.

The door closes with a click, and I'm left with the silence of the room. I run my hand through my hair, sighing. How could I do that with him? What the fuck am I going to do when I go back home?

I've just risked not only my life but my mom's and siblings'. I'm so fucking stupid. I get up with another sigh, needing another shower before bed.

After showering and drying off, I try to resist the urge of snooping, but it only lasts for a couple of minutes. I look through his bedside tables. I don't find much in the first one, except for a very pretty dagger.

The handle is gold with carvings and words that read *forever & always*. I place it back where I found it and notice a necklace that I'd missed. It's got a gold chain with a dainty tear-shaped emerald in the middle, surrounded by sapphires.

The emerald is the size of the top of my pinkie. It looks sentimental, so I gently put it back in its place. On the other bedside table, there's a picture of Eli, Matteo, Lucio, Mara, Mariana, and an older gentleman who looks like the older version of Eli. Eli? Since when did I start calling him that?

I rub my hand down my face. Jesus, I need to get a grip. The man gave me one orgasm and I feel comfortable calling him by his nickname.

I pick up the frame to take a closer look. They all seem so much younger. Emiliano looks like he's in his early twenties. Mara and Matteo both look so young, they must be around thirteen in the picture.

Lucio's quite tall for his age. Mariana and the older version of Emiliano are both looking at each other, smiling blissfully. They appear so happy and content. As if the world can throw anything at them, and they'll be able to handle it with ease.

I bite the side of my cheek, wondering if my family could've been like this if Dad wasn't so power hungry and corruption didn't run so rampant in his blood that it poisoned us.

I'm sure the older man in the picture was just as corrupt, but the love that is clear in his eyes probably helped keep it away from his family.

I run my thumb over Emiliano's face, drinking in his boyish smile. He must've been around my age, but you can tell he was already a Made man with blood on his hands.

I startle when I hear a loud groan. Setting back the photo on the side table, I take a step toward the door. There's another groan as I inch closer. I place my ear against the door and cradle it with my hand to try to hear better.

"Fuck-oh my-Jesus." Oh my God, is that Emiliano? What is he doing? His voice is trembling, and his groans are low and deep. My other hand reaches for the handle. I debate whether to crack the door open a bit to see what he's doing.

The door silently opens, and I try to see through the slit. The scene in front of me makes my blood heat and my cheeks flush instantly. My chest heaves as my breathing picks up. Emiliano is splayed on the couch half naked, his hand pumping his cock up and down. Fast.

I crack the door open a bit farther, curiosity getting the better of me. His head is thrown back, his breaths so loud I could hear them from where I stand. My breath hitches when his eyes meet mine and he doesn't stop, but he slowly strokes his cock.

"This is what you fucking do to me," he groans, pre-cum leaking from the tip of his thick, long cock. It's veiny and huge. I feel my thighs press together as my center throbs with pleasure. The corner of his lips quirk in a smirk before his eyes become hooded and he continues to stare at me as his fist keeps stroking.

He comes with a guttural groan, his hips pumping upwards a few times before he's spent. His hand and cock are covered in cum, and it slides down his cock, pooling on his hand. Emiliano grabs a couple of tissues from the coffee table and cleans himself up without getting up, and I stand still, seemingly frozen.

He doesn't look my way as he continues to clean up. Shaking myself out of my haze, I step into the living room carefully, and he turns to me. He watches me through a hooded gaze, his teeth sinking into his lip.

"I'd fuck you so hard if I thought that you are ready. Fuck, are you wet, baby?" he asks, and I can feel my core pull taunt with desire.

My heart stutters at the sight of him. His hair disheveled, shirtless, all his tattoos on display. I trace each one with my eyes, committing each one to my memory. My favorite is the two snakes on the sides of his abs with their forked tongues out. When I step closer, I notice the fangs have beads of venom covering them. I reach the edge of the couch in a couple of steps without taking my eyes off of him. When my eyes make their way down to his cock, they widen as I take in his once soft flaccid cock has become hard as rock again. My tongue darts out quickly as I wet my lips.

Emiliano growls, "Don't fucking do that when you're looking at my cock, or I'll find that tongue a better job to do." My hand reaches out involuntarily, but he grabs my wrist softly, stopping me. My eyes flicker to his face. "I didn't say you could touch it." He doesn't let my hand go, instead tugging me on top of him. I land between his legs, my center on his warm cock and my face inches from his face.

His eyes twinkle with mischief and my heart stutters at the light smirk that touches his lips. My hands rest on his chest and his on my hips. As I study his face, minty breath fans across my lips.

I'm so close I can make out a faint scar on his eyelid, his blue eyes with small specks of green. His eyes fall closed as my finger traces the scar on his face.

"How did you get this?" I ask.

"When I was five, I was riding a bike down the streets in New Hampton. I didn't see a rock on the ground," he whispers back as he lifts a shoulder. "I toppled over and cut my eyelid on something."

"Did you bleed?" I ask, and a ghost of a smile touches his lips once more.

"A lot. When Ma saw me, she thought I popped my eye out."

That doesn't surprise me. Mariana seems to be the kind of mom who would be overprotective of her kids.

His hands move up to my waist and he circles me with his arms, pulling my body flush against him. Emiliano is all hard muscles, his cock pressing against my center persistently. I pull my bottom lip in between my teeth, biting back a moan at the feeling of him.

"I told you not to leave your room," he says, and I nod.

"I know, but then I heard…" I start, but then I stop, and he quirks an eyebrow as if he knows what I'm saying and wants me to finish. My face heats once again. "I heard you doing what you were doing," I confess, and he gives me a teasing grin.

"And what is it that I was doing?" he asks, and I roll my lips between my teeth, debating how to respond.

"Masturbating," I whisper. He makes a sound at the back of his throat, his light blue eyes darkening to a navy, threatening to swallow me.

"Give me your lips," he mumbles. I inch toward him slowly, my body hyper aware of each breath he takes and each movement. I feel lightheaded when our lips are barely an inch away.

One of Emiliano's arms leaves my waist, and he grabs the back of my head with his hand. He pulls on my nape till our lips finally touch. His kiss is lazy, unhurried, and all the same intoxicating.

He swallows the moan that leaves my lips when he nips the corner of my mouth. His tongue demands entry, and I part my mouth slightly. With a groan, his tongue strokes mine.

His hand slips into the joggers I'm wearing, and his fingers reach my slit, teasing. Groaning once he feels how wet I am, the hand at the back of my head trails down and joins the other.

His tongue swirls around mine as his fingers slowly part my pussy lips, and he slips one inside, slowly, almost at a tormenting speed. My fingers sink into his chest as I tug at his bottom lip with a frustrated growl, needing more.

He chuckles into my mouth before he thrusts his finger fully into me, causing me to jolt on his lap. My walls clench around his finger, and he breaks the kiss, keeping his mouth a breath away from mine.

"So wet. I thought you hated me?" His lips move over mine as he speaks each word like a taunt. A gasp escapes my lips as he curls his finger, and I feel my slickness coating my thighs.

"Fuck you," I moan, and he chuckles darkly before adding a second finger and pumping them slowly, his other hand trailing seductively to my clit.

"On the contrary, I'm fucking you, ragazza mocciosa," he says, and just when I can feel my orgasm on the brink, he slows his thrusting, slowly dislodging his fingers. A sob breaks from my chest, and he breathes an amused sigh.

"Aww, was my poor ragazza about to come?" he mocks. My stomach tightens at his dark tone and a curl of pleasure swirls around in my stomach. I try to push my hips back to slip his thick fingers back in. A loud smack echoes around the room, my ass stinging. My eyes widen at the realization that he just spanked me.

"You answer me when I ask you a question. Understood?" He raises an eyebrow. I swallow, nodding frantically. I know my mistake after he spanks me again.

"Yes," I breathe. His hands smooth over the stinging area before they move back near my center.

"Do you want to come?" he muses, his light touch making me tremble.

"I do." I watch the dark amusement in his eyes.

"Then beg."

My breathing catches and my fingers dig deeper into his chest. As I rub against him, I'm sure he feels how hard my nipples are, beyond turned on.

"Please, let me come." I don't know how it's possible, but I go even more red, and my cheeks feel as if they're on fire.

"Please, let me come on your fingers," he corrects.

"Please, let me come on your fingers." Begging definitely wasn't something I thought could turn me on, but my body disagrees as slickness trails off my thigh.

"Fuck me thirty ways till Sunday. If you beg like that, I think I would burn the world for you."

I don't have time to process what he just said because he sinks his fingers into me and thrusts harder and faster than before. The room spins as I ripple around his fingers and low heat pools into my lower abdomen.

I bury my face into his neck, arching slightly into him. He doesn't slow down, drawing out my orgasm and soaking his fingers with every drop of me as I moan and whimper. Emiliano's fingers leave my pussy with a pop, and through hooded eyes, I watch him suck his fingers like I'm a delicacy. My breath fans across his throat, rapidly slowing down. In the next blink, he flips us around so quickly that it disorients me.

"I want you to sit on the edge of the couch for me." He rises as he pulls his boxers and joggers over his still hard cock. I don't know what I should do in this situation. He's already given me multiple orgasms and has gotten nothing in return.

"What about that?" I ask, jutting my chin at his dick, slowly sitting up.

"We'll deal with that after I'm done getting another orgasm out of you." He slowly kneels in front of the couch between my legs. I shake my head.

"I don't think I have another in me." Even as I say that, I scoot to the edge of the couch, and he grabs my waist.

"Yes, you do, because you love being a good girl for me."

Goosebumps pebble my arms and another wave of shame washes over me at how much I like hearing him call me a good girl. His good girl.

This is so wrong, and I don't think I should be doing this, but something deep within me eats up every word he says, every touch and every look. I think I might have an obsession with the man kneeling in front of me.

"Up," he orders, and as I lift myself up a bit, he yanks the rest of the joggers down, leaving my lower half naked to the cold air.

His tattooed hands trail up my leg, from my calf till they stop at my thighs, pressing softly. A viper's head is in the middle of his hand, in an attacking position with its fangs out.

They look so large against my thighs, and he moves them between my thighs parting them and making my heart race. His gaze burns its way to my center and my nails sink into the couch. Emiliano presses his lips starting at my thigh, moving upwards, stopping before he reaches my slit and doing the same over on my other thigh.

This time, he doesn't pause; he continues his trail of kisses till he reaches my slit. He uses his fingers to part my pussy lips, his tongue peeking out and slowly running along my opening and then flicking my clit. The room fills with my moans.

"You have to be quiet. We don't want someone to come see why you're being loud. If we were in my room, then that wouldn't have been a problem, and God, am I a fucking glutton for your moans," he murmurs against my skin. I whimper as he nips the inside of my thigh before going back to lapping at my wetness. He delves his tongue deeper into my slit and I have to cover my mouth with my palm to stop myself from moaning even louder than I was.

"Don't stop- oh God, please don't stop!" My chest heaves as my breathing picks up. Emiliano presses his thumb over my clit as he flicks his tongue. I feel myself drip over the couch, but I can't focus enough to care.

"This pussy is mine. Your orgasms belong to me and only me. I don't give a fuck about anything else," he murmurs into my wet folds.

My fingers dig into his skull as I press myself against his mouth and feel his chuckle vibrate through me. I throw my head back as my back arches off the couch slightly, my vision blurring, and all I can hear is static.

"Fuck yes, that's right, come on my tongue, ragazza. So wet and so delicious and only for me," he growls, lapping up at my slit. I watch him, still on his knees in front of me with a satisfied smile, as if he's the one who got the most pleasure out of my orgasm.

I give him a lazy smile as my breath slows, letting myself stay in this moment of euphoria for a little longer.

CHAPTER 16
EMILIANO

Valentina's chest moves rapidly after the second orgasm washes over her, her body slightly arching off the couch. I watch her come down from the high. Her face is slick with a light sheen, and her eyes are so bright they almost seem unreal.

She has a lazy smile, and when she stares down at me, she looks like a queen on her throne. I don't break eye contact as I slowly bring my fingers to my lips, smelling her scent. She's a mixture of sweetness and something earthy.

I slip my fingers into my mouth, and her lips pop open, her gaze on my fingers. Cleaning my fingers off, I swirl my tongue around them. She swallows, trying to gather her thoughts as my fingers slip out of my mouth. My cock strains against my joggers, demanding relief.

"I'm going to fuck your mouth," I tell her as I get up, her face positioned at the perfect height to take my dick between her pouty lips. Her eyes filter to the tattoos on my knees, working over the bleeding skulls. I brush my hand over the crown of her head, sinking my nails into her black waves. She gasps when I tug her head back, something akin to pleasure passing over her dark eyes.

"Are you going to let me fuck your pretty little mouth, or are you going to keep staring at my tattoos?"

Her eyes widen, her lips slightly parting as she struggles to not look at my throbbing cock. I tug on her hair again, and her teeth sink into her bottom lip. Reaching my other hand out, I tug her lip out from between her teeth.

"Answer me, Valentina. A man can only take so much temptation."

She inhales sharply as her eyes snap to my covered cock, her pink tongue darting out to wet her bottom lip. *Fuck.* I tilt her chin up to force her to look at me.

"I'm going to go easy on you since you don't have any experience," I say softly.

She narrows her eyes.

"Maybe I do," she challenges.

An amused huff escapes me, even as I feel a surge of possessiveness to find the fucker and kill him, or her. I quirk an eyebrow at her, and she shrugs.

"Okay, maybe I don't, but you didn't know that."

I run my hand through her hair, wrapping the strands around my fist and tugging slightly.

"Maybe you're right, but I could tell," I admit, and she bites that plush lip again.

"Don't do that if you want me to be gentle," I warn. Her eyes become pools of darkness, almost black, and the small seed of possessiveness inside me over her seems to grow.

The dark desire to completely corrupt her, destroy her, and make her mine all at once seems very appealing.

"Maybe I don't want you to be gentle," she whispers.

"Fuck," I groan, but quickly add, "No, you can get hurt. We don't want that now, do we?"

"Take my pants and boxers off," I order, and she follows my instructions, slightly fumbling. Her fingers graze my sides, unsure. She may think she's not being obvious, but I can tell by the way her eyes move up every time her fingertips brush my hips. Once both my pants and boxers are at my ankles, she leans back, but I stop her with a tug on her hair. I push her face toward my cock, holding her only an inch away. I can feel her breath on it, and I clench my teeth as my muscles pull taut, trying to restrain myself from shoving my cock down her throat.

"Lick it." I loosen my hold on her hair, and she moves forward eagerly, her hands resting on my tights and her fingers sinking in. Valentina opens her mouth and her tongue peeks out, lightly stroking my cock. I suck in a breath when she repeats the motion, using more of her tongue.

"What do I do now?" She looks up at me through her lashes.

"Open your mouth and try to take it in as far as you can," I instruct her. "Make sure to not use your teeth."

Her lips wrap around my tip, tongue swirling around it. I unravel my hand from her hair and rub my thumb across her jaw. Valentina's eyes flutter up before she takes more of me in her mouth.

"That's it, you're doing so well," I praise, and she hums as her eyes glaze over. My hips thrust forward involuntarily, and two fat tears drop down her face. I wipe them with my thumbs. "Breathe through your nose. Slowly." She gags when she tries to take more of my cock, and I grasp her shoulders holding her in place. My breathing is uneven, stuttering at how amazing she feels.

"You don't have to take me fully in," I tell her. She pulls back till her lips are just wrapped around the tip of my cock before taking me back in.

"Fuck, just like that," I moan. She repeats the motion for a couple of minutes clumsily, gagging and slightly shaking. Once I'm sure she's became accustomed to my size, I grab her and fuck her face, speeding up.

More tears flow down her cheeks, her hair fanning around her shoulders. Valentina moans around me and my groans echo in the room. My abs tighten as the wet heat of her mouth engulfs me wholly.

"Fuck yes, such a good girl. You look so pretty with tears running down your face." I brush my hand down the side of her face and her fingers dig deeper into my thighs, nearly breaking the skin. "I'm close, so fucking close. Get off if you don't want me to come in your mouth," I warn, but she continues to move up and down my cock, licking and lapping at it. I fist my hands in Valentina's long hair, rocking my hips. As I pull out, she sputters and inhales deeply before I thrust in again. I use her tongue for friction, fucking her mouth thoroughly.

"You're taking me so well. These pretty little lips were made for my cock, *ragazza mocciosa*," I groan. Her eyes brighten, and my lips lift in a twisted smirk. "You love it when I call you that, don't you, *ragazza mocciosa?*"

She doesn't answer with words, but her tongue laps my cock, offering additional friction that drives me over the edge. I come down her throat with a deep groan, and she tries to swallow as much as possible, her throat moving while she looks up at me.

This woman will be mine, one way or another. I'm not letting her go. She's already sunk her talons in way too deep, and I don't want to dislodge them any time soon. When I pull out, some of my cum drips down her lips and chin, and she licks them while still staring at me. I can feel myself harden at the view, but when the living room door handle jiggles, our gazes snap to it.

"Eli, are you in there? Valentina?" Fuck. It's my ma. I look back down at Valentina and quickly pull my boxers and pants up.

"Listen, you answer her. Tell her you want some alone time and will come out when you feel ready."

"What if she asks me about you?" she whispers back.

"Say you don't know where I am," I tell her. She nods before clearing her throat.

"Hey, Mariana, it's just me in here. I'd just like to spend some time alone," Valentina says.

There's a beat of silence before Ma speaks up. "Are you sure? I don't want you isolating yourself just because my son is an asshole."

Valentina gives me a smug smirk, and I send a scowl back at her.

"It's fine. He doesn't scare me, but thank you for your concern," she tells my ma. I study her face, her brows furrow and a cute pout settles on her lips as she watches the door. We listen carefully, but we don't hear her leaving.

"Do you know where Emiliano might be?" Ma asks. Valentina's eyes dart up to mine before she quickly looks back at the door.

"No. I don't," Valentina quickly answers. I hold my breath, waiting to see if Ma believes Valentina.

"Of course, you wouldn't know. Mara, Clarissa, and I will be in the living room if you'd like to join us."

I look at Valentina, trying to gauge if she'll go to see them, but she sees me watching her and shakes her head.

"I'll keep that in mind, thank you, Mariana."

Ma's retreating steps slowly disappear. I wait for a couple more minutes before I sink back to my knees. Valentina frowns at me, a confused look on her face.

"What are you doing?" she asks.

"Saying thank you for that," I say, kissing my way up her thigh.

"For what?" she breathes out.

"For being such a good little girl, and for that, you'll get rewarded."

I sink my teeth into her delectable thighs, running my tongue over the bite mark before moving to her already sobbing pussy, *my pussy*.

I glide my tongue over her wet folds before parting them with my hands and sinking my tongue deep inside her. Valentina's whimpers turn into moans, and I press my face into her pussy, feeling the vibrations from her sweet sounds.

"Fuck, baby, you're soaking wet. So wet that I want to keep drinking from you," I groan into her.

She rakes her hand through my hair and tugs slightly as she pushes herself farther onto my face. I sink my fingers into her thighs as I keep them open. Her walls clench around my tongue, which means she's close. I remove one of my hands, but I don't stop lapping at her, thrusting two fingers inside her wet heat. She moans, and looking up, I see her bottom lip being tugged between her teeth, holding back to stay quiet.

That has me thrusting my fingers in at a savage pace, moving my mouth to her clit. Lapping at it causes her to gasp.

"Oh God, I'm close," she sobs, and I go faster, more savage. She comes with her hands clenching my shoulders, pushing me impossibly closer to her center. I don't stop when she comes, going harder, thrusting my fingers even deeper till the palm of my hand presses into her skin.

"Emiliano, I don't think I can go for more," she pants.

I move just far enough to say, "I know you can, and you will. Don't stop me, please."

"I -" She doesn't finish because she moans as my fingers curl, rubbing her walls. Her head is thrown over the back of the couch, her hair all over the place, the baby hairs sticking to her forehead that's slick with sweat. It doesn't take long for her to come over my tongue and fingers again. I move back to watch her try to catch her breath, a smug smirk on my lips.

"You were saying," I say with a chuckle.

She pushes back a stray hair that fell over my forehead when I was going down on her, watching me with droopy eyes.

"You were right," she breathes out, and I give her right thigh a kiss, sliding my hands up to grab her waist. I give a squeeze before getting up and plant a kiss on her forehead before I settle next to her on the couch and turn the TV on, unsure what she likes. A rerun of *Friends* is playing, and when that appears on the screen, she grabs my forearm.

"Don't you dare skip *Friends*."

"How dare you think that I would ever skip a *Friends* episode?" I turn to her, the TV remote still in my hand. She gives me an amused smile before she turns her face back to the screen. Ross and Rachel are, of course, broken up in this episode, and we both sit in silence as we watch. Pulling my phone out, I decide to go over the contract that Silvio sent over from my meeting with that asshole Stefano.

"It seems like you guys are getting the short end of the deal," she says, and I turn my head to see Valentina staring at my screen. Biting the inside of my cheek, I debate whether to ask her to elaborate or to tell her to not involve herself in my business.

"Why do you say that?"

Her eyes are still on my screen as she begins to talk.

"Well, first off, it says in the renewal clause that you guys would need to pay a 10% increase to the original cost and that the termination can be under two reasons, the first being the expiration of the contract, or investors pull out before profits can be made, which will mean you guys will have to pay 100 million dollars."

I place my hand over my mouth, pretending to scratch my jaw, when in reality, I'm hiding my amusement at the fact that she has managed to catch mistakes that my team had clearly glazed over. Valentina's eyes move from the screen to my face when I don't say anything.

"Did I say something wrong? I'm sorry if I stepped out of line." Her words cause all the amusement I feel to vanish and a sourness twists like a dagger in my abdomen.

"No, no. Don't apologize. You've actually picked up on something that my supposedly great legal team hasn't," I tell her. Valentina is about to say something, when my phone rings, and I clench my teeth as I slip it out.

"Yes, Romiro." I really want to shoot the fucker now.

"There's an emergency. Lucio was injured when he was racing in the Czech's territory. We need you in New York," he tells me in a rush. Fuck!

"Call the airport and tell them to get the jet ready in thirty minutes." I end the call and slide my phone back in my pocket. My eyes return to see Valentina regarding me carefully.

"I need to go get something done. I need you to stay in my room and wait for me. Understood?" I tell her.

She nods, but I squeeze her chin between my thumb and forefinger. "Okay. How long will you be gone?" she asks as she stands up. I bend down, my lips ghosting hers.

"Miss me already?" I ask, amused.

"Fuck off," she mumbles before I kiss those words right out of her mouth. My tongue thrusts inside her welcoming heat, and I devour her with savage need. Valentina tries to kiss me back with tentative strokes, but it's impossible to keep up with my pace, not when I have every intention of consuming her whole. She whimpers against my lips, and I have to remind myself that I need to leave, or I'll fuck her on the couch. I rest my forehead against hers as I try to catch my breath. My hands stroke the sides of her face, my eyes closed.

"I'll be back soon," I tell her before leaving the room with my heart in my throat. Quickly making my way down the marble stairs, I slip out the front door without looking back once. My car roars to life, and I speed down the gravel path till I approach the gates, waiting for them to slide open. I reach the airport in record time and head into the back room of the jet to shower and change.

By the time I'm done, we're halfway to New York, and I decide to call Romiro.

"How's Lucio?" I run my hand through my hair as I sit near the window.

"He's fine, he just had a bullet go through his shoulder."

Ma's not going to like that. Fuck. I don't like it either, but this is our life.

"Gather our men. We're killing some fuckers tonight."

"Will do. When are you landing?" he asks. I look at the digital map showing where we are.

"In about twenty minutes."

"I'll come to the airport," he says. I motion for the flight attendant to come over.

"Sure, see you, Rom." I end the call.

"Yes, sir, what would you like?" Her voice is steady, but I can tell she is afraid, her eyes straying away every couple of seconds as her hands shake.

"Get me some water and something salty." I rub my hand over my lips. I can still smell Valentina on them. Fuck.

"Right away, sir." The flight attendant scurries away quickly.

After she brings me the water and some crackers, the flight goes by very quickly and we land in New York. Of course, to no one's surprise, the weather is fucking shit.

It's down-pouring when I spot Romiro standing near the car with an umbrella and his long trench coat, his blond hair sticking to his forehead. My driver hurries toward me with two umbrellas, one in his hand and the other he's using. I mutter a thank you when he hands me the other umbrella.

"Where's Matteo?" I ask Romiro as he makes his way around the car. The rain is so loud that I can barely hear myself speak.

"He stayed with Lucio in his apartment," he tells me once we slide into the car. Some raindrops fall on the brown leather seats, and I press the button to lift the divider between us and the driver.

"How did Lucio get shot? Why the fuck did no one stop him from racing in the Czech's territory?" I ask. Romiro rolls his shoulders, his face twisting in contempt.

"We were at the OX, but Lucio decided to head out to race with some guys. They'd been racing in Damian's territory. Lucio's car was shot at the most and he's lucky that he'd managed to get away with just a bullet through his shoulder."

I run my hand down my face. Someone is fucking with us and it's someone on the inside.

"They need to fucking stop breaching their territory," I say, and Romiro nods in agreement.

"I mean, we've warned Lucio about this before, but he just doesn't listen." He shrugs. I button up my suit jacket as the car comes to a halt.

"The family's moving back to New York in two weeks. It's time we're back to our city," I inform Romiro before stepping out of the car. It's game time, New York.

***

Romiro and I are sitting in my penthouse, shuffling through the paperwork for the Diamond. The only light illuminating the room is from the lamp on the table in front of us. After we'd checked on

Lucio and Matteo and decided to have them return to New Hampshire, we decided to stay until we'd sorted some shit out.

"I want another meeting with that asshole Stefano," I say, not looking up.

"What for?" he asks. My eyes briefly flicker to Romiro's face before going back to the papers.

"The contract puts us at a disadvantage. I don't understand how our team hasn't caught that. They've had three weeks to look over the damn thing."

"And I'm guessing you were able to spot them?" he probes. I bite the inside of my cheek, debating whether to tell him it was Valentina who pointed it out.

"No, Valentina did." I look up to see a smug little smile on his face.

"No fucking way." Romiro leans forward, getting in my space.

"What is it, fuckface?" I ask.

"It's interesting that just because you guys are fucking, you feel comfortable enough to have her look at important business documents."

"You're a little asshole. Go back to reading through the damn papers." I'm halfway through a sentence, when my phone pings. "Rom, check who's messaging me." I jerk my chin to my phone on the table as I continue to read through the reports for the last two months.

"Dominico's awake and he's apparently going insane trying to leave the hospital."

Romiro and I stare at each other before throwing the papers on the table and grabbing our jackets and our phones, heading toward my elevator.

"Call the doctor and inform him to try to hold Dom in there for as long as possible," I tell him. He nods and pulls out his phone. We reach the parking garage and take our cars. "I want him awake, so make sure they don't try to sedate him."

Romiro nods, sliding into his car. We take the backstreets of Brooklyn to avoid most of the traffic.

There are nurses standing, gossiping outside of Dom's private room, and Rom and I can hear him from down the hall. I fling the door open and step in.

"Get the fuck out of my way, or I'll blow your goddamn puny brain out of its skull." Dom's throwing shit at the doctor, who's trying to dodge it. I don't think Dominico has ever been this unhinged; he's always stayed calm and collected.

"Dom. Calm down," I bark. His wild eyes come to me, looking darker than normal.

His eyes narrow as he growls, "Where's my wife? I tried calling her and got no fucking answer. That shit *never* happens." I can feel Romiro and the doctor stare at me, waiting.

"Everyone out. Romiro, make sure no one is in the hallway," I order. He nods before dragging the doctor out with him and barking at everyone to leave. Dominico and I stare at each other for a beat, his good hand clenching at his side while the other is in a full arm cast.

"She's dead." I don't sugarcoat my words, and Dom knows it, but his jaw locks and his eyes narrow, disbelief shining through.

"What the fuck do you mean she's dead?" he asks. I walk further into the room, stepping over some broken vase.

"Thalia was in a critical condition, two months ago. The Terranova clan had attacked the store she was in and was shot by them," I tell him. His face turns into a snarl.

"And what the fuck has the Camorra done to retaliate?" he demands. I raise an eyebrow at his stupid question.

"We're dealing with the Outfit," I tell him, and he scoffs, before wincing in pain.

"How long have I been out for?" he asks, and I hold up three fingers.

"Three months," I say, and he mutters a "fuck" under his breath before sitting on the edge of the bed. "Get changed so you can go home. I need my Consigliere." He looks back at me, his eyes empty, but he doesn't reply.

"I'll see you soon, Dom," I say before moving toward the door. I shut it behind me and motion for Romiro to follow me.

"So how did he take the news about Thalia?" Romiro looks concerned.

"Better than I expected." I shrug. "Just leave it, Rom."

We head out of the hospital and decide to go back to my apartment. My phone rings in the car and I see that it's Joseph Terranova.

"Joe, you have some nerve calling me after killing my cousin's wife, the Camorra's Consigliere. I'm not responsible for what he'll do," I say, and he huffs out an ugly laugh, only to start coughing at the end, probably all that cigar smoking he loves to do.

"Come on, Folonari, she was just in the wrong place at the wrong time," he explains.

I grit my teeth, trying to stop myself from driving to his place and putting a bullet through his head for being at "the wrong place at the wrong time."

"You know as well as I do that what you just fucking said is bull-shit," I growl.

"Cut the shit, Emiliano, you and I both know that I couldn't do jack-shit about it. My brother runs the show, not me." Orlando Terranova. Fuck-face is yet another thorn in my side. A thorn I plan to take out soon enough.

"What the fuck you calling me up for, then?" I ask, and he doesn't say anything for a beat.

"I'd like to borrow some money," he finally says.

I run my tongue over my teeth. Joe's a snake to everyone, especially his own.

"How much?" I'll play the long game since the little Terranova clan wants to play the short one.

"Two hundred grand." His voice comes out too eager and grates on my nerves.

"Done. I'll have the money transferred within the hour." I cut the phone call short before he even tries to reply. The car comes to a halt in my apartment's parking garage, and I step out, waiting for Romiro to pull in.

His speeding car jerks to a stop next to mine, the engine probably sizzling hot because of how fast the asshole likes to drive. He gives me a grin as he steps out, and I shake my head at him.

CHAPTER 17

VALENTINA

By the time I was done showering and changing into another pair of Emiliano's clothes, my thoughts had cleared and the panic set in. What if he uses this against my Dad to humiliate him? What the fuck was I thinking?

Doing that with him after the nightmare I had... I'm so fucking stupid. I can't believe that I've put both my sisters', brother's, and Mom's life on the line for some short-lived pleasure.

I trudge down the marble staircase as I make my way toward the kitchen. My stomach has been growling non-stop, demanding food, and my dry throat wants water. This time, when I enter the kitchen, it's not empty.

There are three women there. One with a short silver bob, one with shoulder-length black hair that has streaks of pink in it, and the last one has long platinum-blonde hair and a slender, tall figure.

"Can I help you, dear?" The one with the short silver bob is the one to ask me as she walks toward me.

"I was wondering-" I'm cut off when my stomach loudly grumbles, my cheeks burn, and my palms become slick.

"Oh, just a second, dear. I'll grab a couple of things for you.

Would you like a drink as well?" Her eyes are so kind and gentle as she regards me.

"Uh… yes, please. Thank you…" I trail off.

"Lydia, my name is Lydia," she supplies as she heads to the pantry.

"Thank you, Lydia," I call after her. I notice that the woman with the platinum hair is watching me with narrowed eyes. I don't cower, nor do I avoid her stare, and her face twists in a snarl.

"You know that he'll discard of you once he's done fucking you," she says. My fists clench as I try to not flinch at the tone of her voice.

"Of course, you'd know about being discarded." My reply is sharp. I don't want to fight with her, but I'm not going to let her walk all over me. Whoever she is, she clearly thinks she holds some special place in the Capo's life. I don't care enough to fight with her about it. But if she wants to attack me and slut shame me for something that hasn't even happened, then she's got something else coming towards her.

"Ginevra, leave the poor girl alone. Aren't you married? Act like it." Lydia walks back in with a small tray of cheese, bread, and jam. She places a pitcher and a small cup on the tray. Ginevra gives me one last glare before going back to look over the pots on the stove. The girl with the black hair and pink streaks throws me a curious look before going back to her work. Lydia heads my way with a soft smile and hands me the tray.

"Thank you." I grab the handles of the tray.

"You're welcome. I didn't quite catch your name."

"Valentina, but you can call me Val, if you'd like," I say, and she nods.

"Leave some space for dinner. We're making Pasta alla Genovese, Sfogliatella, and Casatiello for dinner." She tells me.

I give her a smile and make my way back to Emiliano's room.

I eat till my stomach no longer hurts and is comfortably full. In the corner of Emiliano's living room, there's a cream bookshelf with gold lining the edges. It looks like it has around sixty books, all ranging from dark literature, some classics, and to my surprise, fantasy.

I wouldn't have thought of him as an avid fantasy reader, but there's at least ten fantasy novels on his shelf. I pick the one which has the most worn-out edges, running my finger on the spine.

The Name of the Wind. I flick through the pages and notice some of the words are underlined or highlighted. The door opens, and I turn around to see who's come in.

"Hi, I know Mom said that you wanted to be alone, but I just wanted to check on you," Mara explains as she shuts the door behind her.

"I'm fine, thank you. It's okay, don't worry about it. I enjoy your company, not that I don't enjoy your Mom's."

Mara nods as she watches me with a playful smile. She notices the book in my hand.

"Emiliano loves that book. I remember when I was younger, I used to see him always carrying it with him," she tells me, and I gobble up that piece of information, because to me, he's still just the Capo of the Camorra.

"I didn't think he'd be a fantasy reader," I say. She heads to the couch, and my throat closes as I watch her getting closer. Once she reaches it, she heads to one of the armchairs.

"Yeah, I can see why you'd say that. He's honestly become a different person in the last three months," she says as she settles in. I tilt my head, confused by what she means. Her gray eyes widen as she looks at me before her eyes dart around the room as if she said something that I am not meant to know.

"Is there a reason he likes to read fantasy?" I ask. Someone like Emiliano doesn't just randomly pick up a fantasy book one day and decide to become obsessed with it till the book spine becomes worn.

"My nonna on my Mom's side was an avid fantasy reader, but she also liked to collect rare fantasy editions of books. I never met her, but I heard she and Emiliano were very close till her death," she tells me. My thumb lightly feathers the worn-out spine of the book as I imagine a young Emiliano reading with an older woman. I bite back a smile. "Do you think you'll be going back soon?"

My eyebrows pull together as I regard her, trying to figure out if she knows about what happened. No, I'm just being paranoid.

"No, I don't. Why?" I ask, and she shrugs.

"I heard my brothers talking about demanding someone in exchange for you."

My stomach drops, but something stronger swirls in my chest. Suspicion. I take some steps closer to Mara. Why is she telling me this? Did someone put her up to this? I chase those thoughts away as I sit on the couch and face her.

"Do you know who they might be exchanging me for?" I ask, hopeful that she might have overheard that as well.

"I think his name was Guiseppe, if I didn't hear wrong. But I'm not sure, sorry."

This is what Dad must have been screaming at my uncle about. Giuseppe must have snuck into Camorra territory, causing this attack.

"Do you have any sisters?" she asks, changing the subject. I study her face, finding nothing but pure curiosity.

"I have two and one little brother."

"What're their names?"

Her questions aren't anything to be suspicious of because anyone can figure out what she's asking just by searching our family name on the internet.

"I have a sister who's a year older than you and her name is Violette, and the youngest one is Monica, and our brother's name is Marcello," I tell her. She rests her chin in her palm.

"Marcello is such a cute name." She sighs, and I nod.

"Yeah, I guess it suits him in a way." I feel my eyes begin to sting as my mind drifts to my siblings. I wish I could see them.

It's nearly been two weeks since I've been taken, and I have never gone this long without them. Mara gazes at me with a look of understanding. A tear slips out and my hand moves quickly to wipe it away. Her eyes soften as mine dart away from her stare.

"I have an idea," she whispers. I look back at her sharply.

"Please tell me you're suggesting what I think you are suggesting?"

This could be my only chance at escaping both the Outfit and the Camorra, two birds with one stone.

"I know a small passageway that my nonna used to use when I was a child and practically no one knows about it." She pushes back the strands that fall over her face as she leans closer.

"What about CCTV, guards?" I ask her, and her face lights up with a convincing smile.

"CCTV was never installed there, and the guards don't know about it either. It's practically run-down and looks like a bunch of ruins."

"Okay, but what's the plan?" I can feel the swarm of butterflies in my stomach taking flight and even nibbling at the edges of my stomach.

"I'll come get you at some point when the coast is clear and take you there. There'll be a bicycle ready for you and a GPS device that will lead you to the closest dock. I'll iron out some more of the details and tell you the rest as we make our way to the exit."

I spend the time between now and dinner just reading. I decide against reading *The Name of the Wind* and instead pick up *Pride and Prejudice*. Even if I've read it close to a hundred times, I'm never bored of it. I love Elizabeth Bennett but, honestly, I read the book for the sole purpose of reading about Mr. Darcy.

He's such an intriguing character, and I love how Elizabeth and him slowly come to understand each other. By the time dinnertime rolls around and Mariana knocks on the door, asking if I want to come join them for dinner, I am nearly halfway through the book. I have to resist the urge to decline the invitation to dinner just to finish the book.

I place the book down on the coffee table and head to the door. Mariana stands to the side with a bright smile on her face, which I return. "Mara told me you were reading, so I decided to leave you till dinner was ready," she says as we begin walking toward the staircase.

"Thank you for being so kind. You have no reason to do this."

She waves her hand around. "Nonsense, you are innocent. I can't stress that enough. You should not be held accountable for your family's decisions or mistakes."

I push my hair back. I understand and agree with what she's saying, but somewhere in my head, something tells me that the other shoe will drop, and they'll show me how they truly think of me.

We reach the dining room. The walls are a green mossy color, the floors a cream marble with silver accents. In the middle, there's a long dining table that holds about twenty people, made out of a large cut of wood with beautiful dark swirls. I spot both Mara and Clarissa sitting on the opposite side of the table, so I'm guessing it'll just be those two, Mariana, and me. I can't help but feel a flicker of disappointment, but I quickly brush it off as I settle into the seat next to Mara, and Mariana settles next to Clarissa.

Lydia serves the food and gives me a wink as she fills my plate.

"Mara, have you decided what you want to do after you're done with school?" Mara turns her attention to Clarissa and tilts her head to the side.

"I'm not sure. I'm thinking about maybe doing some volunteering at some shelters once we're back in New York." She takes a sip of water, her fingers tapping the rim after she put the glass down. "If that's anytime soon."

"Mara," Mariana warns without looking up from her plate as she cuts a piece of her food.

"Mom, you know we've been trapped here for the past three months. The only reason Dad died wa-"

The clank of cutlery cuts her off, and Mariana pushes her chair out, getting up.

"Enough. Mara, I've told you this already. Your brother makes the decisions now. and what he does is for the best. Not for him, but for all of us." Mariana reprimands. Mara's chin wobbles. and her fist clenches on the side of her plate. I watch Mara as Mariana sits back down and begins to quietly speak with Clarissa in hushed voices. My hand covers Mara's, squeezing slightly, and she gives me a wobbly smile.

"You'll be okay, don't worry," I whisper as she bites her lips, contemplating what to say.

"I don't know, I guess I just feel very cagey. We can't even walk around the property without twenty guards trailing behind us."

I study her face, and I can clearly make out the undereye bags beneath her concealer and the fear behind her glassy eyes. I wonder if she can see the exhaustion on my face and the yearning to go back home in my eyes.

The rest of dinner is spent speaking in quiet voices, but the tension between the Mom and the daughter is very obvious. Once we're done with dinner, we head into the living room and dessert is served with some espresso. Mara doesn't touch her espresso.

"I don't like bitter food or drinks unless they have chocolate in them, and even then, I can barely stomach it." She gathers her blonde hair in her hand and puts it up into a ponytail.

"Oh, you would love Alov's cafe. Their pastries are to die for." The cafe is just around the corner from our penthouse in Minneapolis, so Dad allows us to go there with one of our bodyguards.

"I wish I could visit it, but..." She shrugs one shoulder, and I nod in understanding.

"I'm going shopping tomorrow. If you want, I can ask Eli if you could come with me to get some clothes," she suggests. I look down at the oversized joggers and hoodie that I'm wearing. I don't think I've ever worn clothes that were four sizes too big.

"I hope I can, but if he doesn't agree, could you grab me some basic clothes to wear? I'm a size 8. I'll pay you back once I go back to Chicago."

She takes a bite out of the Sfogliatella, some of it getting stuck around her mouth.

"No. Don't worry about the money. I'll get you some undergarments as well."

After telling her my sizes and finishing dessert, I decide it's best I go back upstairs. Mariana stops me halfway to Emiliano's room.

"Hey, Val. I can call you Val, right?" She touches my arm lightly.

"Yes, of course. What's up?" I ask. She gives me a wide smile, her smile lines more evident in her kind expression.

"If you want, I have another room that's ready." Her eyes search my face to see what my reaction is. I should accept it. Staying in another room is for the best because that man clearly messes with my brain worse than any drug my family distributes. If I stay in another room, I'll be able to lock myself in there and avoid being alone with him.

"I think it's best if I wait until your son comes back, just in case he doesn't agree," I say instead. Mariana's eyes narrow, assessing my face before she nods.

"I don't want to force you into doing something, and then end up having him take it out on you." She walks me to the room before telling me goodnight and leaving. Sleep evades me and I settle in front of the fireplace on the couch to finish reading.

When a knock sounds from the other side of the door, I get up and make my way toward it. I open the door and find Mara standing there. She raises her index finger to her lips in a shushing motion, motioning for me to follow her. The hallway is eerily quiet, and I my stomach cramps at the prospect of being able to get away. Do I really want to leave? I mean, I want to leave and get away from my Dad, but... I shake my head. I should ignore the feeling that I'm betraying Emiliano. He's not someone I should feel a sense of loyalty to. Mara twists her head to look back at me and motions for me to hurry up before turning back around. We reach the stairs, and she turns to look at me again.

"There's a secret passageway. Eli knows about it, but he doesn't use it. No one has really used it in about four years now." She tries to keep her voice as low as possible as we slowly make our way down the stairs.

"Don't you think it would be better if we act natural, like we're going to the kitchen or something? Then we can say we weren't doing anything wrong if someone catches us. If we keep acting like this, they'll think we're up to something," I whisper back. She stops at the last step and looks at me, before giving me a small smile.

"You're right. Come on, it'd be better if we didn't get caught at all."

She turns to the left of the second floor, leading me down a hallway I haven't been in. The walls are different, fuchsia with swirls of black that create a look of overgrown roots coming from the ceiling. And instead of marble floors, a lime green carpet is in its place. The place resembles something out of Willy Wonka's Chocolate Factory, with all the bright colors. We walk for two minutes, not talking to each other, but I can hear Mara muttering something under her breath. The hallway comes to a dead end with a large painting of a woman on the wall. Her eyes seem to glow like azure stones, her lips turned down in a frown. She looks young, but mature, as if she's reaching her late thirties. She's wearing a silver cocktail dress, and her hair is twisted in blonde curls that resemble gold rather than actual hair.

Mara steps toward the painting and grips the sides of it. She slides her hands up and down the frame, before something clicks softly. Stepping back, she pulls the right side of the painting with her and it opens like a door, revealing a small hallway in the wall, with light fixtures embedded in the ceiling.

"My nonno built this when the mafia had an all-out blood war with the Russians. He hid the entrance behind a painting of Nonna," she tells me as she steps back and turns to face me.

"I don't know how to express this, but I'm so grateful for this, Mara. Really, thank you." I grip her hands in my own before I pull her in for a hug.

"You didn't do anything wrong, Valentina. Why are we the ones who always have to pay the price for the mistakes these men make? They always have to blame someone for their own shortcomings, and it's unfair. To you, and to every person out there. If I could help at least one person, then I've done some good." Mara squeezes me tighter before pulling back. "Now come on. We have to get you out before someone comes back looking for you." She moves toward the secret entrance and manages to pull herself up into the small hallway. Motioning for me to move closer, she grips a metal bar embedded into the side of the small hallway before she extends her other hand to me.

It takes a bit of an effort to get myself up there, even with Mara's help, but once we're both in there, she moves to the side.

"Could you stand over there? I need to close the entrance door and make sure it's secured."

Once I'm out of her way, she pulls the back of the painting into place, which takes her a couple of seconds to do since the back seems to be made out of metal. The door latches with a hiss, engulfing the entire space with the orange hue of the lights in the ceiling. It takes a bit for my eyes to adjust to the change in lighting.

"Come on, we have to be quick. I don't know what my brother would do if he caught us."

The hallway is wide enough for Mara to walk past me, hunched over, to avoid bumping her head on the low ceiling.

"How long will it take for us to get outside?" I ask as I follow behind her. The farther we go down the hallway, the more damp the walls appear.

"I can't go with you the whole way through, but I'll get you past the confusing hallways that span the entire estate, and then you'll be on your own till you reach the outside. Once you see the outside light, you'll be just outside the estate gates, so be careful. Even though there aren't any cameras installed over there, there's still a chance my brother's guards will catch you," Mara explains as she continues to walk ahead of me. My nerves rachet higher at the possibility.

"What do I do when I get to the dock? I know you've already done a lot for me, and I'm grateful, but I'm not familiar with New Hampshire," I ask, pushing a stray strand of hair out of my face.

"When you get there, a boy with cotton-colored hair should be waiting for you at dock number 6. He'll take you anywhere you'd like to go." Mara stops in front of me before turning her head to look at me. "This is as far as I can get you. If I'm gone any longer, they'll find us." She nods ahead of her. "Keep going forward, and you'll reach the exit in about twenty minutes. I'll try to create a distraction."

"Thank you, Mara. I'm so grateful for your help. I understand that you've put yourself in an awkward position with your family just to help me, so thank you so much." I step closer, and we both hug each other in the small space available.

"Go, you need to leave as soon as you can. Be careful, the hallway becomes narrower than this, but the ceiling gets higher," she whispers into my hair, which urges me to move around her and start walking toward my freedom from this world. I can make out her retreating steps and then the silence.

I grip the wall of the hallway, as it is getting hard to see anything. Squinting, I finally make out the shape of a door with some light peeking through the sides. Hope fills me with energy and something else like excitement and nervousness for the future. I wish I didn't have to choose between running away from the grasps of the Outfit, the Camorra, and my family. But I guess that isn't in the cards for me. Once the Camorra returns me to the Outfit, there will be no way in hell that I'll be able to get away. Security was already tight before the attack and now I can't imagine how hard it would be to even breathe without that being reported.

I hate this shit, I hate it so much. Why do the men in our family get to do whatever the fuck they want? How come the Camorra can establish themselves as ruthless rulers, but treat their women better than the Outfit, who pride themselves with their honor? The hypocrisy that has prevailed within our family will be the end of the Outfit itself. Dad is trying to prevent it, but going with the same old traditions will only intensify the destruction. He may not realize it, but the Outfit will get what's coming its way. And I'll relish the destruction of the very foundation of their ancient traditions.

As I stop in front of the door that will lead me to my freedom, my breath catches and I look back at the hallway. *Bye, Emiliano.* I push on the latch, and the door slowly creaks open. Orange, I'm surrounded by a forest of trees, leaves crunching beneath my feet filling my ears as I run in the direction Mara directed me. It's a blur from there. When I come to my senses again, I'm in front of the road, a bike hidden near the tree to my left. I don't waste any time thinking as I pick it up and take it to the roadside. I debate whether that's wise, then instead take it back to the grass area, making sure that I stay close to the forest edge.

I ride the bike for what seems forever, but I don't stop. Everything around me is a blur as I cycle faster and faster, my chest rising so quickly I'm scared I'll collapse. In the distance, I can see the ocean, which means I'm close. When I see the entrance of the dock, I slow down and relief fills me, but that is soon crushed.

Because right in my line of sight, I see a red Maserati. And who is leaning on the red Maserati, with a lit cigarette in his mouth? Who else other than Emiliano Folonari?

With my pulse pounding in my ears, I drop the bike and make a run for the dock. Maybe I still have a chance at getting away from all this crazy shit. That hope is crushed in less than a minute as the breath is knocked out of me when Emiliano's arm wraps around my waist and he lifts me effortlessly.

"Be a good girl and follow me to the car like a civilized human being," he whispers into my ear. His tone is harsh, cold, and uncaring.

"Let me go, Emiliano." I don't look at him, my eyes still longing to see the man with the cotton-colored hair, my salvation. "Please?" My voice breaks on the word, but he doesn't answer me.

"I'm sorry, ragazza mocciosa, but you know I can't do that." He presses his lips to my ear, a sweet caress if only my eyes weren't filling to the brim with tears. My nails dig into his arm as vengeance singes my blood. I don't know where to direct my anger.

Emiliano practically drags me to the car, throws me in the back passenger seat, and slams my door, locking it. I sit there, shaking and numb, as he slides into the driver's seat. His eyes cut to mine before they return to the street, and he starts the car without saying a word.

We don't speak the entire way back to the mansion, and soon enough, the gates are only a couple of feet away and they creak open for us. The car comes to a halt, neither of us making a move to get out. I can feel Emiliano's eyes on me, and I return his gaze in the rear-view mirror.

"How could-" He pauses before starting again. "Do you understand the danger you put yourself in when you decided to run away?"

His eyes are hardened, but a gleam of vulnerability shines there. I swallow the sudden guilt filling my veins like a traitorous poison.

"What you don't realize, Emiliano, is that you and my Dad are the real dangers to me, so no, I don't understand."

I catch the hurt in his arctic eyes before they become vacant of all emotions. He gets out of the car, and then he's dragging me to his room.

The door closes with a click, and I am back to exactly where I started. Emiliano advances on me like the predator he is, a determined look on his heavenly face. How can someone so devilish look so angelic? The backs of my knees hit the couch. and I tumble backwards with his arm encircling my waist, his face inches from mine.

"You think I'm a danger to you?" Emiliano's voice is full of emotion, which takes me by surprise. Anger and something akin to hurt there as well, maybe sadness. "I would never hurt you, Valentina." His voice is low with his admission, as if someone will hear him. I rest my palms against his rising chest, his heartbeat a drum that matches my own.

"I am your enemy. That is the reason you took me from my family," I remind him, and his eyes soften as they take in my face.

"You are so much more than that," he says before turning cold and distant all over again. "But you tried to run away." Emiliano shoves me onto the couch. "It's time for your punishment." His words confuse me, and then he kneels in front of me, his hands pulling my jeans down along the way.

"What are you doing?" I ask him, nerves making my voice raspy.

"If I make you feel uncomfortable, or you no longer want to do this, then just say 'twist,' and I'll stop. You won't come until I allow you to, and if you come without my explicit instructions...let's just say, you'll regret it." He yanks the jeans and panties down, ignoring my gasp.

His tattooed hands part my legs, lips leaving a blazing flame across my thighs as he kisses his way to my center. I don't think I've ever seen a sexier man in my entire life. Jesus, why does this man look this exquisite on his knees? He blows a breath over my pussy.

And a small chuckle leaves his mouth when I suck in a sharp breath. Brushing two fingers over my wet folds, I whimper as I move my hips upwards to push his fingers in.

"So wet for me, and here I thought you fucking hate me," he says, amused. "Move another inch, Valentina, and I'll spank you till your ass is covered in blood." I don't know why, but his warning causes goosebumps to skitter across my arms and down body, my stomach clenching at the timber in his voice.

Bringing his face forward, he flattens his tongue against me. The slow laps along my wet folds drive me to the brink of madness, and I fight the urge to push myself farther into his face. Instead, I lace my fingers through his silken hair, my head falling to the backrest of the couch.

"Eyes on me, or I'll fuck you to within an inch of your life and it won't be with my cock." Emiliano taps my thigh, and I snap my eyes back to his. They hold me captive as he continues his torturous rhythm. "Beg me, beg me to let you come." His command is clear as day, even though his face is buried in between my thighs.

"Please, let me come, I'm begging you." I tug at his raven strands, and I can feel the smirk that paints his lips as they rest against me.

"No," he answers, before his teeth sink into the side of my inner thigh. I throw my head back on a half moan, half scream. The pain is quick to dissipate, pleasure taking its place as his tongue soothes the bite before he goes back to lapping at my pussy.

A low hum builds in my lower abdomen, so close, but so far away. Emiliano sinks his tongue inside me, swirling it around before he groans in approval.

"So delicious, so mine. Your taste is the best taste I've had the honor to have in my mouth. But you go and fucking ruin this perfection by trying to get away." His strong hands press against the flesh of my thighs, and I'm sure there will be bruises tomorrow, but the pleasure is too much for me to care. "Tell me you're mine, tell me that I'm the only man you'll let have you, own you, mark you, fuck and degrade you as I please. And I'll let you come."

My chest heaves as I tug even more at his hair, writhing against him.

"You lied two seconds ago. How do I know you'll let me come this time?" I pant. His lips are feather light as he kisses my inner thighs again.

"I swear on my honor, Valentina." This time, he does something that makes me release a strangled noise as he flicks my clit with his tongue more than once.

"I'm yours, I'm yours."

"Say that you're my property. Mine to fuck and mine to do as I please."

"I am Emiliano Folonari's property. I am yours to fuck and yours to do what you want with," I breathe out in a rush. That is enough to spur him on because he not only delves into me with his mouth, but he also adds his fingers, two and then three, to be exact.

"Let me tell you this, Val, if you try to run again, I'll pump you so full of my cum till it leaks out of you for days," he growls against my center. "Come for me, Val, come for me and let me taste your sweet release." His words send a hot trail of fire across my skin, and I come with a loud moan, but Emiliano doesn't stop until I'm completely spent.

He stands and tugs my panties and jeans up to my knees. My face flushes red when I see something glisten on his chin, and I realize it's my arousal. I turn my head to look anywhere but at him, but he places two fingers under my chin and turns my attention back to him.

"I think we're way past you being shy." His fingers move back and forth over my cheek, his eyes glazing as if he's thinking of something else. He shakes his head before he says, "Get some sleep. I need to find out how you got out. And don't try to do that again."

By the time I wake up, it's around noon, if the clock on the fireplace is anything to go by. A groan leaves my lips, as trying to move my stiff neck is a mistake. This is what I get for sleeping on the couch. My back hurts like a bitch, and my limbs feel like I haven't moved them in a century. They're so sore that even when I run my palm over my calves, it barely registers. I can't stand on my feet without wincing as I try to make my way into the bedroom to get to the bathroom.

My mood only worsens when I finally see the state of my hair. I try to free some of the knots by threading my fingers through them. But it doesn't help and my fingers get stuck in different sections every time.

I rummage through Emiliano's bathroom drawers, finding a bunch of miscellaneous things. Toothpicks, floss, shaving cream, nail clippers, some scissors and a couple of razors. Opening the cabinet below the drawer, my nose wrinkles when I spot a red thong. Gross. I shut the cabinet and move to the other side of the two sinks.

When I find a brush in there, I take it without looking further. I've traumatized myself enough for the next lifetime. I also don't feel like examining whatever ugly green monster decided to peek out from the depths of my mind. Biting my lip, I swallow my scream. I don't know why brushing my hair hurts, even as I start from the bottom of my hair.

After enduring the pain of pulling out what seems like half of my hair, I hop in the shower. When I first took a shower here, I was surprised to see that Emiliano uses a strawberry-scented shampoo and conditioner. I thought someone like him would use something like *fresh fall.* Whatever the fuck that means. I grab the loofah that I got from one of his cabinets and lather it with the body wash. It smells exactly like him, which causes my skin to tingle and my stomach to clench. I ignore the feeling.

Once I step into the bedroom, I notice it's been cleaned up and some bags are set in the corner. Mara was probably not able to convince Emiliano to let me go with her if the bags have the clothes she offered to get me, especially after the stunt I pulled yesterday. My suspicion is confirmed when I rummage through the bags to find two sets of jeans and some cute tops, two pajama sets, some underwear, bras, and a cute pale blue dress, all in my size. I settle on some blush-colored panties and a matching bra. Then I grab a pair of black joggers and the matching hoodie before leaving the bedroom. My stomach grumbles, and I decide to grab the tray of food from last night and take it downstairs.

My mood takes an ugly turn once I enter the kitchen and spot the woman from yesterday, Ginevra, standing close to Emiliano with one hand resting on his chest. Her finger is making small circles as she speaks in a hushed voice. They don't seem to notice me, and my throat tightens. I try to swallow to get some self-control back, but it does nothing. This isn't the way I should be reacting. I breathe in deeply and gently place the tray on the island table, and ignoring them, I turn to face Lydia who's just come out of the pantry.

"Hi, Val, would you like me to prepare you something?" she asks me as she moves around the kitchen with a soft smile on her face. I can see that Emiliano has pushed Ginevra away from him because she stands scowling at me while he's leaning on the counter and watching me. I follow Lydia around the kitchen.

"Could you just show me where the bread and jam are?" I ask, and she nods and walks toward the marble counters lining the wall that faces the garden. I go to follow her, when a large hand wraps around my wrist. I turn to see Emiliano still leaning on the counter with an amused look in his eyes, but otherwise his face is a mask of indifference. I narrow my eyes at him before trying to yank my wrist out of his hold. It doesn't work. He pulls me closer to him and we stand face to face.

"Lydia, could you please toast two pieces of bread with some jam on the side and put it all on a tray to have Ginevra bring it up to my room?" he says while still assessing me. I continue to scowl at him, trying to free my wrist from his grasp. Emiliano slowly stands up without letting my wrist go and drags me along, all the way back up to his room. He only releases me once we're inside and he's sat in one of the armchairs. I cross my arms over my chest, glaring at him, standing between his legs. He watches me with a slight smile on his lips, his dimples winking at me.

"What do you want?" I ask. His smile widens, and my heart does a weird flutter.

"You're jealous." He leans back, his thumb brushing his clean-shaven jaw lightly.

"I am not. I don't get jealous, first of all. Second of all, there's nothing to be jealous of and, besides, why should I be jealous?" I argue. The smug bastard laughs. I must be starving because my stomach feels all fuzzy. "I want to go back to Chicago. When can I-" I'm cut off when he grabs my arm and yanks me to straddle him on the armchair. My legs land on either side of his hips, my chest pressing against his and my hands landing on his shoulders. His hands grasp my hips, squeezing slightly.

"You're not going anywhere unless I decide so," he growls, with a look of cold anger. I press his shoulders back to get up, but he snakes his arms around my waist and pulls me flush against him. Leaning forward, he runs his nose down my throat, inhaling deeply.

"You smell of me."

"I used your body wash, sorry," I mumble. His lips lightly kiss my throat.

"Don't be. I think I prefer you smelling like me than anything else," he whispers. My lips part on a low moan comes out when his tongue slowly trails up my neck before he bites it. A knock breaks through the little bubble around us, and I begin to wiggle around to get free, but he just holds me in place, not allowing me out of his arms.

"Who is it?" He doesn't make a move, his head still in front of my neck and his fingers still sunken into my sides.

"Ginevra. I have the tray you asked for," she says from the other side of the door, and I roll my eyes as I push harder on his shoulders to get free. His hold tightens.

"Stop moving, or I'll fuck you just like this in front of her," he warns.

"Come in, Ginevra." The sound of the door opening and closing echoes in the room. My back prickles with the sensation of someone watching me. I hear the clatter of plates on a tray as they get closer.

"Do you need anything else, boss?" she asks. Emiliano doesn't stop his light kisses on my neck, causing me to sink my teeth into my bottom lip to stop myself from moaning. I feel one of his arms move. The sound of retreating steps and the door closing is all that I hear after that. He pulls back, regarding my face.

"Ginevra is just one of the maids here."

It feels like I'm rolling my eyes a lot around this man, and when I try to get up again, this time, he lets me. The tray is placed on the coffee table, and I stomp my way to the couch near it.

Once I sit down, and my eyes dart back to Emiliano, I find him watching me once more, his thumb toying with his bottom lip. I scowl, but it has no heat behind it because that's all going to my cheeks. He slips his hand into his suit pocket and pulls out a tiny medicine box.

"What's that?" I ask. His eyes flick from the box back to me, and then down the length of my body, leaving a hot trail behind. Emiliano looks like he's ready to devour me in a beat. My skin pebbles and my neck feels weirdly warm.

"Birth control. It's a patch."

My eyes narrow into slits as I cross my arms over my chest.

"What for?" I ask.

He gives me a smug smirk before twirling the box between two fingers.

"For when I fuck you." This man has such a filthy mouth, he'd make Lucifer blush.

"Who said anything about you fucking me, let alone without a condom?" I ask. His cold eyes drag over my face, gauging my feelings. The smug smirk is replaced by cold indifference.

"I'm clean, if that's what you're worried about," he tells me. I'm inclined to believe him, but after what I saw in the kitchen, I think he might be a bit of a man-whore.

"How the hell have you stayed clean if you don't even use a condom?" I ask. A corner of his mouth lifts in a smirk.

"I've never not used a condom, and everyone I've been with physically had been tested beforehand. And you were begging me to fuck you a couple of hours ago, or have you forgotten?" he teases.

"I guess being Capo has finally driven you to madness," I say, rolling my eyes. He runs his tongue across his top teeth, like the predator watching its prey.

"No, the only thing that has driven me to true madness is your insistence on delaying what is going to happen. Now eat, and if you keep rolling your eyes, I'll make sure they'll stay there permanently when I fuck that attitude out of you," he says, and my stomach flips. I take a bite out of the toast as I give Emiliano a glare. "Eat up, *ragazza mocciosa*, because once you're done, I'm filling you up with something entirely different."

The insinuation isn't lost on me, and I choke on the bite of toast I'd taken. He gets up and pours me a cup of water before handing it to me, rubbing my back as I gulp down the water. I huff out a breath once I finish the glass, his hand still rubbing soothing circles on my back.

I shuffle across the couch, away from his touch, and focus on the tray. He doesn't comment or touch me again, keeping his distance, but I can feel the weight of his stare.

"What makes you think I'll agree to do anything with you?" I know I'm only saying that to provoke him, but he doesn't know that.

"Bullshit. What changed?" he asks.

I turn to look at him, to make out his expression, but his face is an unreadable mask. I shrug.

"You're just not my type. And I don't like tattoos. You have a lot of them." A fucking lie. He gives me a look that says he doesn't believe me, and I give him a look telling him I don't give two shits.

"Stop lying. I can still fucking smell you on my hand, not my fingers, my fucking *hand* because you were so wet. For me."

My entire face feels like it's on fire, and I stuff my mouth with the last piece of toast to avoid saying anything. I dust off the crumbs off my fingers, lips, and joggers before standing up. I quickly make my way to the bathroom, but I don't reach it because Emiliano follows close behind me, locks the door, and grabs me by the waist.

CHAPTER 18
EMILIANO

The door locks with a click, and I circle my arm around Valentina's waist, effectively stopping her from running into the bathroom. Valentina wiggles in my hold, but I don't budge.

"Stop trying to run from me," I say. She glares, sinking her fingers into my arms.

"Let me go, asshole. I'm not running from anything," she seethes. Picking her up, I throw her over my shoulder. One arm over the back of her thighs, I walk us to the bed as she wiggles around.

"Stop fucking moving." I slap my other hand on her ass, and she lets out a low moan. When she sinks her nails into my back, it barely registers. She glares up at me once I drop her on the bed. I swear to God, it feels like all I do around this woman is get a hard-on.

"Now, tell me what got you so pissed?" My eyes narrow when she doesn't respond, instead turning her head to the side to avoid looking at me. Stepping closer, I nudge her thighs open.

"Fuck off. I just don't want to be near you. Is that so hard to comprehend because of your small brain?" Her tone oozes condescension. I slowly bend until my face is the same level as hers.

"I think we both know, ragazza mocciosa, that nothing about me is small."

Her eyes widen before she scowls once more. As she goes to stand up, this time I let her.

The bathroom door slams shut behind me, and the sound of water fills the room. I sigh and run my hand through my hair before leaving my room, heading to my office. My phone rings before I even manage to sit in my chair.

"Folonari, I hope your little brother got the message to not step foot on our fucking streets again." Fucking Damian.

"And I'm guessing you fuckers are calling to ask for forgiveness for attacking my brother."

He barks out a humorless laugh.

"You Italians are always full of so much shit that you can't even see past it," he spits, his thick Slavic accent coming out.

"You know, I just might tell the Russians to wipe the fucking floors with you smug Czech fucks," I say, and I can hear some shouting, but it isn't English.

"Listen, Folonari, keep your little circus on your streets and they'll stay alive." The fucker hangs up. Instead of smashing my phone like I want to, I text Romiro.

ELI

Burn one of Czech's warehouses. I want it gone before tomorrow.

ROM

Have you gone insane???? I thought that we agreed to sit with the elders to talk about what their consequences are for attacking Lucio?

ELI

Just fucking do it!

ROM

Whatever, asshole

I pocket my phone, when a knock sounds at my door. I rub a hand down my face. I can't catch a fucking break, can I?

"Come in," I call out. The door swings open and fucking Ginevra comes strutting in. She stops at the edge of my desk with a coy smile. "The fuck do you want, Ginevra?" I ignore her lifting the screen of my computer. Ginevra moves around my desk, coming to stand next to me, while I continue to stare at my loading computer screen.

"I saw that you'd left soon after you'd dropped off the Outfit's whor-" She doesn't get the rest of her sentence out, because I get up and grip her neck so hard that I probably cut off her circulation. But I don't let up even as her face reddens.

"Don't fucking call her a whore. I hear another word out of your fucking mouth about her, and I'll cleave your tongue right out of your mouth." I let her neck go, and she drops to the ground, gasping and coughing. As I turn back around and sit behind my desk, I can hear her inhaling sharply and coughing some more. "Now get the fuck out before I cut you limb by fucking limb."

She gets up and grips the edge of my desk to steady herself, then slowly makes her way to the door, gripping onto the chairs on the way, trying to stay upright. I slam my computer shut once she's out of my office. Leaning back into my chair, I let out a long sigh and put my hands on the back of my head.

I don't know what the fuck I'm going to do. To get our revenge on the Outfit and fulfill my promise to my soldiers, I need to give Valentina back. The fucking thing that's messing with my head is that a part of me doesn't want to send her back, and it's growing every day.

Fucking fuck. No, I can't have her; she's part of the Outfit. Making up my mind, I slip my phone out of my pocket before I change my mind. I decide to call the Capo.

"Have you decided what you want to return my fucking daughter to me, you sick bastard?" Alvize Moretti has always had a short fuse, and it's never worked in his favor, not in our world and not in the business world.

"I want your nephew." Silence, then I hear some cursing.

"Which nephew are you talking about?" Moretti's acting stupid, as if that shit would buy him time to come up with something.

"Cut the shit, Moretti, I want your nephew, Giuseppe."

Some more cursing, some in English and some in Italian.

"I'm not giving you my fucking nephew, Folonari. Anything else, I'll give you."

I grit my teeth.

"You're in no position to negotiate. You either hand over Giuseppe, or I'll keep Valentina here until kingdom come." I end the phone call without waiting for a reply. I can't believe the bastard thinks he has any room to negotiate. Instead of heading back to my room like I want to, I go to make some food. The kitchen is empty just like I'd expected it to be after lunch was done. I open the fridge door and grab some of the Sfogliatella Lydia made.

Pulling out a stool out, I sit at the island table, enjoying the silence. Once I'm done, I wash the dish and then my hands before heading back to my room to grab some clothes. When I reach my room, I don't find Valentina anywhere. Changing out of my suit, I quickly make my way downstairs. The living room, kitchen, and garden are empty, so I head to go look in the den. I can make out some voices from the long hallway, near the kitchen.

The distinct timber of Valentina's voice becomes clear once I get closer to the gaming den. Valentina, Mara, Matteo, Romiro, and Lucio, whose arm is in a sling, are all scattered around the room with gaming controllers in their hands and eyes glued to the screen. Valentina and Romiro are sitting on the couch, their eyes narrowed.

Mara and Lucio are sitting on the floor in front of them, while Matteo sits in the corner watching them with a bored expression. The carpet muffles my steps as I make my way into the gaming den. They don't see me because the lights are dimmed, the screen providing illumination. Matteo spots me first, but the others don't, not until I stand in front of the gaming screen.

"Oh, what the fuck, Eli, get out the fucking way." Lucio waves the arm holding the controller around.

"What the fuck are you shitheads doing?" I ask, and Lucio groans. Mara sighs loudly, and Romiro leans back with a smirk on his face. Valentina doesn't answer, seeming to have retreated into her head. "Is one of you fucks answering me, or should I wring one of your necks?"

I flick my gaze to Matteo, but he just leans back into his seat, stretching his legs.

"I thought you had better reduction skills as our Capo. They're clearly playing a game," he mutters dryly. Lucio barks out a laugh and throws the controller on the floor.

"I can see that, smartass. What the fuck is she doing out with the rest of you?" I don't have to say who "she" is because they all look at Valentina, who's glaring at me like she wants to burn a hole between my eyes.

"We came by your room to see if you wanted to join us for game night, but found this surprise in there instead." Romiro shrugs. I can tell he finds this shit hilarious.

"You three fuckers, I want you in my office tomorrow morning at nine, no later than that."

Lucio yawns before arguing, "You know I need my beauty sleep, and I don't wake up till twelve."

Romiro bends over and taps him on the shoulder.

"It's okay, pretty boy, one day won't hurt," Rom teases.

Lucio swats at Romiro's arm. "I'd believe you, if you didn't resemble Chucky's bride."

Mara slaps Lucio over the head. "Tiffany deserves some respect."

Valentina looks like she's about to die, holding in her laugh.

"That's enough, you dumb fucks. Valentina, upstairs." When she doesn't move to get up, I add, "Now."

She rolls her eyes before walking past me, muttering under her breath. Romiro snickers and whispers in Lucio's ear, who looks like he's been told he'll get a machine gun for Christmas.

"Wanna make a bet, Esposito?" He cranes his neck backwards. I narrow my eyes at them, before walking toward a scowling Valentina.

"Sure, I bet you a thousand that they're fucking already," Romiro says. I stop dead in my tracks and turn to look at Romiro and Lucio, who are ignoring me.

Lucio counters with, "Nah, fuck that, make it a hundred thousand, and I bet that he won't give her back to Chicago."

"You two little fucks think you're funny? Drop this, or I'll drop you in the middle of the fucking Atlantic, dead." I don't wait for them to reply and storm out of the room, Valentina hot on my trail.

The door slams behind me as I make my way to the couch, turning on the TV. I lean back into the couch, watching the news anchor woman talk about some Russian mobster being arrested. Valentina comes to stand in front of me, arms crossed and eyes molten like honey on a warm summer day. My eyes trail the length of her till they reach her gaze once more, her nostrils flaring a little.

"Why was she touching you in the kitchen?" she asks, and I give her a puzzled look, utterly confused, but she doesn't elaborate.

"Who?" I ask her as I lean forward, placing my elbows on my knees. It dawns on me who she's talking about when something flickers in her eyes. "Ginevra." A renewed scowl rests on her face when Ginevra's name leaves my mouth.

"Yeah. Her," she replies with disgust.

"No one you should feel the need to ask about." My answer doesn't seem to appease her as she drops her crossed arms, hands fisting at her sides. But Ginevra is quickly forgotten when the news anchor woman says:

"Valentina Moretti, the daughter of Alvize and Diletta Moretti, has been missing for two weeks, with no leads as to where her location may be. If-" The TV shuts off and silence fills the room, as Valentina and I watch each other. Her eyes look glossy from where I'm staring at her and her chin wobbles before she clenches her jaw.

My face becomes unreadable when she asks. "When will you send me back to my family?"

I stand abruptly, and she has to take a step back so we're not pressed up against each other.

"You'll go back to the Outfit when I decide it's time. Stop fucking asking me."

She follows me as I make it to my room, pushing the door open. I grab a set of pajamas, gray boxers, and a blanket.

"Emiliano, this isn't fair on me-" she starts, but I cut her off.

"Tough shit, sweetheart. Life isn't fair, and I sure as fuck am not. So, deal with it."

The room is silent as I continue to rummage through my second drawer, when she sniffles, once, then twice, and a third time. My throat tightens and a weird sensation fills my chest. I should probably call Callahan. The bathroom door closes softly, and I feel like a huge asshole for some reason. I'm knocking on the door before I can think better of it.

"Valentina, listen, I know that wasn't exactly nice. Come out, I want to talk." Nothing. "Valentina?"

"Fuck off, I'd rather speak to the devil than you," she says with a shaky but stern voice, and I can't help but laugh, which causes her to fling the door open.

"Shut up, you don't get to laugh." Her eyes look red, and my face instantly falls. Valentina's eyes analyze me before she decides that she wants to slam the bathroom door in my face. I stick my hand out, stopping her from doing just that. As she tries to push my arm out the way, I don't budge. "Move, asshole."

Pushing the door open with my other hand, I step into the bathroom. Valentina doesn't budge from where she's standing. I move into her space, so close, she has to tilt her head up to look me in the eye.

"Get out." Her words are barely audible as she tries to speak up.

"No. Listen I'm...sorry," I say softly.

Her eyes harden, looking enraged.

"Sorry for what, exactly? Taking me from my family? Being rude and abrasive? Or sorry for the things we've done? Which is it?" Valentina shoves her hands into my chest with each sentence, but on the third push, I grab her wrists into my hands and pull her into me.

"I'm not sorry for what we've done. I'm not sorry for taking you from your family. But I am sorry for the way I spoke to you," I whisper into her ear. She shudders at the tone I use, but doesn't move. "Now you tell me, are you sorry for what we've done so far?"

Her breath hitches, but she doesn't answer. I let go of her wrists and slowly inch backwards. Valentina surprises me when she wraps her arms around my neck and pulls me down to kiss me.

Her lips are as soft as I remember, causing me to kiss her back feverishly. My arms snake around her waist, as one of her hands makes its way into my hair. I groan when she pulls at the strands, my tongue swiping across her bottom lip and her mouth parts slightly. A shiver runs down my spine as her nails rake over the back of my neck,. I rest my forehead on hers as we both try to catch our breaths.

"That wasn't a kiss you'd give to someone who isn't your type," I tease. She sinks her nails into the back of my neck again, not liking my teasing tone.

"Shut up and kiss me," she mumbles against my lips. I pick her up, and her legs wrap around my waist as I swallow her surprised gasp. My arms support her legs as I walk us to my room.

She lands on the bed as I stand at the edge, watching her as she pants, eyes wide and full of lust. When my hand trails up her leg, she fists the sheets beside her. Looking into her eyes, I pause my hand at her joggers' waistband.

"Are you sure you want this?" I ask. Her throat moves on a rough swallow before she nods.

"That's not good enough. I need you to say it."

She sinks her teeth into her lip, contemplation crossing her face.

Finally, she whispers, "Yes. I do."

I drag her joggers down swiftly, my hands reaching her blush-colored underwear. My eyes flicker to her face as I rip them off. Valentina's legs press together on a gasp, her face flushing a matching color.

"Don't do that." I push her legs back open and place my knee on the bed between them. Swiping my finger over her wet folds, I lift it up.

"This doesn't seem like the kind of reaction you'd get from someone who's 'not your type.' Does it?" I ask. She pants a little and her sweet scent fills the air.

"Shut up, you're talking too much and moving too slow," she complains. I huff out a laugh before pushing two of my fingers inside her, eliciting a delicious moan. My fingers thrust as she tightens her hold on the sheets.

"Oh, God," she moans as I curl my fingers, then thrust them deeper. Valentina's moans are a melody to my ears, and that's all I want to hear. I press the heel of my palm to her clit, which has her clenching around my fingers and writhing into me, looking for more as she cries out her release. And I'm about to give it to her.

Shoving my pants down, I position my cock against her entrance, pushing in slowly. Groaning, I feel the remnants of her orgasm around my length, even coating her thighs. Going slow, her small whimpers fill the room, and I feel my control slip, but I restrain myself.

"See? Your cunt is stretching and welcoming me. How sweet of her? She likes it sweet and slow, and what about you, baby?" I grip her by the hips and thrust inside her at a pace that's so savage and unhinged that she moans louder without a care. Slowing down, I ask, "Hmm? Do you like it sweet and slow? Or do you like fast and rough, to be fucked like a good little whore? My good little whore."

Valentina only answers in whimpers, occasionally gasping whenever I hit her G-spot.

So, I do it again and again until her pussy strangles my cock. The slap of flesh against flesh echoes in my room, her rewarding sounds on an endless loop that has me throbbing and ready to explode. When I groan, low and deep, she wraps her arms around my neck and looks up at me with those half-lidded fuck-me eyes. To torture me more, I assume. I clench my jaw, my hands fisting into tight balls as I hold myself back from fucking her so hard she sees the stars. With a grunt, I give in for a second, thrusting into her like a madman, the bedframe hitting the wall, her whimpers turning into screams.

But I won't stop. And I certainly don't take it easy. I release a hip and wrap my fingers around her throat. Her pussy tightening impossibly as I hold her down.

"Do you feel how your pussy tightens around my cock?"

Tears shine in her eyes, and I'm not sure if it's because of my words or her ongoing orgasm.

"You'll let me stuff my cock into this pussy and use you whenever and however I please, won't you? You'll come for me, on my cock, tongue, and fingers because you like being my good little whore." My strokes get faster and shorter, making her head hit the frame of the bed. I pause my thrusting and flip us over so she's on top of me. Her eyes are dazed as she grips my shoulders, her nails digging in and her face wet with tears.

I grab her hips and thrust up into her, watching her perfect body bounce above me before collapsing over me. Her wild heartbeat falls against mine, and she bites my neck as her pussy spasms around my cock.

"Mine, only mine, mine to fuck, my personal cum-whore." I thrust up once more, and when she hides her face in the crook of my neck, I come inside her. My release is long and hard, and cum smears all over her thighs.

Valentina doesn't move. Her frail hands are thrown on my shoulders, and her teary face is still hidden in my neck. We remain like that for a few moments. Me catching my breath from the most powerful release I've ever had, and her body slick with the sweat, before she awkwardly tries to lift herself up so she can make me pull out.

I help her, and she winces, probably sore. My cum smears down her thighs with a small amount of blood. Fuck. I really hope I didn't hurt her. She is on her feet, but wobbles, so I get up and lift her bridal style and lay her down. I make my way into the bathroom, putting the bath's plug in and turning the hot water faucet.

I wait until it's halfway full before going back into the room. I find Valentina still awake, but just barely. I pick her up again, her arms going around my neck. She tries to mumble some kind of protest, but lets me carry her, too exhausted to argue as I set her in the tub. I watch her until she's completely relaxed and go to grab a loofah to help her since she seems to be too tired to do anything. It doesn't take long for me to finish washing her body. I move to her hair, but she shakes her head.

"I don't wash my hair every day; it isn't the best for my type of hair."

Instead, I massage her head, pleased that she likes it when she moans. We stay like that until she wants to shower, both of us enjoying this moment of relaxation. After she's finished, I take her back to the bedroom and lay her down on the bed.

She clutches my arm and whispers, "Don't go, stay here."

I nod. "Go to sleep, I'll be right here." Her eyes flutter closed as I cover her body. I try to make as little noise as possible as I make my way to my closet. Once I've thrown on some boxers, I slip into bed next to Valentina.

CHAPTER 19
EMILIANO

I walk through the living room and open the glass doors, stepping outside. My steps echo throughout the greenhouse as I walk up the spiral stairs to check on the flowers. I drop to my haunches, before slipping a cigarette in my mouth and lighting it. Once I spray the leaves of the Cape bushes, I tend to the rest of the plants, taking one of the violets, wanting to give it to Valentina before going to the stairs. I bend my head down to avoid the lavender flowers when I pass them on my way back down the stairs. My eyes widen a fraction when I spot Valentina standing in the middle of the greenhouse, next to the fountain. She's in a pale blue dress with her hair down, reaching her waist. Her gaze burns my skin as it trails down my body.

"What are you doing here?" I speak around the burning cigarette as I step closer.

"I wanted to know where you went." She looks around before looking back at me. "You keep surprising me. I didn't know you were an early bird." I flick her forehead with my middle finger.

"Don't run your mouth and don't go running around my house without asking," I say, and she fake pouts.

"I'm sorry, master, have I broken the rules?" she says mockingly. I huff out a laugh before grabbing her jaw.

"You like being a smartass, don't you?" I murmur against her lips, but she doesn't answer because I seal our lips together and slip the violet into her hair. She reaches to feel it, but I grab her hand. With a small smirk, her hands roam my naked arms before grasping my shoulders. She pushes me back until I stop on the edge of the stone bench, breaking off the kiss and giving me a peck on my lips before sinking to her knees. I swallow and try to calm my breathing when I figure out her intentions. Her eyes flicker to my face as she sinks her teeth in her lower lip and hooks her fingers in my sweatpants. She looks back down at my crotch, her eyes widening a little when she notices my cock pressing against them. My gloved hands fist at my sides.

"Take them off already, or you're going to burn a hole in them." I reach to take another puff, pressing the butt of it between my teeth when she abruptly yanks my sweatpants down with my boxers. My hard cock smacks my abs, and Valentina runs her tongue across her bottom lip at the sight.

"I'm going to fuck your face if you don't stop moving at the pace of a fucking snail," I say through clenched teeth. She narrows her eyes at my warning before her lips close around the head of my dick. I groan when she swirls her tongue around it before taking more of me in, gagging a bit before continuing.

"Remember, breathe through your nose and take it slow." I run my hand through her raven hair as I instruct her, tugging a little at the roots. Her moan vibrates through my whole body and her eyes glaze over, tears welling before they roll down her plump cheeks. I swipe my thumb across them, cooing, "You're taking me so well."

The humidity clings to my skin and a fine shine slicks my body as I try to hold myself back. I grip Valentina's shoulders and thrust into her mouth, my cock hitting the back of her throat. My groan is drowned by the sound of my balls slapping against her chin. As my body shakes, I try to hold back my ejaculation.

"Move one of your hands off my thigh and lift your little dress."

Valentina follows what I tell her, flipping back her dress, showing her little black panties.

"Move your panties to the side and push in one finger."

More tears roll down her cheeks as she moves her middle finger between her wet folds. Her whimper sends a quiver through my cock.

"Fuck yourself with your finger, but don't come until I tell you."

She plunges her finger deeper into her pussy, shuddering as she continues to take my cock in her mouth. My stomach tightens as I watch her choke on my cock.

"Fuck yourself with another finger." Valentina fumbles to add another finger inside her, the ones still on my thighs sinking into my muscles. My skin sizzles as my hand tightens on her head, my fingers digging into her scalp. She makes a strangled noise at the back of her throat as she struggles to stop herself from coming.

"Don't come until I tell you," I growl. My skin prickles as I feel myself getting close. As my breathing picks up, my thrusts begin to get sloppy, and a buzz settles in the back of my head. I give a couple more thrusts before I tense and hold her head in place, coming in her mouth. My head tilted up toward the ceiling, my vision fading.

When my eyes move back to Valentina, I find her face flushed, tears wetting cheeks, and her fingers still buried in her pussy. I pull back and my cock comes out of her swollen lips with a pop, cum dripping down her chin. My thumb swipes it, and I push it back into her mouth. She moans around my thumb, lapping at it with her warm tongue.

"Take your fingers out and get on the bench." I take my thumb out of her mouth and watch her as she pulls her two small fingers out of her wet cunt.

She slowly gets up to her feet, her dress falling to cover her pussy. I steady her when she sways, and turn us, pushing her onto the stone bench. Valentina wipes the rest of her tears off her cheeks, trying to dry them as she watches me lift my boxers and sweats up. I tug at her little dress, exposing her dark brown nipples.

I kneel, placing my knees on each side of her thighs. Her nipples are hard, looking so beautiful, and I tease one with my finger before slipping one in my mouth while twisting the other. As I swirl my tongue around her peaked nipple, a whimper slips from her lips. I love how she's so responsive to my touch that a mere nipple teasing can turn her into a moaning mess. I bite her nipple before running over it with my tongue.

Her back arches, pushing them farther into my face, another moan leaving her lips. "Oh, God."

I speak against her. "Asking God for help won't stop me from fucking you." I run my tongue over her nipple one more time and then kiss her lips. She bites my bottom lip in a teasing manner, causing me to growl in her mouth. Valentina giggles before sealing her lips to mine, kissing me with a desperation I've never seen from her before. It turns me on even more, and I kiss her back with increased hunger. When I pull back, watching her tear-stricken face, disappointment flashes in her honey-colored eyes.

"Pull the skirt of your dress up," I command.

She swallows, her hands moving to comply. My hand snakes forward, ripping her black panties off, earning a gasp from her swollen lips. Her gasp turns into a moan when I thrust two fingers inside her.

"You're so fucking wet. You want my cock, don't you, ragazza?" I swallow the moaned response, grazing my teeth across her little chin as I pull back.

"Do you feel yourself drenching my fingers? You enjoy fucking the man who took you from your family? You like being my dirty little whore?"

Her nipples rub against my chest due to her chest rising rapidly, and she clenches around my fingers. An amused breath leaves me like a sigh, feeling her soak my fingers even more.

"Do you enjoy being called my dirty little whore, hmm? Tell me, ragazza mocciosa," I demand, our lips a breadth away from each other. Her tongue peeks out and demands entrance to my mouth as I tease her clit with my thumb.

"You're my good little fucking whore, and you're going to come on my fingers, aren't you?"

"Oh, God, yes..." she whispers. "Yes." Her lips hover over mine, parted as her pussy tightens around my fingers. Head rolling back, her hair falls off her shoulders. My other hand grabs the back of her neck.

"Eyes on me, Val. I want you to be looking at me when you come."

Her hooded eyes come to my face, her sweet breath fanning my lips as she rides my fingers for her orgasm. I run my nose down her neck, nibbling on the sensitive spot behind her ear. She presses her lips to my neck, softly kissing and giving me goosebumps. When I pull my fingers out of her wet pussy, her soft moan echoes in my head. I slowly kiss my way down her neck, her breasts, flicking her nipples with my tongue before moving down till I'm on my knees between her legs.

I push her thighs open and lap at her wet folds, pressing my fingers into her thighs to urge her to bring her eyes back to mine. Valentina pulls her bottom lips into her teeth as I slip my tongue inside her, her eyes meeting mine again as she moans. Her second orgasm comes quicker, and she digs her fingers into my skull as she cries out, her thighs clenching around my head. I continue to lap at her wet folds until her legs separate and her breathing slows.

I quickly rise and kick off my sweats and boxers before positioning my cock at her entrance. Digging my fingers into her hips, I thrust inside her all at once. Her body jerks as she whimpers, but her cunt swallows me whole, strangling my cock.

"Fuck. You feel like mine." Thrust.

"My woman." Thrust.

"Fucking mine," I growl.

She nods frantically, and one of her hands grips my shoulder while the other grips the back of the stone bench. Her long black hair tumbles back as her head tilts backwards, tits jiggling from the powerful rhythm of my thrusts. As she arches into me, my lips find hers. My arms circle her waist, pressing her into my chest. I bite her neck before running my tongue over the sensitive skin.

"Oh my God, Eli. Don't stop. Please, don't stop," she begs, and my thrusts turn animalistic, her pussy tightening. The sound of skin slapping on skin so loud I'm sure it can be heard from outside the greenhouse.

It doesn't stop me as I slow but deepen my thrusts, her moans getting louder and more frequent. She pulses around me, her teeth sinking into my shoulder as she comes with a shudder taking over her body. Her hard nipples scrape over my chest as my hips push harder into her thighs before I come in her warm pussy.

I rest my slick forehead against hers, our breathing loud and chests moving in sync. She winces as I move to pull out of her, my cum dripping. I gather it with my forefinger and thrust it back inside her, and she moans before swatting my hand away.

"Don't do that. It's embarrassing." She pulls her panties back on before lifting her neckline back to cover her chest. I watch her, amused, as she smooths her hands over her hair.

"What's embarrassing about shoving my cum back inside you, where it belongs? It's my pussy, remember that, or have you forgotten that it's mine?" I tease, and her face reddens, but she doesn't say anything as she adjusts herself. My phone rings in my pocket, and I reach my hand in and take it out. She watches me pick up the call without looking away from her.

"You want Giuseppe for my daughter back?" Fuck, it's her dad. Her eyes narrow as she takes in my tense shoulders and the frown that has settled over my face.

"Yes, I want Giuseppe to give you your precious little daughter back."

Hurt flashes across her flushed face before she smooths her hand over her dress one more time, then quickly moves to leave the greenhouse. My hand twitches to grab her, but I watch Valentina's retreating back, shaking off the regret that settles in my gut.

"Fine, where do you want to meet?" he asks. I press my eyes closed. This is about our revenge. Mine, my family and the Camorras. Not about her.

"I'll have the details sent to you." I end the call and slip the phone back in my pocket. I watch the greenhouse door for a beat before heading out after Valentina. I debate whether to go and check in my room, but instead I go to my office.

Opening the door, I find Dominico sitting behind my desk, a

vicious, smug smirk across his face. I close the door behind me and walk to the edge of my desk.

"What the fuck are you doing in my chair?" I ask. My tone makes him throw his head back and laugh, the sound hollow and wrong.

"Good to know that you're still the asshole you are, even after fucking the enemy," he says. My eyes pinch at the corners, and my jaw clenches.

"Get out of my chair and you'll do good to mind your own fucking business," I warn. He moves around the desk and plops down in one of the chairs in front of my desk. "Why are you here?" I sit in my chair and lean into my elbows, looking at Dominico.

"Why can't I come see my cugino and Capo?" he asks. I raise an eyebrow, and he shakes his head as he huffs an amused sigh. All his movements seem off, as if he's playing a role. "Fine, that's a lie. I came here because I wanted to ask for permission to get revenge."

I slide my palms over the mahogany wood as I lean back.

"On who?" I know who, but I'm just stalling to turn it over in my head and see if it's worth the risk of more bloodshed in my territory.

"Cut the shit, Eli. You know who. My wife's fucking dead, and I was in a fucking coma for three months, and the Camorra couldn't do shit about it." His face twists in a snarl as his hand lands on my desk.

"Watch your fucking tone, Dom. I'm still your fucking Capo. Sharing a last name won't stop me from gutting you." My threat causes his nostrils to flare, but he leans back in his chair.

"All I want is permission to pursue my revenge on the Terranovas."

I search his face, the scar on his left cheek more pronounced against his pale face.

"No," I say. His lips curl, and I put my palm up to stop him from speaking. "Dom, I'm speaking as your cousin, not your Capo. I can't allow you this."

His jaw ticks before he growls. "You can fucking go after your revenge, but I can't. Honestly, I thought you, of all people, would understand." He stands to his feet, wincing as he moves his injured arm.

"I understand, Dom, I do. This isn't only my revenge. This is the Camorra's revenge not only for my Pop, but my soldiers who lost their lives and families," I say, and his shoulders tense as his face turns blank.

"I'm going back to New York. I'll be dealing with the men down there to prepare everyone for the return of the family." He flicks a piece of lint off his jacket before heading to the door.

"Dom?" I call after him. "I'm glad you're back." He pauses with his grip tightening on the doorknob, but doesn't turn to face me.

"Yeah...it's good to be back." The door shuts behind him with a click and the silence settles in each corner of the room like a blanket. I close my eyes, trying to clear my thoughts and focus on one thing. The clock on the wall behind me ticks the minutes away as I bite the inside of my cheek. I run my palm down my face and decide to text both Matteo and Romiro to come to my office.

I tap my pen against the table as I wait. It doesn't last long, and I get bored, so I drop my pen on my desk and move to my window. Fuck. Dominic had a full view of Valentina and I in the greenhouse from here. Of course, the fucker said what he did when I walked in. The possessiveness over her makes me want to go and gauge his eyes out for looking at her. Even if it was from afar. I run a hand through my messy hair. After I'm done with Romiro and Matteo, I'll probably go back to my room. There's a knock on the door before it swings open.

"What's up, fuckface?" Romiro says. He places his hand on my shoulder, standing beside me.

"Go sit the fuck down, Romiro, you too, Matteo," I order. Matteo shakes his head at Romiro's antics, and Romiro gives him a shark-like smile before taking a seat next to each other as I settle back at my desk "Moretti has agreed to our terms."

I regard my brother and best friend. Matteo's face stays passive and his eyes as blank as they usually are, but Romiro's smile slips off his face.

"Romiro, set up a meeting spot that's secured and ready to go. Matteo, send the Outfit the address, also monitor the area on surveillance, and make sure that they aren't going to try an attack on us."

Matteo nods his head once.

"I'll send them the location before you guys get there in an hour. I'll also have the place set up for any attack they might try."

He gets up and looks to Romiro, but Romiro stays sat, staring at me.

"You go ahead, Matteo, I'll be out in a bit. I need to speak to the Capo first," Romiro tells him, and Matteo looks between us before shutting the door behind him. I lean back in my chair and cross my feet at the ankles while I study Romiro.

"So, you're sending Valentina back to the Outfit." He's not asking, but stating a fact. I search his face, trying to figure out what his thought process is. He already knows the plan.

"Yes. Is there something I should know about?" I ask. He leans forward and shrugs. A twinkle enters his eyes.

"I just thought you were more of a Matteontic than this little shitstorm."

I narrow my eyes at him before shaking my head.

"Cut the shit, Rom. I don't get what you mean."

He gives me a wink and leans back into his seat, looking relaxed.

"Come on. You don't actually think we didn't know you two were fucking like rabbits."

I rub my temple as my eyes close for a second.

"What do you mean by 'we'?" I ask, and he shrugs.

"Me, Mara, Matteo, Lucio, and now Dom," he counts off. I lean forward and cradle my head in my hands. "Dom texted me before you did. Real classy, fucking in the garden's greenhouse."

"Does Ma know about this?" I ask him with a groan. My eyes flick to his face, and he shakes his head.

"Her poor, conservative heart won't take it," he finally tells me.

I roll my eyes at his stupidity.

"Shut up. We both know that's not why she'll be pissed."

"Whatever. She'll be pissed, regardless. But now she won't know because Valentina is going back to her family, and everything will fall back in place." He shrugs. A nagging voice at the back of my head tells me that no, everything will not fall back in place. Valentina and I have gone too deep and now we're completely and utterly fucked.

"Yeah. I guess that's true. Don't you fuckers have something to do?" I say, and he pushes to his feet.

"Aww, I know you love me."

My face wrinkles in disgust at the absolute audacity of this man who considers himself a fucking Camorrista. He laughs, shaking his head before turning to the door.

"Just don't forget yourself as Capo, and we'll all be with you in all the decisions you make." A knowing look passes over his face before he nods once and slips outside. Instead of staying in my office, I head to my room to talk to Val.

The door to my living room opens without a sound, and I step in. The silence is deafening, as if there isn't anyone in here. As I step inside, I scan the room. Nothing seems out of place, but I know in my gut that it's too empty and she's not here.

I reach my room door in three strides and pause in front of the door before twisting the knob and flinging it open. Empty. I don't know where the fuck she went, and I really don't understand why she isn't in here. Unless... No, fuck no. She's been desperate to go home for the last couple of days, as if she's a psych patient. And she did try to run the first time, but this time, she won't be able to get away. There are guards everywhere, surrounding the perimeter, so if she tries to even leave through an exit, they'll bring her back to me.

I sigh and close my bedroom door behind me. This is for the best. She can stay wherever the fuck she is, and I'll stay the fuck away until it's time to give her back to the Outfit. I head into the bathroom, my clothes hitting the floor on my way to the shower.

The steam from the shower slowly fills the bathroom and the boiling water pummels against my back. I stare off at the tiles as I wash my hair. I close my eyes as I imagine what would happen if...if I don't go through with the revenge.

I'd keep Valentina, we'd get married here in the back garden. I can see her walking down a pale green carpet, wearing a simple white dress, holding a colorful bouquet with the most gorgeous smile on her face.

Romiro, Dom, and my brothers stand beside me, while my sister, Alessia, and Ma stand on the opposite side. Everyone's eyes are on Val as she floats like an apparition down the aisle.

Then, after we marry, we'll go on a honeymoon somewhere she'll love. And a couple of years down the line, maybe a family of our own. Val, me, and our kids, a dream.

A knot finds its way in my throat as the vision slowly fades.

* * *

THE LAST TWO DAYS PASSED IN A BLUR AS I'D HURRIED MYSELF IN getting everything ready to move everyone back to New York. Valentina and I had managed to avoid each other. She'd spend time with my family during breakfast, lunch, and dinner and spend the rest of her time in my ma's guest room. Today's going to be a different routine, however. Because today is the day we'll be completing the plan. The knot that had wiggled its way in my throat a couple of days ago has only managed to get bigger with every minute that passes.

I find Valentina, Mara, and my ma all sitting together in the living room, making something. I ignore the curiosity at what they're doing. Rounding the back of the couch, I come to a stop beside Mara, who's next to Valentina. Mara looks up and narrows her eyes before deciding she's tired of fighting and gives me a small smile. The girl has always reminded me of a ray of sunshine, even when she's pissed. Valentina ignores me as she concentrates on the task in her hands. I clear my throat, but only Ma and Mara are the ones who look at me.

"Valentina," I say. She slowly turns her head around, and she has her best poker face on, but her expressive eyes betray her. She's upset. Upset and pissed. I ignore the voice begging me to comfort her. "Get up, we're leaving," I order. She presses her lips into a tight line, her eyes wandering to the side before they flicker to my sister and ma.

She gives them both a weak smile and hugs them tight. They hug her back, Mara and Ma giving her a squeeze and whispering something in her ear before letting her go.

The room is quiet and something heavy settles over us as Valentina steps away to come with me. Ma gives me a look that tells me she knows about what's transpired over the past couple days. I ignore it and walk ahead of Valentina, listening to her quiet steps behind me.

She's wearing another pair of sweats, this time a pair of purple sweatpants with a purple hoodie. We head toward the hallway she was staying in when she first got here. I open a door and step in, holding it open and waiting for her to walk in. As she does, she avoids looking at me. It irks me, but I leave it alone, not wanting to argue with her. Especially not when this will be the last time I'll see her.

I'll never see her again.

My throat tightens at the thought, but I ignore it.

There's a large table in the middle of the room with six chairs around it. On the table, there's a box placed on the edge closest to us. We both stay quiet as I open it. A replica of the dress she was wearing on the night of her kidnapping is in the box. Her eyes flicker with recognition when I hold it up, and her jaw clenches as I extend it toward her.

"Change in here, I'll be out there. Be quick," I tell her.

She snatches it out of my hand, and I don't wait for a reply as I slam the door.

CHAPTER 20
VALENTINA

Today I'll be going back to my family. I should be happy, thrilled, and I try to trick myself into believing that I am. But my insides feel hollow. I watch Emiliano's retreating back, and I flinch when he slams the door behind him. Swallowing down the hurt and blinking away the burning tears, my hands become slick with anticipation. I try to swallow again, but my tongue sticks to the roof of my mouth. I don't know how the fuck I'm going to be able to explain my lack of virginity when I go back, because as soon as Nicholas realizes that I am not a virgin, I'm sure he'll do something in retaliation.

I look down at the dress. It's an exact match to the one that I was wearing the night I was taken. I clench my fists, trying to stop myself from shaking. Placing the dress on the table, I push down my joggers, then pull my hoodie over my head, my arms and legs prickling as the cold air cools my warm body. I step into the dress, sliding my arms through the straps, but when I reach behind me to try zip it up, I only manage to get halfway, even after struggling with it for a couple of minutes. Opening the door, I find Emiliano standing against the opposite wall, his eyes on his phone screen.

"Are you done?" he asks. I narrow my eyes. I guess we're both not looking each other in the eye.

"Umm." I don't know what to say. His eyes snap to my face, and he scans me from head to toe, confusion crossing his gaze before he shuts it down. "I need help zipping the dress up."

He dips his head once. "Turn around."

I move my hair to the side as I turn, and he takes a step closer. His breath fans the top of my head and his warm fingertips ghost over my back. I feel his finger and thumb trap the zipper, his thumb caressing my skin as it ascends. My chest moves slightly faster than it should, and it feels like it's taking too much effort to breathe.

His breath ghosts the shell of my ear as he rasps, "All done."

I do what feels like the most impossible thing in the universe and step away from Emiliano. Taking a deep breath, I close my eyes for a second before opening them and turning around. Emiliano's hands are clenched at his sides, but his face gives away nothing.

He opens his mouth to say something, but he clamps it shut and heads toward the door of the hallway. I hurry behind him, taking a step back when he abruptly stops in front of the door, his hand on the knob in a death grip.

He inhales sharply before opening the door, then we make our way out of the house and down the steps.

I spot Romiro and a tall, large man stands next to him. Once we get closer, I notice that the man has curly dark hair and his eyes are the color of whiskey, his skin tan but his face pale; a scar running down his cheek adds to his dangerous aura and his arm is in a cast. Even though he is laughing, something dark lurks in his eyes and red rims around them that make him look sick.

Emiliano comes to a stop next to them, clapping each other on their backs. I stop a couple of steps away, cautious and suspicious. Romiro looks at me and gives me a small smile with a wink. I return his smile with a weak one.

"Well, well, if it isn't the most beautiful girl in the Outfit." The gravel crunches beneath the man's steps as he comes closer to me. I notice he has a strong alcoholic smell. Clenching my fists, I try to stop them from shaking. "I'm Dominico Folonari, Consigliere and cousin of Eli," he introduces himself, extending his hand, and I just watch it. My eyes flicker to Romiro's and Emiliano's faces, finding them both watching us with strained looks. I shake his hand, not wanting to be rude, and he squeezes my palm before letting it go. I rub it, trying to soothe the pulsing pain.

"Leave her alone, Dom. It's not her fault her ass of a cousin put you in a coma," Romiro says. He scowls, turning to look at Romiro.

"Mind your fucking business, Esposito," Dominico growls.

"Enough. You get in the car, and you two get in the other car." Emiliano points at me first. Pressing my lips together to stop myself from snapping at him, I open the backseat door, when his hand slams it shut. "You're sitting in the front."

My nose scrunches in disdain, but I do what he wants. They speak in hushed voices, but the car door muffles what they're saying even more.

I lean my head on the window and watch them. My breath catches in my throat when Emiliano's face breaks out in a genuine smile, and he laughs at something Romiro said. I face forward and avoid looking at them again until he opens the car door, and the smell of musk and cinnamon fills the space.

We sit in silence for a couple of seconds before Emiliano shifts and starts the car ignition, but the car doesn't move. The driver's window rolls down, and I can see from the corner of my eye that Romiro is in another car with his arm resting on the door, window rolled down. They mutter something to each other before Romiro drives down the gravel driveway toward the gates.

The car finally moves, and Emiliano drives in silence.

"Are you not going to blindfold me?" I ask as we speed past the gate's entrance, Emiliano ignoring me. I sigh and look out the window. I'm surprised to find more houses in a similar style to the Folonari's house, all far apart with acres separating them. I guess when I tried to escape, I left from a different street.

"No. The Outfit isn't stupid enough to risk breaching my territory twice, and even if they try, they won't know where to go, because you don't even know which part of New Hampshire this is."

He's right. I'm not exactly the biggest fan of geography; I prefer history anyway. The drive is long, and we both refuse to talk to each other, tense air filling the silence. Soon, my eyelids begin to feel heavy, and I keep yawning every two seconds. I'll just close my eyes for a bit.

The car comes to a sudden halt, and I jolt up, looking around.

"Well, that was fast." Emiliano huffs out an amused breath, and I turn to him, narrowing my eyes.

"What?" I ask. He shakes his head, a small smirk on his lips.

"You slept for four hours," he tells me. My eyes widen, and he laughs at my reaction before opening his door.

"Stay in here and don't get out until I come to get you."

I look out the window and see that we've stopped at some sort of parking lot that's surrounded by warehouses. Romiro and Dominico are both leaning on the car they came in, positioned diagonally to the one I'm in. I fight the urge to get out of the car and instead wait.

The three men stand near the car I'm in, but only Romiro and Dominico have a gun drawn in their hands. Two cars come creeping in from the other side of the parking lot and stop a couple of inches away.

I hold my breath as the car door opens and my Dad steps out, in a suit, his gray hair slicked back and his belly protruding over his black dress pants. The other car doors fling open, and four bodyguards pile out and stand close to Dad with guns drawn.

Behind him, the passenger door opens, and Angelo steps out of the car next, swiftly walking to the trunk. The driver's door also swings open and Dad's other guard follows Angelo.

I cover my mouth with my palm as Angelo and Giovanni pull out a tied man with a black bag over his head. They drop him in front of Emiliano's feet. Dad's mouth moves, but I can't hear anything from this far and the car door doesn't help either.

Romiro steps forward and grabs the bag off the tied man's head. I gasp into my palm, watching a beat-up Giuseppe slowly blink up at the three men above him. Emiliano turns to the car I'm in and walks toward it, my heart suddenly flying to my throat at what's coming.

He flings the passenger door open and pulls me out by the arm. I wince at the force of his grip, which he notices and loosens it.

"Valentina." I fight the urge to hurl at the fake tone Dad uses when he says my name.

"I'm sorry, *amore*," Emiliano whispers in my ear, low enough just for me to hear, and I feel tears welling in my eyes. He doesn't get to call me that when he's giving me back.

I force myself to swallow the knot that had formed in my throat as he throws me toward my Dad. Dad's hands grip me by my upper arms, and he shoves me toward Angelo and Giovanni. I stumble, but Angelo catches me.

"Angelo, take Valentina to the other car and make sure they get her out of here" my Dad orders. I bite my tongue to stop myself from arguing. I let Angelo drag me to the other car, and I try to resist looking back, but once I reach the car door and it opens for me to get inside, I rebel. Emiliano's icy eyes meet mine, and they soften a fraction before his face hardens and his eyes flick back to my Dad's.

I swallow and bend my head to slide into the car, the cool leather seats gliding against my warm skin. The car door slams and the silence envelops me into its bitter arms. The guards join me, one besides me, one in the front passenger seat, and one driving. I look to where Emiliano, Romiro, and Dominico are standing to find all of them staring at my Dad with their guns drawn as they watch him get back in his car. As the car begins to move, everything outside becomes a whirl of dull colors as I try to decipher what is what.

The sound of the air conditioner fills the private jet as we step onto it. We'd reached New Jersey state half an hour ago, and once we stepped out the cars, Dad hadn't spoken one word to me. My palms feel slick as my anxiety worsens over the next couple of minutes. I settle into one of the seats and Dad's guard stands waiting for him to do the same.

Dad's narrowed eyes flicker to me before he settles into his seat and leans back, asking for the flight attendant. "Get me some scotch, no ice."

I lean back in my seat, my muscles all scrunched up and are wound so tight that I think I might snap any second. I stay like that the whole ride back to Chicago, anticipating Dad's wrath, but it never comes, not when we're in the jet, not when we're in the car on our way to our house, and not when we enter the house. Mom, Violette, Monica, Marcello, and Nonna all stand in front of the door. Their faces are full of hope, but something broken lingers in their eyes. I run to Mom, who holds her arms open and squeezes me in her embrace.

I feel everyone else joins in, even Nonna, and Marcello hugs my legs. All the tears that I had bottled up come pouring out of me as an ugly sob leaves my lips. Mom's shoulders shake as she buries her face in my hair.

"I was...I was so scared that I'll never see you alive." Her voice breaks, and she pulls back her palms, cradling my face as she scans me from head to toe for any injuries.

"Valentina, my sweet girl. Those barbarians didn't torture you, did they?" Nonna's voice is full of disgust as she speaks about "them," as if they're not the same as us.

"No, Nonna they...they didn't torture me." I decide against telling my family that, instead of torturing me, they treated me with kindness and respect.

"Let the girl breathe. I'm going to my office," I hear Dad grumble as he heads up the stairs, his steps echoing around the large entrance hall.

"Come along, we need to get you ready for when you meet your fiancé and his family in a couple of days." Nonna pulls me from Mom's embrace as she drags me toward the stairs.

Fiancé...I don't want a fiancé, not the one my family had chosen for me. I look back and see that Lottie looks dejected and Mon whispers in her ear. Marcello looks at us, his eyes still haunted. Mom just stands there, her face sagging. She looks as exhausted and ill as ever. Nothing has changed...but me.

By dinnertime, Nonna finally decides to let me go to my room. I close the door behind me, and a yelp leaves my lips as I turn to find Violette sitting in one of my chairs. I rush to her, and we collapse into an embrace, both of us silently crying as we feel the despair of the last couple of weeks.

"I didn't think that I..." Her breath catches as she tries to stop crying to get her words out. "I didn't think I would see you again. Everyone was saying that the Camorristas are all monsters and that you weren't going to come back."

I swallow the urge to admit the truth to Lottie, and instead choose to stay silent, even as the guilt eats at my insides. She pulls back and grasps my hands, pulling me toward the two chairs facing each other.

"Did anything happen while I was gone? Did Dad hurt you guys?" I ask her, and she shakes her head.

"No, he was too busy freaking the fuck out and killing a bunch of people for the shitty security that night." Her blue eyes bounce around the room before coming back to me, her lips rolling together.

"I also got..." she trails off and I grab her hands.

"What? What did you get?" I ask. Her hands shake slightly in mine before she squeezes mine and pulls back.

"I got engaged to one of Dad's business partners."

I grit my teeth, feeling responsible for this predicament that Violette got placed in.

"How old is he?" I ask. Her nonchalant face doesn't trick me. I know she's nervous.

"He's twenty-three. His name is Massimo." She gives me a small smile.

"Have you spoken to him? Is he nice to you?" I ask her, and the tops of her ears turn a light pink, which gives her away.

"Yeah, I guess you can say he's nice." Her fingers twirl around each other. I don't think I've ever seen my sister visibly nervous.

A loud bang hits my door, making us jump, and Nonna shouts, "Come down for dinner!" We huff a laugh before making our way downstairs.

I stand near the stairs that lead down to the party, and stare at the reflection of myself in the mirror, running my palms over my hair.

I look the same as I did before I was taken by the Camorra, but I don't feel the same. Everybody tries to tell me and show me that everything is the same as it used to be, but nothing is.

I can feel it, in the way that Mom cries when she thinks that I left the room, or when Lottie and Mon whisper among themselves before asking me about the Camorra, and Marcello continues to look more and more emotionless as each day passes.

I can hear the buzz of the little get-together downstairs. My fiancé and his family are all there with my family. I swallow the lump forming in my throat, my skin feeling slightly slicker than I'd like it to.

I grip the railing as I take each step. My chest tightens as the image of Emiliano filters in front of my eyes, and I blink it away. I won't think of someone who'd give me up so easily. He doesn't want me, so I shouldn't want him.

I hate my dad. I hate him with such burning passion that maybe one day the flames will either swallow me whole because of my hatred, or it will burn all those around it. I clench my fists as I try to calm my breathing, the flames of rage flickering against my abdomen. Tears sting my eyes, and the acid burns my throat as the sobs fight to break through.

Death has never seemed so appealing. I just want to be happy, is that really too much to ask for? Straightening my dress, I suck in a deep breath. I might have entertained escaping this life before the Capo of the Camorra had taken me, and then my heart, but now I have people I need to protect, I can't be selfish. My sisters need me, my brother needs me. They deserve better than this shitshow of a circus my dad calls a family.

My heel clicks against the last step of the stairs, and I steel myself. I wish I had the courage to run away, but I can't do that. Dad would kill my sisters and my Mom and then me once he got his hands on me.

This will determine my future. The sound of chatter and laughter gets louder the closer I get to where everyone is waiting.

"I suppose you're one of those ladies who enjoy being fashionably late?" I startle as I spot a man standing off the entrance of the room, leaning into the shadows with his arms folded across his chest. He's tall and broad. A hint of an accent laced around his words makes them sound seductive. I narrow my eyes at him.

"No. I don't like being late, and that was incredibly sexist."

He stands straighter, and I take a cautious step back.

"You're Valentina, correct?" He steps into the light, and I can see that his eyes are a bright green like a cat's, and his hair is as dark as the night sky.

"Depends on who's asking," I counter. His face remains bleak, as if he finds me a nuisance.

"I'm Nicholas Guerrero, your fiancé."

Great, the guy clearly doesn't like me already.

"Sorry. I didn't know who you were," I apologize. I'm not really sorry; I don't give a fuck, and I'm sure he doesn't either. He nods before passing me, heading the opposite way as the party. "Where are you going? The party's in there," I ask.

"That party is boring as fuck. I'd love to stay and chat, but..." Nicholas shrugs, as if he's not bothered to come up with an excuse, and his tone suggests he'd rather do anything other than stay. I watch his retreating back until he turns the corner, then decide to go to the party. The chatter slows, and I can feel everyone's gaze on me. Everyone I know is here, and there are some people I don't know. I spot Violette and her fiancé, Massimo, if I'm not mistaken.

He looks at my sister like she holds the moon and the sun in the palms of her hands. Lucky bitch. Nonna's the first one to get to me as she loops her arm with mine. She's in a soft gray dress and her hair is twisted into one of her elegant hair buns.

"Valentina, I'd like to introduce you to Gloria Guerrero. She's Nicholas' stepMom." She gestures toward a woman who we come to a stop in front of. Gloria is wearing a long maxi violet dress, and her ginger hair is down in beach waves. She gives me a smile full of teeth and she looks at my nonna.

"Oh, you did say she's beautiful, but the photos don't do her justice."

I fight the urge to roll my eyes and decide to tune out their little talk. I manage to pry my arm out of Nonna's grip and excuse myself.

I take a couple of steps toward an empty corner and grab a flute of champagne off one of the trays the servers are carrying around on my way. I only manage to take a sip before both Mia and Violette swarm me.

"Are you two here to ask me about the Camorra? Again," I say. Mia gives me a sheepish smile, but Lottie just shakes her head.

"Come on, Val. You refuse to say anything about what happened, and everyone's worried," Violette complains. Mia steps closer to me, her fingertips grazing my upper arm carefully. I shake my head, my grip tightening on the stem of the champagne flute.

"You guys need to leave me alone. I don't want to talk about it. It's time that we all move on with our lives. I have a wedding to plan for." The knot in my throat tightens further, but I swallow a gulp of the champagne. Mia presses her lips together, and Lottie's giving me a look that I ignore.

"You know you're not the only one who has to marry someone you don't want to."

I tip my glass at Violette, feeling annoyed by her tone.

"No, I'm not, but the fact is, I'm the one who has to marry someone who will take me far away from my family, and I have little time to get to know him."

Violette doesn't say anything because Mia grabs her shoulder, shaking her head, as if they're in an alliance or something. By the time we're sitting around the dinner table, I've downed two more glasses of champagne, and my head feels lighter.

Dad sits at the head of the table with Antonio Guerrero and Gloria Guerrero to his left. The chair to his right is empty, and I'm sitting next to it. I suppose it's where Nicholas would be sitting.

Nonna is sitting to my left, but she's speaking with whoever is on the other side of her.

"Where is Nicholas?" I can hear Gloria whisper to one of their guards over the sound of everyone talking. The guard whispers something in her ear, and she nods, a grim expression on her face before she sees me looking at her and a dazzling smile replaces it. I return her smile and look back down at my empty plate.

We're still waiting for Nicholas, who graces us with his presence with a tall woman walking behind him. She walks with an air of confidence that I can feel from where I am sitting, her long red hair swooped to the side.

Her long wine-red cocktail dress flows behind her as she takes the empty seat beside Gloria, who whispers in her ear. Nicholas takes the seat beside me, not sparing me a glance before he begins to talk with my Dad and his dad about some shipment.

I look back toward where the woman is sitting and find her watching me, her hazel eyes slightly narrowed before she gives me a soft smile, going back to talking to Gloria.

"Nonna, who's that woman sitting next to Gloria?" I ask quietly. Nonna looks at me and then the woman sitting opposite her.

"That's Sofia Gonzales, the Lawyer for the Guerrero family."

"She looks really young," I comment. Nonna nods before turning her sharp eyes to me.

"Valentina, I want you to keep out of their family business. Understood." Her fingertips dig into my forearm.

"Yes, Nonna." Her tight grip disappears.

"Good," she whispers before turning back to her conversation with Nicholas' nonna. I lean back into my place and clench my fists. I don't talk to anyone as the servers move around the table, placing our food in front of us, and neither do I engage with anyone as we begin to eat. When we're done, I stand near the doors, waiting for the time I can slip away and no one will take notice.

"I'm Sofia." I look up to find the woman from before standing directly next to me with a smile on her face.

I swallow the piece of delizie al limone down before replying,

"Valentina, nice to meet you." Her hazel eyes are sharp, assessing everything about me from my soft pink dress that reaches my mid-thigh, dagger-shaped earrings, to my black Jimmy Choos.

"I like your dress. It's a very unique color." I don't know if she thinks I wore this to catch Nicholas' eyes or what, but I accept the compliment nonetheless.

"Thank you. I don't think I've seen any woman being involved in the..." My hand moves around in a circle motion. "Well... you know," I say, and she nods, an amused smile on her red lips.

"Organized crime business?" she supplies, and I nod, flustered. Clearly, the three champagne glasses I've had affected me. Our conversation is cut short by Gloria, who comes strutting over and accidentally—not accidentally—spills some wine on Sofia's dress.

"Oh, I am so sorry, Sora."

Sofia narrows her eyes at Gloria, who's wiping her palm over her dress.

Sofia mutters with a blank stare, "It's fine. Excuse me, Valentina." She rushes past me, and I see that Gloria looks suspiciously pleased with herself. Nicholas rushes past me, following Sofia, which causes the smug smile on Gloria's face to drop. Sensing something weird is about to happen, I quickly excuse myself and decide to head to my room. But once I reach the end of the hallway, I hear two people talking. I slowly peek around the edge and spot Sofia and Nicholas close to each other.

"Leave me alone, Guerrero. I don't need you trailing after me like some puppy when you have a fiancée." Sofia's voice is harsh, and she's pushing one hand against Nicholas' chest. He grabs her wrist and pulls her to him, his other arm going around her waist.

"Sofia, come on, you can't be serious about this. I told you I'll find a solution for this." They're both staring at each other intensely and don't notice me. I cringe when he leans down and kisses her. Great, my fiancé is hung up on someone else. At least I'll know who he'll be with if he stays out late once we're married. I twist the ring on my middle finger, debating whether I should go back to the party or just walk by them. It's not like I'm heartbroken and was expecting great love.

After all, I wasn't exactly thinking of Nicholas when it comes to the person I want to spend the rest of my life with. I shake my head, not wanting to think of him. Nicholas and Sofia rip away from each other at the sound of my heels tapping against the marble floors.

Nicholas' face is set in cool indifference, but Sofia looks guilty and as if she's made the biggest mistake on earth. They both stare at me, expecting me to stop and say something, but I just keep walking toward the staircase.

"Aren't you going to say something?" Sofia's voice stops me, and I turn my neck to look at both of them.

"No, I don't care what you two do. Just leave me out of it."

I don't wait around for what they have to say, and instead make my way back to my room. Tonight is definitely one of the most exhausting nights I've ever had.

I'M IN THE GARDEN, WALKING OUTSIDE OF THE MAZE INSTEAD OF INSIDE. My eyes sweep across the tall hedges until I'm staring at the gray clouds above.

"All you ever do is go out and walk around in the garden or read. You never talk with us anymore." Violette's voice comes from behind me. I close my eyes, squeezing them shut.

"It's not like I don't want to spend time with you, guys. I do, Lottie. It's just..." I swallow, struggling to finish my sentence. Violette's hand lands on my shoulder.

"Val, you know we're here for you. Mom, Monica, Marco, and me, we are all here for you. You don't have to keep things to yourself." The leaves crunch under my boots as I turn to face Violette. Her bright blonde hair is swept to the side in a long braid and her blue eyes are lined with her black liner. She drops her hand from my shoulder and slips it into the pocket of her red coat.

"I know all that, I do. And I'm grateful to have you all, but I'm just not ready to talk about...everything."

Her eyes search my face, her eyes narrowing slightly before she nods.

"I get it. Last time we were all together... You, Mon, and I." My brow furrows, surprised that Violette is willingly talking about the day we were ripped from Mom's arms and taken by the four traitors. She shrugs. "We're worried, that's all." I wrap my arms around my stomach, my eyes falling to the grass.

"Can we please talk about something else? Everyone ever talks about is the abduction and I'm sick of hearing it."

Violette is quiet for a second, and when my eyes make their way back up to her face, she sighs.

"It must've been awful."

I roll my lips between my teeth, not wanting to lie. It wasn't awful. In fact, it was the most freeing time of my entire existence, but now the anxiety of the consequences of what I've done is making me question everything.

"Hey, you didn't tell me that you were going to come out here with Val."

Violette turns her head to look back at Monica, and I give Mon a sheepish smile.

"I came out here alone," I tell her. Monica huffs out a breath.

"Oh, I know. The whole house knows. Mama and Nonna are both watching from the kitchen window."

My head whips to the side, and I spot both my mom and Nonna trying to appear like they were talking to each other.

"How long have they been standing there for?" I ask, turning my head back to Monica, expecting an answer.

She shrugs. "I don't know, maybe half an hour."

I groan, rubbing both my hands over my temples.

"Do you guys want to go to the coffee shop that's opened around the corner?" Monica suggests, and I look over at Violette to see what she'll tell Monica, but Violette just stares at me.

"Fine, whatever, but you know we can't leave until we tell Nonna or Dad, and have security following us," I say, and Violette rolls her eyes.

"As if that protected you last time," she mutters under her breath. I playfully bump my shoulder into hers as we make our way up the large marble stairs. Monica keeps to the end with the wall, clinging to the railing.

"How's your fiancé treating you?" I keep my voice low enough, not wanting Mon to hear us.

A slight blush covers Violette's cheeks and over the bridge of her nose, but she shrugs, "He's nice, I guess."

I bite the side of my cheek, trying to figure out how she really feels about Massimo.

"You have a crush on him, don't you?" I ask.

Violette whips her head my way as we come to a stop in front of the large door leading into the house.

"Val, do you realize how ridiculous that sounds? How can I have a crush on my fiancé?" she says as she shakes her head. I give her a shove.

"It's not impossible. Besides, it's not like you guys are marrying because you're in love," I tease her. Her lips twist as she regards me with narrowed eyes.

"It's not like you're marrying for love either, Valentina. Don't forget that our marriages are for the benefit of the family," she retorts, offended. I run my hand through my hair.

"No, maybe I'm not marrying for love either, but let's not tell lies. Both our marriages are to benefit our Dad, not the family or the Outfit."

Violette's eyes widen, and we both look to see if Monica heard us, but we just find the door open. I take a step toward the door, but Violette grabs my arm.

"I don't know what has happened to you, Val, for you to forget that it doesn't matter whether our marriages benefit the Outfit or our dad. Because Dad is the Outfit, and the Outfit is Dad. You think anyone would dare question that?" She sinks her nails into my arm. "Grown men have done less and suffered greater consequences."

I yank my arm out of her hold and slap her hand away.

"Scared, Violette? Or are you trying to piss me off?" I taunt. She crosses her arms over her chest.

"I don't think you remember what Dad is capable of," she says firmly.

Acid burns my throat, and my nails dig into my palms. Instead of retaliating, I decided to go inside.

"Val, wait, I didn't mean it like that."

I don't answer her, and she keeps following behind me. Our footsteps echo around the hallway as we make our way into the kitchen.

"Val, come on."

Mom and Monica are standing at the counter, but Nonna is nowhere to be seen.

"What's happened?" Mom makes her way toward me, her eyes frantically checking me, and then moving to Violette behind me. I step around Mom and make my way to the fridge, grabbing a bottle of iced coffee.

"Nothing," I reply simply, closing the fridge and facing my Mom. Her eyebrows are pinched as she looks at me and then at Violette.

"Are you sure, cara?" she asks, and I give her another nod, before going back to my room.

***

I dust the lightest layer of pink blush over my pale cheeks. They're usually tan, but I've been feeling sick as of lately. Pulling down the sleeves of my dress, I watch as Violette slips into my room and silently closes the door.

She turns and sees that I'm watching her, giving me a sheepish smile as she says, "Nicholas is downstairs." I raise an eyebrow and she adds, "He also brought you some roses." A sour taste fills my mouth as I put the blush brush down and turn to look at my sister.

"I have to go. Don't want to keep him waiting," I mutter. As I pass by her, she grabs my arm.

"Val, you don't have to fight this marriage, you can embrace it. You never know, it might be a good thing and not something bad like you think."

I don't look at her, yanking my arm out of her hand and walking to the door.

My hand rests on the door handle as I say, "It seems your fiancé has already turned you into a hopeless Matteontic."

The door shuts behind me with a silent thud and I head down the stairs. I can hear Dad and Nicholas speaking, but I can't make out what they're saying exactly. They both stop and turn to look at me when I reach the last step, my heels echoing against the marble floors.

I give them both a smile, but it feels forced. I just hope it doesn't *look* forced. Nicholas' face remains vacant of any emotions as his eyes stay on mine. He has a bouquet of red roses in hand, and he's wearing a white dress shirt and navy dress pants. His hair is pushed back in an effortlessly loose hairstyle. It makes him resemble Prince Eric from the Little Mermaid but with green eyes.

"Drive safe and get her back home before midnight," Dad says to Nicholas, who gives him a nod before handing the roses to one of the maids and heading to the entrance doors. Dad's hand snakes out and grabs me when I try to walk past him. "Behave yourself, and don't do anything that might annoy Nicholas." His tone carries an unsaid threat, and I give him a curt nod as he releases my arm.

Nicholas holds the door open for me and gives me a curious look as I walk past him. I ignore it and continue toward what I assume to be his car. His driver opens the back door for us, and I slide in, Nicholas sliding in after me. The drive on the way to the restaurant is spent in silence, neither of us wanting to engage the other in idle conversation.

We come to a stop in front of The Daisy, which is known for its cutesy but intimate atmosphere. I slant Nicholas a look as we both step out; I'm trying to figure out why we're at this restaurant. Especially when he already has eyes for someone else. My question is answered quicker than I thought it would be because more than one blinding flash of light goes off and the shouts of the paparazzi fill the air. Of course, it's a publicity stunt. I'm not mad because I care, but I wish he had the decency to tell me beforehand.

Side by side, we walk toward the entrance. Nicholas maintains the constant constipated look on his face, and I have a small smile on mine. Once we reach the entrance, two guards open the glass doors for us, and the muted beige carpet muffles the sound of our steps. The hostess greets us with a smile before she leads us to our table that's not far from where the paparazzi are seated, but it's private enough that no one can hear us talk.

Nicholas pulls out a chair for me, and I can hear the clicks of the cameras go off. We don't have time to even go over the menu before a waiter comes our way to ask for our orders. I order the steak and mashed potato on the side, medium rare. And Nicholas orders some Wagyu with asparagus. I guess we both know to be as bland and boring as possible when outside.

Once the waiter is gone, Nicholas turns to look back at me and asks, "How do I know that you're not going to go yapping your mouth about what you saw at the party?"

I narrow my eyes at him before shooting back, "I'm about as happy as you with this marriage arrangement; however, for me, my survival depends on this shitshow working out. I won't say anything if you can keep yourself out of the tabloids. At least until we're married because, after that, my dad won't give a fuck what you do."

He raises an eyebrow and says, "Well, that's settled. You'll mind your business, and I'll mind mine once we're married, but until then, let's keep our interactions to a minimum. I don't exactly feel like going out on dates with someone I don't enjoy the company of."

"Ditto," is all I say before the waiter brings out our dishes and wine and we eat in silence. The only sound is the clinking of our cutlery.

Nicholas takes me back home just before eleven-thirty, and I manage to avoid everyone on my way to my room.

2 MONTHS LATER

Soft cries echo in the large cathedral. Nonna's dead. She had a heart attack, and it was Nicholas and Sofia who had 'found' her. They say they found her, but I know that she probably saw them together and her heart couldn't take it.

My sisters and Marcello are sitting on the pew behind us. Nicholas is sitting right next to me between my dad and I, and Mom is next to Dad, but I can make out her soft wails. The priest stands at the front of the Church, droning on about the afterlife and how Nonna lived a good, honest, and a happy life as a believing woman.

I almost laugh at how much of a lie and joke it all is. Nonna wasn't honest or happy, and she certainly wasn't good. Once the service is done, we all make our way to the graveyard for Nonna's casket to be buried.

"What happened? And don't bullshit me like you're bullshitting everyone right now." Nicholas stares ahead, not sparing me a glance, the ever-resting bitch face in place. "Nicho-"

"Sofia and I were speaking about what you had seen when your abuela walked in, all blazing eyes, and threatened us." His cool baritone voice cuts me off. I narrow my eyes and my teeth grind together; I don't believe one fucking word out of his mouth.

"She saw you two doing something, didn't she?" I'm not asking him, just stating a fact. He slowly turns his head, his green eyes drilling a hole in my forehead as he tries to understand why I'm speaking to him.

This is our third conversation since we met, and from what I can tell, this marriage is going to go up in flames as soon as the ink is dry on the paper. He's been avoiding me, not that I mind it, and no one is pushing for us to talk, so we're fine to keep to ourselves. Until the wedding. I clench my purse and look straight ahead.

Nicholas and I don't speak after that and go on about the funeral proceedings as if we're not meant to marry in a couple of months. The wedding was postponed due to Nonna's sudden death.

Six months, and I'll be married to a man I barely know, can barely stand the sight of, and feel absolutely nothing for, but what do I matter in the big plan of my Dad's big criminal enterprise.

The next day, Gloria, Nicholas's stepMom, is at our house with her husband, but Nicholas isn't here. Gloria sits with me and Mom while Mom sends Violette and Monica out.

Violette leaves without any pushback since she has a date with her fiancé, but she doesn't want to call it a date. Instead, it's a "meetup"—whatever the fuck that means. Monica, on the other hand, seems to want to be involved in the wedding planning, not affected by the funeral we had yesterday.

"Yes, we'll have a wedding dress shopping day maybe next month."

Mom's hand squeezes mine as she agrees with whatever the hell her and Gloria are talking about.

We're sitting in the guest living room. The gray armchair is so uncomfortable that I shift around every couple of minutes, earning me looks from Gloria and Mom. I ignore them and stare off in the distance, wondering what everyone in the Camorra is doing.

I hate myself for it, because all I can think of is Emiliano. All I dream of is him. He consumes my every thought. I need to snap out of it.

I'm getting married in four months, and it's not to him.

CHAPTER 21
VALENTINA

1 month later

"Valentina, mia cara. Are you okay? Are you feeling okay? You've been zoning out a lot since..." Mom doesn't finish what she wants to say; she doesn't have to. I understand what she means. We're headed to the wedding dress stores in the city.

"Yes, Mom, I'm fine. I just don't...I don't really have anything to say." I shrug my shoulders, hoping she'll buy it. Her eyes briefly close as she sighs before she opens them again and nods.

"You'll tell me if something's bothering you, right?" she asks. I would never do that to my Mom. She already has enough on her plate.

"Yes, Mom, of course." The car comes to a halt, and the doors fling open, our bodyguards scouring the surrounding area. Perrin's bridal shop has a cute look to it, and I'm sure that Gloria doesn't like it by her sour expression when she steps out of the car behind ours. The glass doors have an arch of different flowers, mostly orange and yellow, but some reds peek through. The guards push the gold hardware on the glass doors and hold them open for us.

Stepping inside, the vibrant orange carpet muffles the sound of our heels. The walls are a mix of orange, yellow, and pink, like a water marble with gold accents, making it look vibrant and inviting. Gloria looks around with disdain before stepping forward. Two attendants stand to the side with bright smiles on their faces.

One of them has a beautiful Afro and the other has a pretty scarf on her head.

"Hi, I'm Valentina, and we're here for our first wedding dress shopping appointment," I say. Recognition crosses the face of the girl with the scarf.

"Yes, we have you booked in for the day. I'm Inara, and I'll be your assistant, and this is Dorothy, my trainee. She'll be assisting you as well." She gestures to the woman next to her, and I give them both a smile, trying to be as friendly as possible. "Would you like to follow Dorothy to your waiting area." She waves to my mom and Gloria, who both follow Dorothy to an open space with a gray carpet and gray chairs. Inara looks back for me to follow her.

"Is there a style you have in mind?" she asks as we stop, and I look around.

"I like simple dresses, but I really like glitter and sparkles as well."

She taps a finger on her chin, her eyes narrowing on the row of dresses.

"How about you have a look around here, and I'll grab some of our one-of-a-kind dress designs from the back." I nod at her, and she gives me a smile before heading down the row of dresses. Flipping through them, I sigh heavily when I can't concentrate because of the pulsing migraine. I press my eyes closed and count. One, breathe, two, breathe, three. Releasing a another breath, I open my eyes and flip through the princess silhouettes. I pause on a pure white sweetheart neckline with sheer off-the-shoulder sleeves. I try to get it out but fail, and one of the attendants comes rushing to pull it out for me.

"Thank you," I say. He nods, holding the dress over his arm.

"I'll place it in the dressing room for you, Miss Moretti."

Inara comes toward us, pulling a rack with a couple of different dresses in garment bags.

"Did you find any that caught your eye?"

"Yes. This one seems to be my style." I gesture to the dress in the male attendant's hand. She smiles at him and thanks him for helping me before grabbing the dress and hanging it on the rack handle. We make it to the waiting area, and both Mom and Gloria are sitting, talking to each other in hushed voices.

"Oh, have you found any that you think are suitable for the wedding?" Gloria asks me when I walk by them to follow Inara.

"Yes, I did. I'm just going to try one on, and we'll go from there," I tell them both. She nods and turns back to my mom, who gives me a smile before going back to their conversation. I step into the changing room, which has a floor-to-ceiling wall mirror, the lighting bright enough to blind anyone.

A round table and a small stool are in the corner of the changing room. Some white clips are placed on the round table, and Inara pauses next to it with the rack, unzipping the garment bags before looking back at me.

"I've unzipped all the dresses. Try on whichever one you'd like. If you need any help, I'll just be outside. Tap on the door, and I'll come in."

I thank her as moves past me and out the door, shutting it gently behind her.

My head drops between my shoulders, and I look at my reflection. The thick concealer is still intact, none of the exhaustion showing, and the blush adds some color back into my pale face. Looking back at the dresses, I sigh once more and begin to strip. I pinch my arms, and the weight gain is noticeable. I really need to get my anxiety under control, or I'll have an unhealthy obsession with food again.

The dress I picked is really pretty and has a very elegant look to it, but I can tell that it isn't the dress for this kind of wedding. I knock on the door twice and step back. Inara opens the door, poking her head in.

"What can I help with?"

"Could you please put the clips in the back of the dress?" I ask. She nods with a kind smile, and I turn around. She steps closer with two clips in her hand after grabbing them from the round table. Once she's done, she looks at me through the mirror, and I run my palms down the front of the dress.

"I like it, but I love the silhouette more than anything else."

"Yes. A-line silhouettes are very popular with our young brides. If you'd like I could pull out some more dresses," she suggests, but I shake my head.

"No. The ones we have out are fine for now. Thank you."

She smiles and moves to the side so I'm able to leave the dressing room. Gloria and Mom are both still talking, but they pause and look at me as I step toward the podium positioned in front of a long mirror.

I face them, unsure how they feel. Mom's eyes are glazed over, her fingertips pressing to her quivering lips. On the other hand, Gloria assesses the dress with narrowed eyes before shaking her head.

"It's too simple. Valentina, I'm sure you'd find a more suitable dress from Vera Wang or Schiaparelli," Gloria says. Mom looks apologetic, as she probably thinks that this is the dress I want.

"I think we'll find something we can both agree on in this boutique. But I agree this dress isn't exactly suitable for a wedding between our families." I step off the podium and head back to the dressing room, but Gloria's voice stops me.

"You could try to lose some weight before the wedding. You look quite pudgy."

My eyes sting and my fists clench around the dress as I try to calm my breathing. The room falls into a tense silence, and I look back at her.

"You might want to keep that kind of 'advice' to yourself, because I'm a healthy weight for my height."

I don't wait to see her reaction and trudge toward the dressing room, Inara following behind me. The rest of the fitting goes by in a quiet blur, nobody agreeing on any of the dresses. That is, until we get to the second-to-last dress. It's sparkly with a V-neckline and beautiful, sheer, off-the-shoulder puff sleeves.

When Inara comes into the changing room, she pauses for a

second before asking me, "Would you like me to get the matching veil for the dress?"

She hurries off after I nod, only to come rushing back in a bit out of breath. She comes up behind me and places the sheer sparkly veil in my bun, adjusting it until she deems it perfect. The veil is long and drags behind me as I make my way to the waiting room and stand in front of my mom and Gloria, who are both silent.

"It's perfect," Mom and Gloria both say at the same time. They sound almost breathless, and it honestly makes me glad that they love the dress.

"Yes, it is. I think this is the one,"

My wedding dress is picked. Soon, I'll be marrying the future drug lord of one of the most notorious Colombian drug Cartels in the country.

Six months later

Today is my wedding day.

The whole house is in wedding mode, and everyone is freaking out. I can hear my wedding planner screaming down the hall from my room. My hairstylist, Melissa, is working on getting my up-do perfect and making sure that it'll last through the fourteen-hour wedding day. It's only 7:30 and we have around two hours before the wedding ceremony.

Mom's running around like a headless chicken, trying to make sure that Violette and Monica are ready. She's also chasing Marcello to get him to put on a tie, but he keeps dodging her; that is, until Dad gives him a look that could make a grown man shit himself.

The last couple of steps for my look are lipstick, dusting off the setting powder, and setting spray. With Melissa nearly done, she rushes over to the other girls to get them ready before they leave to go to the church.

"Come on, Monica. You don't need that much makeup, sweetie, you're fourteen." Mom urges Mon to stop trying to add more makeup, but she doesn't listen.

"I'll see you at church, Mom. I'm going to go change in the other room." I kiss Mom's cheeks, and she pulls me into a hug, sniffling.

"When did my little girl grow up? I remember when you were a little girl running around, asking everyone to play with you." She pulls back, dabbing the corners of her eyes with the edge of her fingers.

I give her a small smile, wishing I can be that young again and not feel like the weight of a mountain rests on my shoulders.

"Don't cry, Mom. I'm getting married, not dying," I say. Although I'd much rather the latter of the two.

"Yes, I know. I just want you to be happy. Are you happy, sweetie?"

The knot in my throat intensifies, and I really don't want to lie to my mom, but I just nod my head and kiss her cheek. Her palm cradles my cheek for a second before she turns to my sisters.

"Come on, girls, we need to go, and Marcello, come on, caro amico, we have to go to the church."

They all rush out the door, the makeup artist and hairdresser behind them. I stare at the closed mahogany door for a beat before going into the second room to get dressed. The only people in the house now are Dad, me, and four bodyguards. Everyone else is at the church and most of the guards are guarding the church with Guerrero's guards.

It's quiet. It's almost eerie how quiet it is, but I shake it off and try to ignore the small lead ball in the bottom of my stomach, telling me something is off. I open the closet door that holds my wedding dress, heels, Nicholas' family heirloom necklace, and the long veil. I had the dress designed to have a zipper on the side instead of the back since I wanted to get dressed by myself, refusing to have anyone in here with me.

The dress slips on easily and the zipper glides up smoothly. I take the white kitten heels out of their box and place them on the ground, lifting the dress. Putting on the shoes, I move to the necklace and then the veil. The sound of my heels against the marble floors echoes around in the room as I go to stand in front of the long mirror. In the reflection, I find something that resembles me, but it isn't really me. It doesn't feel like me.

The girl in the mirror is groomed to perfection, as an instrument for her family's plans, but that's not who I want to be. What scares me the most is the fact that I look so...empty. My eyes bleak, as if life had been drained out of them, and that's how I'd been feeling the last few months, like I've been floating through life, not really living.

My heart aches, entire body aches, and existing alone hurts like a thousand knives. I fight the urge to cry as my eyes glaze and the familiar sting takes over. My throat tightens, and the noose that has been around it since I'd left...New Hampshire has finally become too tight to breathe, and my limbs feel too weak to stand. I don't fall, I won't fall. I'll stand straight and tall, and whatever this fucking life throws at me I will take.

I don't need anyone.

But I'm jolted within the next second, my emotion switching to shock.

My eyes widen as I look in the mirror again and see the only person I have wanted to see. He stands behind me in a black suit, his hands in his pockets like he has all the time in the world. His face softens at the look in my eyes. I don't turn around.

"You look breathtaking, ragazza mocciosa," he whispers. My teeth grind together at the softness of his voice, at the adoring look in his eyes.

"What are you doing here? Today, of all days?" I ask, heart racing, and his eyes harden at the roughness of my tone, his tattooed hands sliding out from his pockets.

"I've come to take back what's mine."

I scoff at that, even as my stomach swoops like it's fighting against me. His eyes narrow as he steps closer.

"And what would that be?"

I stiffen when he leans forward, his eyes still on mine, but his lips near my studded ears.

"You," he whispers as I look up at him. I fist the skirt of my dress, vibrating with immeasurable amounts of rage.

"I'm nobody's property, least of all yours. What are you doing here, Emiliano, on my fucking wedding day?" I demand, and he grips my chin, forcing me to turn around to face him. His eyes search my face, looking increasingly displeased with what he sees before his eyes soften again, just a fraction.

"I...I don't know how I was able to leave you for so many months. I don't know how I was able to stay away from you. I'd dream of you every night and nothing else. You haunted my every thought. *Every* fucking thought. Awake or asleep, I couldn't escape you. I didn't want to escape you. I don't know how I was able to breathe without you. You are the air I need. A life without you is not a life. Not one worth living," he says. I search his face, trying to find any hint of deception, panicking when I find none.

"What are you thinking? Do you know what will happen to you if they find you here? Do you know what my Dad will do to you if he finds you here?" I ask. His arms wrap around my waist, bringing us closer.

"I don't care. I'd rather risk everything to even have a chance with you, and whether I die trying to, or survive to get us both out of here, then I'd take it." He's insane. Oh. My. God. This man is actually insane and he's in my room only hours from my fucking wedding to another man. I swallow roughly as nerves ripple through my body.

"What do you mean by that?" I ask him. He rests his forehead on mine, his bright blue eyes locked in on my gaze.

"It means that I am irrevocably, painfully, and so delusionally in love with you, Valentina Moretti, and want you to come with me back to New York."

My chest swells at his words and my body breaks out in soft sobs as I bury my head into his neck.

"Don't cry. Please, don't cry. I'm sorry. I wanted to come earlier, but I needed to gather my thoughts. I was so confused. I thought what I wanted the most was revenge," he explains. I half laugh, half cry.

"Thought?" I ask, looking up at him.

"Yes, I thought that I wanted revenge. But what I truly want is you."

I quickly sober up, realizing that my Dad will be up here any minute now.

"You need to leave. Like, now." Shakily, I push at his chest, but he doesn't move.

"We. Valentina, we need to leave. I'm not leaving without you." I press my lips together, and my brow furrows as I fist his suit jacket.

"You asshole. You can't just come here and crash a wedding after giving me back and really expect me to want to go back to New York with you," I argue, but Emiliano's hold only tightens on my waist.

"I'm taking you with me, whether you like it or not, Valentina."

My jaw ticks and my eyes narrow.

"No. You gave me up. You don't get to decide when you want me. I'm not a fucking toy you can jerk around, Emiliano."

He sighs, lips pursing before he continues. "Please, come home with me. I miss you, please. You are the best thing that has happened to me," he pleads. Home? Is Camorra territory really home to me now?

"I am home, Emiliano," I say, a bit hesitantly. He shakes his head, his jaw clenching.

"No, you're not. Please, just come back with me and let's talk."

I open my mouth to reply, but the door to the room bursts open, and my Dad stands there with a gun raised and a snarl twisting his ugly face. Emiliano quickly draws his gun out from his waist holster.

"I see you, Camorra bastards, like to breach my fucking territory." Dad throws the insult at Emiliano. He faces my Dad, pushing me behind him, aiming his gun. Fuck. I told him to get out of here. He slips me his phone, his messages with Romiro open. I quickly shoot a text to Romiro, telling him what's happening.

"It's not my fault your territory isn't properly protected." Emiliano shrugs nonchalantly. I pull at his suit jacket to tell him to stop provoking my Dad. He knows my dad has a short fuse.

"You fucking brat might have been able to get away with it last time, but this time, you won't. I'll dismember you to the point your own family won't recognize you."

My stomach churns at my dad's threat, because I know he'll make true on it. After all, he only got his cruel reputation after years of torture and death. The sheer white curtains that cover the open balcony door blow in as the soft breeze drifts into the tense room. Romiro sends a text, which tells us that they're outside the balcony and will be up in two minutes. That could be two minutes too fucking late. My dad and Emiliano are in a standoff.

"Valentina, come here." My dad's voice booms, but Emiliano's arm sticks out, trying to prevent me from moving. I push past it and stop between my dad and Emiliano, the silence thick enough to cut through with a butter knife.

"No, Dad. I'm leaving, and you can't stop me."

His angry eyes focus on my face as he snarls, "You fucking whore. I didn't raise you to betray me. You will not be leaving. You will stay. Do you hear me? You will stay here and marry Guerrero's son and do what I say."

My hands tremble at my sides as I shake my head, fear gripping me, but I push through. "No. I will not." He points the gun at me, and before I know what's happening, Emiliano has pushed me out of the way of the gunfire and taken a bullet to his abdomen.

He falls to the ground with a thud, and I scream, my stomach dropping. No. No. This isn't fair. Hot tears run down my face as I watch Emiliano wince as he tries to stand up. My dad advances on us, his hand grabbing my hair and he pulling me up. Romiro bursts through the open balcony door in that moment with Lucio behind him, both of them with their guns drawn.

"Put the girl down, Moretti, or I'll fucking shoot a bullet right between your beady little eyes," Romiro demands. Dad's grip tightens, and he pulls me up in a headlock. The feel of the cool metal against my temple makes me pause.

"You fuckers need to get off my property and out of my territory before I blow her fucking brains." Dad pushes the gun's mouth farther into my skull, emphasizing his threat. I claw at his thick fat arm, but he just pushes his arm into my throat. When I look down to see if Emiliano is fine, I only see a patch of blood. Romiro's face is twisted in a look that can only be described as a pure boiling rage. I only notice a fraction of a nod before I hear the sound of a gunshot that makes my eyes ring and the warm feeling of something splattering on the side of my face.

Emiliano has killed my Dad. On my wedding day.

Dad slugs off behind me and drags me down with him. He lands with a thud, and I manage to push his arm off me before I fall to the floor.

Morbid curiosity gets the best of me, and as I'm about to turn to look, Romiro warns, "Don't look back or you won't be able to sleep." My head snaps to the front, and Romiro huffs out an amused laugh before he sobers up. "We need to get out of here. Lucio, help me get Emiliano. Val, go to the balcony. Matteo is waiting down there for you."

I look back at Emiliano, who gives me a meek smile, his face ashen. I reach for him, but he shakes his head at me. My nerves are running rampant as I move to the balcony and look down to find Matteo down there. He gives me a wave before pointing at a rope that's hooked to the balcony rod. I swallow as I feel my throat go dry before quickly taking off my heels, throwing them down and aiming far from where Matteo is standing. Next, I rip off the bottom half of my dress. A groan from behind me makes me rub my hands together and grab the first step on the ladder to climb down. I try not to think about what has just happened. Looking back up, I find Lucio beginning to climb down, and I almost slip. I don't know how Emiliano is going to get out of there.

"Jump," Matteo instructs me, and I find that I'm only a couple of inches up from the ground. I can tell I'm slowing them down, so I quickly close my eyes and jump. I land and manage to fall on my back, a couple of feet away from where Matteo is standing. I quickly get up, grab my heels, and put them on.

"Come with me," Matteo instructs once I'm near him. He quickly walks ahead of me toward the fence that separates the garden and the forest.

"What about them?" I ask. He doesn't look back as he grunts.

"They'll be fine. We need to get you out of here first." I quickly walk after him to catch up. He stops before the fence and turns to look at me. "I'm going to climb first and then pull you up."

He doesn't wait for me to agree, and he climbs until he stands on the stone part of the fence. Extending one arm, he grabs the fence with the other. Matteo manages to pull me up the second time after I'd slipped the first, and we drop over to the other side. Romiro, Lucio, and Emiliano make it to the fence by the time we're on the other side. Matteo begins to walk, and I follow after him, looking back a couple of times to make sure that the other three are following us. We get to the road where a parked car is hidden from view.

Once we've all quickly piled into the car, the drive begins. It's only a matter of time before everyone figures out what has happened. I hope my sisters, brother, and mom will be okay since Dad is now dead. I'm sitting next to Emiliano, who's sweating like he's run a marathon, his white shirt soaked in his blood. Romiro is sat next to him as Matteo drives the car as fast as he can.

"Matteo, drive till we reach Ohio. We need to get the bullet out."

Matteo at Romiro's instructions and turns back to the road. Romiro presses a piece of fabric to Emiliano's wound, and Emiliano winces. I really hope we can make it out of Outfit territory before everyone figures out what has happened. The wedding should have started by now, which means everyone just thinks that Dad and I are a little late, unless the guards in the house have alerted everyone.

We make it to Ohio in under five hours and manage to get Emiliano to one of the Camorra's hospitals in time.

"He needs a minor surgery. The bullet is still in there and we need to get it out."

The doctor talks to Romiro and both of Emiliano's brothers. Emiliano is asleep, hooked up to an IV and a heart monitor.

"Okay, do it as soon as possible," Romiro tells the doctor, and so do Lucio and Matteo. The doctor drones on about something else before rushing out of the room. I'm clutching Emiliano's hand as the hot wet tears roll down my cheeks.

"You fucking asshole, you better wake up soon so I can kick your dumb ass. Why the fuck would you do something as stupid as jump in front of a bullet?" I ask, and Romiro's hand lands on my back as he tries to soothe me.

"You know why, Val, come on. It's the same reason he breached Outfit territory for you."

I sniff, trying to compose myself.

"Yeah, I guess I do," I mutter.

He needs to wake up. He shouldn't get to tell me he loves me and then fucking die.

CHAPTER 22
EMILIANO

Darkness is all I see, and the throbbing pain in the side of my abdomen feels like shit. I can hear someone talking near me. Actually, no, it's an angel talking with me. Did I fucking die by a fucking Moretti's hands like my Dad? I groan, and all of a sudden, something grips my hand.

"Oh my God, Eli. Wake up. Are you awake? Romiro, go call the doctor, he's awake." She squeezes my hand, and my eyes fling open, only to fall shut again as the blinding white light stings my eyes. I try to open them again and blink away the black spots.

"What's my name?" I croak at Valentina, who's standing next me with a worried look in her eyes.

"Emiliano?" she says sweetly.

I clear my throat.

"No, the other one," I say, and she rubs her fingertips across my forehead, pushing back the hair that had fallen on it.

"Eli?"

I close my eyes and sigh in contentment.

"You're so dramatic for a Capo, you know," she teases, her eyes full of adoration and something I'm scared I'm mistaking. A doctor with white hair and a thick-rimmed pair of glasses on the edge of his nose comes barging in, with Romiro behind him, giving us a shit-eating grin.

"I'm leaving after you do a checkup," I inform the doctor, whose eyes widen, and he looks from Val to Rom, and then back again, before clearing his throat.

"I would strongly advise against that." He pushes his glasses up the bridge of his nose.

"I don't fucking care. I'm leaving after this. Romiro, go get the discharge paperwork done."

Romiro looks conflicted for a second before nodding and shutting the door behind him. Val looks at me, concerned, but doesn't say anything as the doctor checks my vitals. Once he's done, he sighs as he stands at the edge of the hospital bed.

"You're doing very well and will probably be fine to leave, but please rest up for the next couple of days and make sure to drink plenty of fluids," he advises. Val assures him that she'll make sure I do that before thanking him and closing the door after he leaves.

"Where did your wedding dress go?" I ask. She's wearing a pair of mom jeans and a white short-sleeved shirt.

"Got rid of it. I couldn't exactly stay in that thing for two days straight and be comfortable with the looks I got. Especially with blood stains and rips on it."

I laugh, but wince once the pain got a bit too much. She hurries to my side.

"Oh my God, you need to be careful," she fusses. I grab her hand and pull her closer.

"I'll be fine as long as you're here. You're like my special healing potion," I croak, and she rolls her eyes.

"When did you get this cheesy? It's gross. Stop it." I laugh at her teasing, and her little grin widens into a full-blown smile.

Romiro, of course, decides to walk in at that moment.

"Ew, can you two not stay the fuck away from each other for at least a couple of hours, or do you have to fuck like rabbits?" His nose wrinkles in disgust, and Val rolls her eyes at him this time.

"We're doing something called cuddling, you drama queen. I'm not sure you know what that means," she says. Romiro flips her off, and she gives him two birds, making him laugh and shake his head.

"Where's Lucio and Matteo?" My voice is still a bit hoarse, but it doesn't hurt.

"They're at the airport waiting for us."

I slowly get up from the bed, and the room spins for a bit. Valentina grabs me to help, and I give her a grateful smile and press a kiss on the side of her head. Romiro rolls his eyes before helping us.

"Come on, let's get you love bunnies back to New York."

It's been a couple of days since we got Valentina out of Outfit territory and made our way back to New York. I look at the alarm clock on my stand, which reads 6:30 a.m. Valentina and I had fallen asleep while spooning, which means she still has her back against my front, and my morning wood strains against my boxers. Val groans as she fights the urge to go back to sleep, and I decide to help her. My arm snakes to the front of the long shirt she's wearing—my shirt, to be exact—and lifts it slightly, exposing her bare pussy. Well, it's technically mine. I dip my fingers through her folds, slightly brushing her clit, and a moan vibrates through her whole body. I feel it as she arches her back into me.

"Eli. What are you doing?" she moans. My breath feathers the shell of her ear, and her skin pebbles with goosebumps.

"Getting my first snack of the day," I say. She huffs a laugh as she rubs one of her eyes with her fist.

I rub her clit until I feel her become slick, and then dip two of my fingers into her until I bury them knuckles deep.

"Oh my God. Eli, I'm really sore," she complains, but pushes her ass into me. I kiss the side of her face.

"I'm sorry, ragazza mocciosa, you can't blame me. You're like a drug I don't want to quit. I can't quit, even if I wanted to."

She moans as I slowly thrust my fingers into her. I speed up once I know I've hit her G-spot. Her hand snakes up and her fingers sink in my skull as she rides my hand.

"Are you going to come on my fingers like a good little whore? Hmm?" I ask. Her moans turn breathless and her body jerks twice before her pussy walls clench as she orgasms. I pepper kisses over her sweat-slicked face and down her neck, then slowly pull my fingers out of her once her breathing evens and bring them up to my lips, groaning as I taste her on my tongue.

"I love you," she mumbles sleepily, and I go rigid for a moment before I relax as I realize that I've been waiting for her to tell me.

I watch her in awe as she drifts back to sleep, her small palm resting between her cheek and the pillow, long black hair splayed, and I have to muffle a laugh at the small snores that leave her parted lips. She always denies them when she's awake, and I don't argue with her because she gets mad about it. I kiss her forehead and decide to go back to sleep as well since I like it better when she's awake.

CHAPTER 23

VALENTINA

Emiliano had some of his men set up a vanity table in his room for me, the dark wood contrasting with the lightness of the space. I'm facing the mirror, but my eyes are on the man I left my family for. His back is to me, and I can clearly make out the various tattoos from where I'm sitting. The two vipers' tails wrapping around his arms and their tails reaching all the way up to his broad shoulders.

"Stop staring at me, or we won't make it to dinner," he warns. I bite back a smile when he turns around. He's fixing the cufflinks that I got him, on the cuffs of his black shirt.

"Is that a threat or a promise?" I ask, dusting some blush on my cheeks. He looks up, a playful glint in his eyes.

"Was it a threat or a promise when I fucked you with the handle of my dagger last night? You tell me," he counters, and my eyes widen, eyebrows rising to the middle of my forehead. Eli's dimples make an appearance when he laughs at my expression.

"Do you have to be so vulgar?" I push my dangling gold earrings through my earlobe, muttering my disapproval. Emiliano comes to a stop behind me, his eyes on mine.

"Are we going to talk about what happened?" he asks. My throat tightens, and I can feel my nose tingling as my eyes sting with the threat of tears.

"I don't think I'm ready for that... It feels like I've betrayed my sisters, my brother, and my mom," I admit to him. His hand cups my chin, turning it toward him.

"Val, I know that you feel guilty for leaving them behind, and nothing I say will make that feeling go away, but I want you to know that I support you and will support you through whatever decision you make. No matter what..." Emiliano's voice is hushed, as if he speaks too loud, the walls might hear.

"I'll always come second, Eli, no matter what you want to believe," I say. He shakes his head, his eyebrows furrowed, as if he can't comprehend placing anything above me. Turning my head back toward the mirror, I brush my ponytail back. "The Camorra."

Emiliano grips both my shoulders, the fabric of my pearly dress scrunching up under his large hands. He leans down, his breath fanning the shell of my ear.

"You will always be first. I risked everything to get you back, and I will risk everything to keep you by my side. You put me over your family, and I'll put you over my oath to the Camorra." His voice is convincing, and my eyes search his, my lips stretching in a soft smile when I find sincerity and love shining back at me.

EPILOGUE
EMILIANO

I've called for a meeting to talk about what will take place with the Outfit after the crashed wedding. Even though it has been a couple of weeks, the Outfit has yet to declare an all-out war for the death of their Capo and the breaching of their territory.

"Everyone, down to the fucking basement, now!"

All my men scurry down to make their way downstairs, but of course, some little shit has to disobey me. And I'm not surprised to see that it is Vincent Colombo's spawn. I don't have the time of day for his dumb fuck of a dad, and I sure as fuck don't have the time of day for dumb fuck junior.

"Vince," Romiro calls him over, and he walks over with a solemn look.

"I suppose there's a reason as to why you thought it was a good idea to disrespect the Capo?" Romiro continues once he's stood in front of us.

"I mean no disrespect to the boss's orders. There is something that cannot wait until the end," he explains, and I narrow my eyes as I watch him. He's fidgety, his legs shuffling, as if he can't seem to stand without feeling the need to move. His eyes are frantically darting around the place, like he's expecting something or someone. To do what? I don't fucking know, but if my gut is right, I won't like any of it.

"Spit it out, Colombo," I demand.

He bristles before he whispers. "My uncles are preparing a coup to overthrow you."

My hand snakes out and grasps his neck, his feet dangling as I pull him up directly in my face. His hands clasp over mine as he tries to pry them, and his legs flail a little as he continues to struggle. Even with his nails digging into my hand, I don't budge.

"What the fuck do you mean by your uncles are planning a coup?" I growl.

His eyes bug out of their sockets, and I loosen my grip a little.

"I swear, I came to you as soon as I found out. They want to get rid of you and replace you with someone else," he chokes out. I search his face for any signs of deception, appeased when I find none.

I drop my hand from his neck, and Vince stumbles to the floor.

"You didn't tell me shit, and if I find out that you ran your mouth to anyone else, I'll start with your tongue. Come by my office after the meeting," I order him as Romiro and I make our way toward the spiral staircase.

Bring it on, fuckers. We're only going to have a field day with them. I give Romiro a twisted smile as we trod down the stairs. Game time.

The End

CHAPTER 20 (ELI'S POV)

EMILIANO

It's been three months. Three fucking months. Three fucking months of pure torture, agonizing pain.

"You need to stop watching everything they post about her. If you're not stalking her on social media, you've been tasking Matteo with hacking the security system of every place she could be at and watching her. It's unhealthy, Eli," Romiro says, but I ignore him as I watch the stupid date Valentina's family set up for her with her fiancé. They have been sitting at their table for half an hour, barely exchanging a couple of sentences.

"Are you seriously going to ignore what he just said?" Lucio asks, his hand reaching for the laptop to close the lid.

I smack his hand away, looking at them as I snarl, "Mind your fucking business. The both of you."

They both sigh and look at each other before Romiro speaks up again. "If you wanted her this badly, why did you give her up?"

"Because she wanted to go back; she wanted to get away from me. I won't have her resent me for holding her back. And it's not a want, Romiro. It's a need, an obsession. She's everything, and without her, everything else is meaningless. If you can't get that, then mind your fucking business."

I slam my palm on my desk, causing my empty cup of coffee to tip over and land sideways. My eyes snap to the screen when I see movement. They're leaving. And he has his fucking hand on the small of her back. I'm crushing that hand and stuffing it right up his Colombian ass.

I make my way toward my office doors, ignoring both Lucio's and Romiro's questions. Their footsteps are loud as they follow me into the kitchen. "Ma wants to see you; you've been in New York for four months, and she hasn't even heard a peep from you," Lucio says from behind me.

I open my cooler, grabbing the two-hundred-year-old Scotch. Lucio, of course, does something stupid and goes to grab it from me.

"Fuck off, Lucio," I say as I place it on the counter and grab one of my tumblers.

"All you do is drink alcohol or coffee and watch the CCTV footage you can get your hands on. It's not healthy," Romiro reasons. I don't respond, instead chugging back the Scotch. I wipe my mouth with the back of my sleeve and go to pour some more, when Lucio grabs the Scotch and pours it down the drain.

I lunge at him, popping his jaw with a right hook, causing him to drop to the floor with a thud. Romiro tries to pull us off each other, but we pummel each other's faces till we're both bleeding and our knuckles are busted. I finally get off my brother and extend my hand for him to get up. He takes it, laughing like the maniac he is. Shaking my head, I walk toward the cupboard near the sink and grab the first aid kit. I slide Lucio some band-aids, disinfectant, and gauze for his fists.

"What the fuck do you idiots suggest, then? Because I'm not going to stop watching her unless she's by my side where she belongs," I say, as I wrap my busted knuckles. Romiro leans on the kitchen island, watching me before he sighs and runs a hand through his blond curls.

"First off, you need to get yourself together. You look like death is on your doorstep. You need to keep up with your training. You're the fucking Capo, for the love of God. Second of all, there's talk about the

Scorpion having an affair with his family's lawyer, who's also his step-Mom's cousin," Romiro tells me. I turn to look at him and try to recoup my thoughts. What the fuck was Moretti thinking giving his daughter to a piece of shit like that.

"Get me Guerrero on the phone," I say before making my way down the hall, toward my room.

"Wait, what?" Romiro shouts behind me, and I turn to look at him.

"I said get me Nicholas Guerrero on the fucking phone."

I don't wait for an answer as I enter my room and close the door.

A week later

It's about time that my family moves back to New York where we belong. Romiro and I are waiting in the limo for Ma and my siblings. It's early January, so the weather still has a bite to it. It's been snowing in New York city for the past couple of days, and to say that I feel like shit would be an understatement.

"Have you managed to contact Guerrero?" I ask Romiro as I watch the landing strip.

"Yes, he's agreed to a call, but only under specific instructions," Romiro says.

My face twists, and I snarl, "The sheer stupidity of that boy is astounding. Like fuck I'm going to let him have his way." I turn to look at Romiro when he doesn't say anything.

Romiro shrugs before he says, "Well, you are if you want to be able to talk to him; otherwise, he refuses to even entertain the thought of talking to you."

My teeth grind together at the thought of even agreeing to play nice with the asshole who gets to live the rest of his days with the object of all my desires, and the fucker decides to fuck it up before it even starts. I run my hand through my hair as I mutter, "What the fuck does he want?"

"He said that he wants no mention of this to anyone, but those who already know. He also said that no one can know what you discuss. The phone call must be from a burner phone that is completely wiped out and disposed of afterwards. Only then will he agree to the phone call." Romiro lists off the Scorpion's demands, and I don't think that anything is unreasonable until Romiro finishes off by saying, "He also said that if this call is about Valentina, he'll shoot you in the face himself."

That fucking ticks me off, and I turn to look outside.

"Get Mariano to call our contact in Guerrero's territory," I order. Romiro doesn't say anything, and we wait for a couple more minutes before the plane from New Hampshire lands on the strip. Mara, my brothers, and Ma all slide inside.

"Hey, Ma," I say, going in for a kiss on her cheek, but she swerves out the way, which has Lucio and Romiro both laughing.

"Don't even think about it. You haven't even bothered to *call* for the past three months, and you have the audacity to say, 'hi, Ma' and try to give me a kiss." Her eyes narrow into slits.

Sending both a glare before clearing my throat and turning back to Ma, I say, "Ma, I'm sorry. I've been busy trying to make sure everything is going smoothly enough for all of us to return to New York City."

She scoffs and turns to look outside, and I decide to give her some space, so I lean back into the Italian leather seat. The drive to the family townhouse in Greenwich isn't long, and the car comes to a halt right outside the gates. Everyone piles out the other side of the car, leaving me and Ma. She goes for the car handle, and when I lock the doors, she whips her head to me.

"Emiliano Folonari, if you do not open this-" she seethes, her fists are clenched at her sides.

"I'm sorry, Ma, I really am," I cut her off. Her eyes soften, and the harsh lines bleed into the smile that takes over her face.

Ma searches my face before asking, "Do you love her?" My jaw clenches, and my eyes filter to the street outside.

I let the silence talk for me, because the noose around my neck has become unbearably tight, and the ache in my chest feels like a thousand gunshots.

"It's okay if you do. Emiliano, love isn't a weakness, nor is it a flaw. Love is strength, kindness. Love is also knowing your own shortcomings and making up for them with your actions, words. If you love her, fight for her," she says, her warm hand resting on top of mine.

"Ma, I don't think you realize what you're saying."

She shakes her head. "No, I know more than you think. If you love her truly, don't go thinking that by letting her go you're showing her that you love her. Unless she told you that herself, but she didn't, and instead of giving her a choice, you took it away from her."

"She doesn't love me. She tried to escape. More than once, she looked for a way out," I reason.

"She wanted to get out because she didn't want to be a trading mare. You can't honestly expect her to willingly sit around and wait for her good-for-nothing Dad to do something."

I'm about to say something, but she cuts me off, "She loves you; I saw how she looked the day you took her to give her back to her Dad. And the days before then, all she ever did was randomly burst out crying and try to avoid everyone."

I swallow, trying to rid myself of the ball that's forming in my throat. The locks click, signaling the end of the conversation. But before Ma gets out, I whisper, "A wedding is sacred. If I take her again, it will be an all-out war. No more dilly-dallying around the threats."

Ma pushes the limo door open, but before she completely steps out, she says, "All's fair in love and war."

A couple of days later

I lean back in my chair at the Diamond, staring at the damn burner phone, waiting for it to ring. The seconds tick away, and when the phone rings at five on the dot, I let it ring twice before picking it up.

"Folonari. I'm not surprised you've wanted to set up a call, but I'm certainly surprised that it's taken you this long to do so." Nicholas rolls the *r* in my surname, and it grates on my nerves, but I ignore it.

"Nicholas, I'd say it's nice to meet you, but I'd be lying. So, I'll just get to the point of this call. I want you to distract the Morettis for long enough for me to get Valentina out."

"Why should I help you take my fucking fiancée?" he asks.

"Maybe because you don't want to be engaged to her. Listen here, you piece of shit. If you think that nobody knows about your little girlfriend, what was her name? Sof-"

He cuts me off, growling, "Don't you fucking dare say her name, or I'll tear your fucking throat out, you dumb fuck. I fucking told you that if you bring Valentina up in this fucking call that I'd shoot you myself."

I scoff as I tap my hand against my desk. "I wouldn't be using this tone if I were in your position. After all, a sniper is positioned right outside your little girlfriend's bedroom window. She's sleeping so she won't feel it."

There's no sound but his breathing on the other end of the phone.

"I'll fucking kill all of you fuckers if a hair on her head is missing," he threatens.

I chuckle before saying, "Then you agree to set up something for me to get Valentina out?"

"Fuck you," he says before ending the call.

I'll take that as a yes.

WHAT'S NEXT?

Thank you so much for reading *Veil of Vengence*! If you liked it, please leave a review.
Your support means the world to me.

Up next is Veil of the Past, it is Romiro's book. I hope you'll join Rom and Alessia in their book!

ACKNOWLEDGMENTS

First and formost this is to the reader, I would like to thank you for picking up this book and reading it to the very end. I am forever grateful for you. Please consider leaving a review.

To all of my alpha readers, Brandy and Sonia. I am so grateful for your feedback.

To all of my beta readers, but especially Melissa, you guys gave me an amazing amount of encouragement and your love for this book really pushed me to go through with it to the very end.

To my Editors Mel and Mackenzie you guys made this book infinitely better, and shaped it up to become what it is today and for that thank you. To my proofreader, thank you for correcting any last errors and making the words flow better.

To my cover designer and the entire group over at BooksandMoods, thank you for your patience and amazing work on the revamp of the cover for book 1 and the cover of book 2. I can't rave enough about how gorgeous they turned out and how in love I am with them. Thank you.

To Elle Maldonado and Gabrielle Sands, thank you for your amazing advice. I will cherish every piece of it, and for that I am grateful.

To my ARC readers, thank you for reading my debut novel and giving this book a chance.

And finally, I want to say thank you to everyone who showed even an ounce of interest in my book, because that is what continued to push me to keep writing till the very end.

Serafina x

ABOUT THE AUTHOR

Serafina Marron is a Dark Romance enthusiast. She enjoys coming up with dark, twisted and delicious villains for her heroins. When she isn't doing that, Sera is usually consuming too much caffeine in the form of energy drinks.

Taking a gap year before studying Computer Science in England, her love for writing had flourished once again.

When she's not writing, you can find her avoiding human interactions as much as possible, listening to explicit songs at full volume, feeding stray cats, and staying up late obsessing over fictional characters.

If you're in the mood to stalk me:
Website
Newsletter
Instagram
TikTok

www.ingramcontent.com/pod-product-compliance
Lightning Source LLC
Chambersburg PA
CBHW061118100726
47911CB00013B/589